Enjoy!

with love,

Jo Lobbato

x

THE WOMAN WHO LOST HER LOVE

JO LOBATO

THE WOMAN WHO LOST HER LOVE

First edition. 09 July, 2020.

ISBN: 978-1-8380912-1-7

Written by Jo Lobato.

For Mum.

"Art is a lie that makes us realise truth."
Picasso

DAY ONE

'So, we're ready. No going back now.' I clip in the seatbelt, taking care to adjust the strap until it feels just right. Not too tight, we'll be here for a while, but not so loose that—

Well. It pays to be cautious.

'Oh.' The bing bong sounds out, creating a flash of red in my mind. I haven't much flying experience, but I know to feel on edge at the alerting noise. Goodness. Does anyone ever fully relax in these over-populated cylinders of recycled air; gigantic pods that propel one through time and space to a foreign environment?

Best not give it too much thought . . .

I place a hand on David's arm. His eyes remain closed. He is keen to relax, but perhaps the bing bong unnerves him, too. No doubt he is imagining himself in first class rather than crushed up here in the – what did he call it? Oh, yes – *riff-raff*. If I were to paint my husband's portrait at this moment, I would make it pinched - screwed up in that way Bertie used to do during a tantrum. A long time ago, of course, but it's hard not to picture our daughter as that adorable little toddler when I summon her face to mind, even now she's in her twenties.

'Oh, goodness me. I'm sorry, darling, I forgot.' I squeeze

David's arm. 'Would you mind getting my compression socks from the bag?'

'They've just put the sign on.' He manages to speak while barely moving his mouth. A ventriloquist.

'I'd rather have them now, and then we can settle in. It's a long flight—'

'O-*kay*.' David makes a show of opening his eyes, before he turns to the suited passenger lucky enough to have been granted the aisle seat. If we'd paid for priority, perhaps we could have selected an outside position, extra leg room ...

David speaks in a low voice, and smart aisle man rises from his seat to allow David to squeeze through.

And, gosh, it is a squeeze. Poor David, he's not escaped the mid-life fill.

Although, 'midlife' is probably generous.

And what is with this suit, Suit Man? It's twelve hours to Singapore and then another eight on to Australia. Surely, it's a little constricted? Perhaps he has a meeting as soon as he lands. He presents as some sort of advertising executive or maybe a—

Oh. I appear to have tuned out and missed what David said. The engine has started to roar, a darkness aroused in my mind.

Right. Search for a focus point ...

Ah. Approaching air hostess.

Suit Man clocks her and returns to his seat.

The woman's shooting pout appears aimed toward the speckles of sweat now spotting through my husband's shirt.

Oh no, hostess, don't go there. You don't want to start your day with that.

'I can't do this,' David says again from his heightened position. The third time he has spoken these words? A peculiar sentence, in his search for socks.

Suit Man lifts his book closer to his face, although I haven't seen him turn the page in a while. The book cover is reminiscent of a Goya painting - intense and disturbing - and I can't help but assume this man probably won't finish the thing. The shelves of his lounge are undoubtedly lined with weighty tomes, doing more to nourish a desired image than feed his imagination. I clamp my hand over my mouth to catch a chuckle. Imagine the people who fall for such tosh, clinking oversized wine glasses on an oversized couch as they discuss the non-fiction bestsellers ...

Don't I know something about Goya? Didn't he have a fear of insanity? Of hysteria, perhaps.

I won't share this fact with David.

'What do you mean? You can't see the socks? They're in the front pocket of my bag. I left them right at the top.' I speak with speed before the air hostess arrives. Maybe I can play the thirtieth-anniversary card on her. I mean, I know people are married far longer but it certainly feels like an achievement. And the hotel manager who offered the honeymoon suite seemed to agree. Although, it turned out to be a pricey agreement and we settled for a standard double. David almost cancelled the entire trip because of it, but—

I've waited years for this. The promise of being shown the world has taken an unexpectedly long time to materialise.

'Don't worry, just sit down.' Hm. There is that awful haughty edge creeping into my tone, reminding me that I am a woman in her fifth decade, embracing stereotype. The words I would apply to myself are adjectives my younger self would have baulked at - uppity, lofty, sardonic ...

I'm too late. The red blotch is creeping up David's cheeks and his nostrils flare. I had hoped this trip could be a chance for us to unwind, connect to that elusive attraction that gets stamped out by work, existing ... The chore of life.

Another passenger has thwarted the air hostess's mission, no doubt a fellow Brit requesting alcohol before we've even left the ground.

Suit Man emits what I strongly suspect is a fake cough.

'David?' I whisper, panic fermenting just above my colon. David is not one to - how do I phrase this? - *lose his shit*, as Bertie would say. That's the term she used in reference to my recent behaviour, anyway.

Goodness. When did I become a woman to Lose Her Shit?

'I can't do this,' David repeats. The tenth time? The phrase is coming out in repetitive waves now. Like that breathing I did during labour. My sister Francis had told me yoga was witches' brew. It was obscure back then, not popular like it is now, but .. . Well, it worked. Bertie's birth had been transcendent. The glimmer amongst—

Everything else.

I find a balance point on the new chin David is developing, my stare landing on a penny-sized patch of greying stubble he must have missed in his morning shave. From my lowered angle, I have a fresh view of the blotched neck, which hangs from his jaw like a half-empty water balloon, quivering as he speaks.

'David, sit down, please. It doesn't matter. I can get the socks later.' David had used this authoritative tone on me last week in John Lewis, and it had worked - I calmed down, and the security guard eventually released his hold.

'David.' Stern now; the air hostess is marching, and they just made an announcement over the tannoy reminding passengers to *Please obey the seatbelt sign.*

Suit Man drops all pretense, as do the surrounding passengers. Gosh. The heat of everyone — all these *bodies*. Beating hearts, gurgling stomachs, siphoning intestines. Grotesque bodily functions. We're all here, crammed in together.

And now, head tops transform to faces as people turn. Mutter. A moving *Marilyn Diptych.*

Discretion is a lost segment of a bygone era.

The engine is roaring loud. My vision speckles.

Goodness. These windows don't open, do they?

David's gaze is also fixed on the window, although I wouldn't say he is looking at it. His eyes seem unfocused. Where once was life is now negative space. I mean, I know all irises are negative space but David's look is . . . A nothingness. Depleted.

'Sir, the seatbelt sign is on, and we need you to please take a seat.'

Oh, bugger.

'Madam.' Ugh. Listen to my voice, flecked with superiority. 'Is the air conditioning on?'

Madam ignores me. David remains vacant. In my peripheral vision, the eyes of the Marilyn's search the scene.

My breath has crept back into my chest.

Concentrate. Rise and fall.

Suit Man faces me. I attempt an apologetic smile, but I grimace, dry lips cracking across beige old lady teeth.

'I can't do this.' David. Again.

I swallow into a scream that threatens to dislodge from my larynx. How long have I been stifling it? My fingernails scratch into my tweed skirt.

Goodness. Tweed? What a ridiculous choice for a long-haul flight. David likes me to look conservative, but I should have had the presence of mind to know I'd be trying to peel it off for the duration of our compressed existence.

I open my mouth but—

No. I can't speak in that way again. David simply needs to pull himself together and bloody well sit down. For goodness sake, what is he playing at?

Finally, my husband shifts gaze from the window to me, as though following a hypnotist's pendant - slow, measured, not entirely conscious.

'I'm sorry.' Hm. He doesn't look sorry. He looks forlorn. Lost. Like that puppy Bertie made us buy that time, his bulging little eyes desperate to know where was home.

The air hostess is talking to David, but I don't hear what she says because my mind is flooded in black and blue and—

Her hand. On his elbow. She steps away and he follows for a beat before he turns back. Our eyes meet.

For a moment there is only him and me and we're back in the aquarium Bertie used to love. We're standing in the glass tunnel and all of our past and future is washing around us in tanks and he has to stay.

He *must* stay, but—

Another step toward the air hostess.

'I'm sorry, Diane.'

He doesn't stay.

We land in Singapore. I'll need to unpeel myself from the seat as I haven't moved in a full twelve hours. I suspect I'm on borrowed time, as they say, because, of course, I never got my socks. But I just could not bear to give Suit Man the satisfaction of my being a Woman With Needs.

I wait, clenching my bladder in my seat, as more and more people leave but David—?

Surely, he wouldn't have forgotten to collect me?

Hm. Perhaps Madam forced him to use the rear doors. She does seem very forceful. She wouldn't even consider my idea of waiting on the plane until it lands back in London.

Right.

He's still not here.

All passengers have now disembarked.

So. I suppose I'll get off.

Reluctantly, I shuffle into the terminal, but it's difficult to spot my husband amongst the crowd. Did I land in a live Lowry painting? Stylised figures with no shadows and no weather here in this cavernous airport which I've now circled seventeen times, but . . . I don't see David anywhere. I am a mere matchstick man in a lofty befuddlement of to-ing and fro-ing bodies, people with places to be and I am—

I didn't sleep. I should have slept. But, goodness, is it even time to sleep? Aren't Australian clocks ahead of the UK? Yet we're not there yet. I've no idea if I should be in night or day or dawn or dusk.

A sense of not here and not yet there.

I am nowhere. With no-one.

I perch on a fixed plastic chair on the outer edge of a restaurant. The most western-looking establishment I can find. A 'diner'? There appears to be sandwiches and tea on the menu, although all tables are piled high with trays of dirty dishes.

I mean, can that girl behind the counter not *see* this mess? Perhaps she should spend less time on her makeup and more time on the hygiene of her eatery.

Hm. This is just a three-hour layover, so perhaps I'll wait to eat until—

Until?

Well. I don't know. I mean, this is David. I know my husband to be solid and reliable and . . . A saviour.

Our saviour.

I'm unsure how long I sit in the cafe. Time takes on an odd quality in an airport. Slippery. Like custard falling through a sieve. I did that once. Didn't turn on my brain, tried to sieve the lumps out of some custard over the sink instead of a bowl, so ended up with only lumps.

That's what I have now. Sticky lumps of time. Useless.

Ah. I appear to have switched off my intelligence again and have rung my sister, in America. 'What do you mean, he's gone?' Francis says.

I explain the facts, which doesn't take long. I'm not sure I've ever felt so devoid of information.

There is a smack of lips on the other end, an indiscreet tut. I imagine Francis opening and closing her mouth, making and reforming a reply. That, or she is mouthing the information to her nosy husband, Roy. Roy has an answer for everything.

But I am still stuck on questions.

'What are you doing?' I close my eyes and think of white. A vast white space, spreading to the edges of my mind. Like the Bolivian salt flats, perhaps. Not that I've been. 'Stop it,' I add. The image has gone.

I open my eyes.

'Diane? What is it?'

Oh! My phone is vibrating, but it's not Francis. It's a message.

David.

My head shakes. I lift one hand to still it.

Then I open the message:

`I'm sorry. I need some time out. I'm sure you understand. I'll see you at the wedding. If you need the details, email Cecelia.`

'Why does he need time out? What does he mean?' This is Francis.

'Hello?'

'Diane? Are you okay? You're making me worried.'

I lift the phone to my ear.

'Diane? Why does he need time out?' My sister's voice seems loud in the quiet of the cafe.

'How do you know what he said?'

'You just read aloud what I assume is a message from David.'

'Oh.' I sound just like her, don't I? It's ... Old.

I am old.

'And you're still on the phone to me. Diane, *please*. Do you know what he's talking about?' And now there's the edge creeping into her voice. An increasingly present element over the last few years.

'I don't know.' I no longer have an edge. I no longer have anything. I don't even have luggage. 'How do I get home? Where's my bag?'

A baby is screaming on the far side of a cafe. The mother plugs one of those awful dummy things in its mouth and, thank goodness, the cry stops.

'The gate number will be displayed on the departure board. I assume your bag will be automatically transferred onto your flight.'

My flight.

I press the palm of my hand into my eyes until I see stars, trying to force the image of Bertie out of my mind.

And I love Bertie. I always want to see her, but—

'No. I can't do it. I should come home,' I whisper.

Bertie will be disappointed. She was so excited for me to visit Australia. She'd loved it when she went. She'd spent so long listing recommendations ...

Not that David considered any of her endorsements. Hostels aren't his thing.

'Diane. Roy and I have been discussing-' *Discussing?* '-And you need to get onto the next flight out to us.'

I stare at the table in front of me. Beige. A chipped corner.

Somewhere, thoughts must be processing. Because, somehow, I speak. 'Yes.'

'We'll collect you. Just tell us the flight details once you've booked. You can stay with us for as long as you need.'

I picture meeting Francis at the airport. The veil of pitying melodrama the only thing she's able to wear around me nowadays. Eventually I'd walk through my front door - the house cold because David refuses to leave the heating on, regardless of the time of year and risk of frost. Empty beds, photos of long-ago memories, the soul gone.

This holiday was a chance for us to rekindle that soul. Rediscover the depths of what makes us *us*, David and I. And yet, for some reason, he wishes to embark on the trip alone.

Three weeks.

Less than three weeks. *Twenty sleeps,* as Bertie would say.

But what if David changes his mind? If I'm in England or America I can't very well respond with immediacy, can I? My husband does not like to wait. If I'm not there at his nephew's wedding, he won't know what to think. I have to show him I am the person he wants to take home. I need him to take me home. I can't go back there by myself. I—

'I need to get on the flight to Australia.'

Silence pulses through the thousands of miles that separate me from my sister. I picture Francis's chin-dipping look to Roy. His eye roll. Head shaking all around.

My own skull mirrors.

Somehow, I stand. I find a departure board.

Jesus. Gate 30.

Thirty years.

'Diane. Let's look at the facts as we have them. I know this is a shock. It's going to be difficult to process, but I'm not sure you can expect David to be there.'

They're giving the final call.

Thirty years.

I can risk twenty sleeps for thirty years, can't I? Break it down, one day at a time. Doable, right?

'Diane?'

Right. All I have to do is find a hotel and lie in the sun.

'I am going to try, Francis. Thirty bloody years. I have to at least try.'

———

I am surprised by my own volition. Finding the gate, boarding this plane. These are not difficult tasks but, well, they're not in my typical repertoire. For Bertie, yes, easy. For David, more so. But, me? I used to want adventure, despite being scared of the idea, but ...

Life happens, doesn't it? Things change.

I was the one to look after the home. The traditional model. It worked for us.

But the seat beside me remains empty, and I wonder what it was I could have missed.

'Are you not a fan of flying, either?' The woman next to me speaks. A gentle voice, northern undertones, her head is resting back but inclined in my direction, cushioned by a mass of unruly hair.

'It's fine.' I lean back in the seat. Position my arms on the rests. It's best not to engage. We have many hours left to fly, and once you begin a conversation, then the quiet is no longer comfortable. Instead, expectant.

I'm always surprised when Francis flies over from the States and declares that she had the most horrendous flight, but it'd been salvaged by having met *a highly interesting woman who had the most interesting history, Diane*.

Interesting for someone as nosy as you, I refrain from saying.

Shouldn't Francis have been more surprised at David's disappearance? Perhaps I imagined it, but the edge in her voice seemed to resemble anger.

Angry at me? For some unfathomable reason, this seems plausible.

I force my fists to unclench and lower my hands into my lap. I pick up an inflight magazine.

The plane jolts. The woman beside me sucks in air. We must be about half way now.

I need some time out. I'm sure you understand.

But—?

I don't understand. I know it's not been easy of late, perhaps *I* have not been easy, but . . . Why wouldn't he mention anything in England? Why would he let me do this trip alone? He must know how hard it would be for me.

'Cute,' comes the woman's voice. She is referring to a large photo in the magazine I am pretending to read. The image depicts a family on holiday. Happy mummy and daddy and two sun-kissed smiling children.

No comment.

'Do you have kids?' she asks.

'One. A daughter.' The family are a matchy-matchy set - all whitened teeth and blue eyes. Scandinavian, I should think. Aren't they the breed of happy human? Capable types. Doers.

'Oh, gosh, I would have loved girls. I have two boys - teenagers now - and - *phew!* - I physically gag when I change their beds. I probably shouldn't do it, you know, we want to encourage independence and all that but if I don't, it won't get done, and then the police will be pressing charges for smell pollution.' A burst of laughter injects shards of pink in my mind. 'Does your daughter live with you?'

'She lives in London.'

'Oh, lovely.'

How long do we have left to fly?

'See with girls you can do the whole girl date thing, and I bet you get into London to see her lots for shows and some such? So wonderful. What's her name?'

'Liberty. But we call her Bertie.'

'Oh, how unusual. Lovely.'

Five hours.

Five hours.

I flick through the magazine. White beaches, turquoise sea. Like I'm looking at the life I was promised.

I glance at the empty seat. I think of Francis.

Gosh. What choice do I have?

'What are your plans for the trip?'

The woman sits up straight, her face open as she turns to me. 'You know, a week ago, I would have been able to provide an hour-by-hour itinerary, but something stopped me just recently, and I thought, *Miriam, what are you doing? You need to be able to take opportunities as they arise, open yourself up to the people you might meet . . .* So, now? I've thrown all plans out the window and have decided to fly by the seat of my pants.' The woman punctuates the sentence with another honk of laughter.

I smile because it's polite, though I'm not entirely sure what this means. Didn't Bertie admit she'd made no advance plans? She had the first hostel booked and then she would *see what happened.*

Goodness, I'd been horrified.

Yet, I don't even have the first hostel or hotel or motel or anything booked because David has the itinerary. And even if I did know, clearly, judging by David's message, he wants me to do my own thing.

A test?

The aeroplane jolts. I reflexively grab the arm of the chair.

'Miriam' ramps up speed: 'I was going to stop in at Sydney and then head up the coast but I've just been reading about this art course that sounds super fun in Byron, and I wonder if I can get a direct bus from the airport and just get stuck straight in, you know? I'm not really bothered about seeing the stuff in between Sydney and Byron and I can always check it out on the way back if I change my mind.'

Byron. Where Bertie had loved most. Didn't she change her flight home to stay there longer?

'Do you know how far Byron is from Southport?' I ask.

Miriam opens the map in her travel guide. She stretches the pages back to show me. 'I'd say that's not that far to drive. If Byron is eight hours from Sydney, it's probably - what? - An hour or so? Why?'

'I have a nephew's wedding to go to in Southport. In three weeks.' At least I know this much.

Oh, wasn't the wedding in some godawful chain hotel where David's family were all to stay together? *Unoriginal*, I'd thought when David told me. *Sounds great!* I'd replied.

'Oh, fabulous. A wedding abroad. Well, you should definitely stop at Byron on the way. I can give you the details of the art course if you're into that sort of thing?'

Goodness.

Byron. Art.

How peculiar that life should unravel at speed with the smallest of alterations.

Or is that altercations?

'Or, you're welcome to come with me?' The woman's voice stretches — a piece of elastic, lengthening slowly. 'I know we've just met, but I think that's sort of how it goes here: Open yourself to opportunity, meet someone, travel, part ways when you become too annoying . . .' She closes with a fire of that chortle like the canned laughter on some ghastly American sitcom - one that someone has turned to full volume and keeps accidentally pushing go.

However. I do find myself giving a genuine smile now. Could this be a *blessing*, as Bertie would say? *Go with the flow.* She says I should do that more.

Gosh. Bertie and her backpack, heading off at the airport. Her face had looked excited and scared in equal measures. Her mouth lifting but her brow flickering.

But Bertie is braver than me - she would not have waited for the flight's final call. She does not hesitate over anything, not once she sets her mind on it.

She loved Byron. I know that much.

And if Byron is near to my destination, then it makes sense to accept this offer, doesn't it? I can travel with this Miriam woman here, find a hotel and sunbathe until I meet David in Southport and afterwards get back to our life of plans and routine and regularity.

'What do you think?' Miriam asks. 'Two women on their own, looking out for each other?'

The family in my lap beam their grins with conviction.

What do I think?

A Woman On Her Own. Goodness.

The Weeping Woman. Picasso.

'Bertie loved Byron when she was there.'

Picasso liked to experiment.

And maybe I need not weep.

'So? You'll come?'

Well. In all honesty, what choice do I have?

———

Bertie would say I *jinxed it* by thinking of how the trip might go wrong. I know she'll say I brought this on myself because of my negative *head space*, but—

'It's not here,' I say. Miriam is beside me. We both face the baggage carousel, upon which only one bag remains. Round and round the orphaned suitcase goes, teasing me every time it comes into view, and I let myself think, hope, for a moment that—

No. It's the same one returning - a ghastly neon pink number that looks as though it may spring open if you poke it, a mere canvas belt strapping the ripe-for-bursting contents together.

'Maybe you should just take that one?' Miriam elbows me in the arm.

'Oh, no, I . . .' I can't bear to imagine what atrocities a suitcase such as that may contain.

'Too late.'

The bag has been claimed, hauled off the carousel by a rotund man who sweats with the exertion of it. And - goodness - his whole family are round. And pink, too. Just like their luggage.

I would chuckle at the image, but—

'My bag is not here.' The orphaned bag has been claimed. Which means there are no more bags. No suitcases left and no chance of my suitcase coming out here.

Goodness. The box. Inside my luggage.

We are standing in this vast baggage reclaim space of Sydney airport, and yet my world is closing in. The walls of my existence slowly collapsing as brick by brick is removed, the support begins to wobble, and soon - boom. It will all fall down.

'I am *Woman with a Bag*. Except I have no bag.'

'Excuse me?'

'Karl Schmidt-Rottluff's oil painting. Before he went to war. Misery. Just . . . misery, Miriam.'

'You've lost me. Look, try not to worry; this happens all the time. I'm sure there is an explana—'

'*Happens all the time?* That's simply not good enough. A large company such as this. These are my things, Miriam. My only possessions. Everything else is—' I shake my head. I can't have lost my bag. The box is in there. I have to have the box.

I lower myself down.

'Oh, I wouldn't sit—'

Oh, goodness. A frightful idea. The carousel is moving, and it wants to take my bottom with it.

Thankfully, Miriam stands in front of me, and I grab hold of her waist. Her hands are full with her guide book and that huge camera around her neck which she is preventing from bashing into my head.

I can't stand up. I can't breathe.

'This can't be happening. The first step—'

'It's okay.' Miriam's voice is gentle, soothing. It sounds like that preschool teacher Bertie had once, she always took the time to come and speak to me, *check in*, as she'd say. I saw her not too long ago, I think. An older woman, even older than me. Hadn't I seen her at—?

Well. No doubt she's elderly now.

'Listen, I have loads of clothes so you can borrow whatever you need.'

I glance up to Miriam's combat trouser and unshapely t-shirt combo; a scent of incense lurks. I close my eyes.

Rise and fall.

'The bag will turn up in no time.'

Rise and fall.

'You can use my things, and we'll find a shop to buy some essentials.'

Rise and fall.

'Why don't you go and talk to the airline helpdesk? I'll arrange our travel up to Byron.'

Rise and fall.

Byron?

Right. Yes. Byron.

Slowly, I lift myself upright.

Goodness. David insisted we have separate bags and, at the time, I didn't question it. But ... had he been planning to leave me here all along?

Thirty years.

'Okay?' Miriam's hand is steadying on my arm.

Rise and fall.

'Okay,' I say.

But I'm a good liar.

The man at the airline desk is a moron. *Help desk*, for goodness sake. 'You are no help; you are offering me nothing.'

The booth of the *help desk* feels distinctly low budget. A cheap knock-off. Unsturdy.

It doesn't fill me with confidence ...

'Mam, I understand this is an inconvenience—'

'This is more than an inconvenience, *Sir*. This is a ... Catastrophe. A goddamn catastrophe.' I look at my hands. 'I apologise for swearing.'

Bertie. This is not my fault. I don't have negative headspace, I have ... Nothing.

The man adjusts himself in his seat. Tell-tale signs of a fake tan smudge around his ears, and I wouldn't be surprised if he thickened those eyebrows with a brow pen. He would fit on that terrible reality show about the people of Essex.

'I'm sorry, but that's simply not a good enough explanation,' I say. Again. I want to deliver my explanation of precisely what that bag means to me. What the content holds, but . . .

I can't bear it.

'Mam, I apologise once more on behalf of the airline, but when we locate your bag, we will send it on. Here is the form you need to fill—'

'Fill in a form and all will be okay?' I slide the paper back across to him. 'How can I trust you ever again?'

'Mam, we need a forwarding address, and we will send the suitcase on as soon as we have it. Usually, they turn up in just a day or two.'

'*Usually?* So, this is a frequent occurrence? Do you not think it might be worth doing something to prevent losing the luggage in the first place?'

The man says nothing.

I suspect he is getting bored.

Gosh. I can't help but think of David. I bet his luggage is fine. In fact, I bet our bags are cosying up together, diverted from Australia to follow David to— Where? Bali? Somewhere else exotic . . .

Side by side.

And I am alone.

'I can fill the form on your behalf. Do you have a forwarding address?'

'Forwarding address?' These words are unfamiliar. It's been a long while since I've had an address that is not mine and David's home. I can barely remember the time. Although I am pretty certain I was less . . . querulous then. With the outside world, at least.

A different person.

'Where are you staying?'

My heart rate has increased. Perhaps I should sit down.

'I . . .' Miriam is in the next section of the airport booking our transfer. She said she would book the hotel, and I don't know . . .

Anything.

'Do you know anyone in Australia that we could send it to?'

'David.'

'Okay, David—?'

Goddamn David.

Rise and fall.

'A chain hotel. In Southport. I am going there.'

'Okay, great. And the name?'

'Oh, it's . . . Erm, something to do with first . . . something.' I touch a hand to my hair.

'The Premier?'

'Yes.'

'Perfect, I'll look up the full address online.'

'But I'm not due there for three weeks.' I wish I were a person prone to severe swearing. Cussing would help me in this instance. Relieve something. Clear a clog somewhere, perhaps.

'No problem, I'll mark it to your attention, and you can get it when—'

'*Three weeks,* sir. I cannot be without my things for three weeks.'

But the man ignores me. He has already found the necessary details and has filled in the form and is passing it over for me to sign.

Good grief.

The pen is a lead weight in my hand, the letters mixing on the page into nonsensical patterns, but I drop the nib to where Sir is pointing, and I scribble my signature.

Gosh. The only thing I have left - my name.

DAY TWO

I'm not entirely sure how this happened, but I find myself - can you believe it? - in a godforsaken hostel. A private room, at least. It was all I could do to walk myself up here last night and climb into bed. I was so exhausted yet, after a brief stint of sleep, I have been awake since four a.m. Jet lag, I suspect. I'm not a fan. Unwanted thoughts always seem unrulier when nobody is up to distract them.

Miriam was naughty to book this shared house. Bertie once told me you could have up to sixteen people cohabiting a room in some battery-packed dormitory, conditions to which I would prohibit even chickens from occupying.

Although, Miriam was extraordinarily helpful in the airport shop where she assisted with my purchase of two pairs of leggings and three fitted t-shirts, along with a pair of flip flops (or *thongs*, as they are, strangely, known here). Miriam also reiterated her offer of clothing, but . . .

I'll try to manage with these few simple items. It's actually rather refreshing to be in new clothes.

And this room is not in bad shape; a striking resemblance to Van Gogh's *The Bedroom*. Lilac walls, wooden floor, small table, two chairs as though I am to expect visitors. But, of course, there will be none.

The space smells of fresh linen, thank goodness. The window is open - it must have been open when I arrived last night - and a breeze saunters in, making the curtain lift and wane, lift and wane, a bottom note of sea salt trickling through the light cotton.

I close the window and turn the key in the lock.

Coming in on the bus last night we'd passed a sign: WELCOME TO BYRON.

Goodness.

Everything Bertie described - the vivid colours, the luscious trees, the cute wooden shacks, the low-lying village feel of the town - transformed from imagination to reality.

This is a town to be painted. A village to be adored. I can see that, but—

But this town is not my friend. This is a place to wait it out. Survive.

I sit back on the bed. Hadn't Van Gogh painted *The Bedroom* when he'd first bought a home of his own?

Yes, I read something of this. The artist intended to capture relaxation, but the viewer senses turmoil. The sharp perspective signifying anxiety rather than peace.

I've always considered lilac walls a peculiar choice for a man. Weren't there three versions of *The Bedroom*? Perhaps Van Gogh changed his mind. My father had had that shed at the bottom of the garden, his *man cave* (before the concept was 'a thing'), and he painted it that colour of drudgery - a dark blue - no wonder he was as he was. Like he had to make his masculinity known by throwing it at a shed, for goodness sake.

We should have understood he was trying to send us a message. Maybe if Mum had let him live in that shed, his subsequent deceit would have been prevented.

Goodness. Has David put me in this position because of—?

No. All too long ago now.

Get through the twenty days, and then I can discuss it with him. Sort this misunderstanding out.

Although, regretfully, there is no pool here for me to spend my days as I was hoping. The hostel is a 'townhouse' located toward the edge of the village which is a five-minute walk away. The beach is there too, so I suppose I'll sunbathe on that instead. I could quite happily lie down for a while and admire the Australian sky - the particular shade of blue is unlike any I know from home. And this is winter.

Although, I suspect, this is to be a season unlike any other.

Gosh, how far away I am from home. Patricia would have gone in today to water the plants. No doubt she will have noticed the curtain I need to restore in the lounge, the plant pot that will need straightening as our cleaner never aligns it quite right.

A family portrait resides on the mantelpiece - me, David and Bertie, smiles. Someone took the photograph at a theme park. One of those garish places full of over-excited children, smells of petrol and candy floss heightening the nausea. Bertie had loved it, of course. Always far more adventurous than I, that child.

Although, the picture . . . David switched it, didn't he? Instead, there now sits a nondescript photo of the lakes. Our summer walks. Attempting to live up to his promise of travel.

And yet—

Well.

I suppose I should leave *The Bedroom*. Think of Bertie.

Brave.

Rise and fall.

I stand. Open the door. Force my feet to walk me downstairs to the 'living room'. Everyone else must still sleeping.

Ah. Good. There is a bookcase behind one of the large sofas. In the opposite corner sits a box of a computer - a relic from the eighties which is just the sort of appliance I used to imagine Bertie emailing me from when she was here. In fact, the antiquated machine looks as though it takes money for, I suppose, internet time.

A sign on the wall instructs me toward the rather generously named 'library', a single bookshelf offering two sides of overflowing dog-eared paperbacks - all the popular titles of the past two decades. The twaddle of the *Should Read* lists. My book club has covered pretty much all of these.

Gosh, what will I tell the book club girls? (*Girls*. The label seems ludicrous all of a sudden. No wonder David would laugh at it. I used to chuckle with him, but now I think of it, was his laugh more of a sneer?)

And the sewing ladies at our monthly 'sewing bee'. *He left you?* I can hear Patricia saying. Always one for an opinion, Patricia.

I select a Costa Prize winner. The book feels worn, used. I don't like to bend the spine on mine. David says I should read on a Kindle - he bought me one for Christmas one year, ever insistent - but I enjoy the feel of a book. Especially nowadays, hardbacks have such beautiful covers. I like to observe what I have read on the shelf. A sense of achievement. Something to show for my time.

But these books tell another story. The hands through which they have passed, the countries they've visited. Most of these books, I should think, are worldlier than I.

I squeeze the novel back in its place and squirt some sanitiser on my palms, inhaling the sterile scent. Mm. Familiar. A comfort in this space where everything is so . . . different.

Not just the scenery or surroundings but the people, accents. I suppose I live in a rather refined area. Goodness. No, I don't mean that.

What do I mean? Shaded?

Insular?

'Good morning.'

Oh! I turn to find the owner of this clipped, deep voice is a woman - young (what else), wearing all black, her long dark hair pulled tight off her face into a high ponytail. Judging by the confident stance, I assume this person is staff, although her sterile appearance is at odds with the shabby-chic styling of the room. The interior decoration is not to my taste, of course - this undone look, not trying to try - but I can appreciate the stylistic value. This lounge has a different finish to the country-house feel of my room. Whoever decorated, clearly has an eye.

Maybe it was this sharp girl in front of me.

I lift my face into a mirroring smile, but she has dropped her gaze to another book I have selected.

Oh, gosh. I'm only bloody holding *Fifty Shades*, aren't I? This is one of the titles our book club has not read, obviously. I know what it is, I . . . I wanted to see what the hype was about. I feel a redness creep up my neck as I recall Bertie's reaction to my joking the book club would read this next. *You're all too tame,* she had laughed.

I look at the young woman in front of me now. Does she think I am tame?

Or maybe Bertie had said *lame*.

'Diane, is it?' Somehow this woman can maintain a pout, even when she speaks. It is somewhat intimidating.

'Dee,' I hear myself saying.

Dee Dee.

Gosh.

I swallow hard.

'Dee, nice to meet you. I am Sofia, the receptionist here. Your friend said you'd like to join the art course?' I am enjoying the distraction of Sofia's professionalism. I find my shoulders pulling back, wanting to be as sure in my skin as she seems in hers. 'I'll need your passport details.'

I glance over at Miriam, who has hauled herself from

slumber at last and is conversing loudly with two girls in the doorway. More fresh faces. Youths. Gap year, I would guess (*gap-yar*, as Bertie says in jest). I remember Bertie's request to travel when she had been only eighteen, but David had insisted university wouldn't wait.

'Let me see if I can find it.' I replace the dirty book to its position. I picture the lace trim nightie sitting in the bottom of my lost luggage and my shoulders round.

I am a fool.

'Oh, Diane, Indie and Lola here were just telling me about a surf trip they're going on tomorrow.'

I hover next to the battered sofa and, despite the sudden heaviness in my legs, I refrain from sitting. What I can't refrain from doing is lifting my eyebrows. *Indie and Lola?*

For goodness sake.

Indie and Lola are all bounce and bust. My own sap and sag amplifies in their company, and yet Miriam is suggesting an excursion with them?

I manage to nod. Even a smile, too. One for you, Bertie.

Maybe I should treat them as I would Bertie. They are a good few years younger than her, and I suspect immature and - what would Bertie say? - *dippy*. I haven't spoken to them directly myself but—

One can tell these things. Bertie read Architecture at King's.

'Apparently, these girls have already done the surfing, and they say it's not scary. The wave is quite gentle here,' Miriam says.

I look down at her hand, which she rests on my forearm.

'You should come.'

'Oh, well, that's kind of you to offer . . .' I can't remember if this one is Indie or Lola, so I skip the name and give an appreciative nod. A sweet girl. Naive, I suspect.

'Ohmygosh, Indie, we should tell them about the bungee jump.' This one - the juicier of the two girls, Lola, apparently, over-annunciates every syllable, her full lips seeming to work unnecessarily hard to form the words. I press my own, somewhat thinner lips, together.

'Bungee?' I try the word out.

As suspected, I don't like it.

Miriam is nodding, but her curls don't move. She has the sort of hair I can't believe has ever seen a brush.

'It's not obligatory,' she says.

Look at them all. The two girls, dripping in innocent excitement, Miriam just about young enough to pass for not-desperate. (I hope she does not go drinking with them. *Binge drinking.* There, I suspect, is the line.) I had been feeling almost okay in my new clothes, but now? Opposite are micro denim shorts, exposed bra straps and . . . I am just a . . . fuddy duddy.

Goodness. Could this be David's payback? This has been the inevitable act, hasn't it?

I am tense. Too tense. My heart lets me know it is beating. How long have I been in this state? Goodness. Years now.

I close my eyes. The box.

'What are you doing?'

Somehow, I'm back in my room. 'I'm going home,' I reply to Miriam, grabbing at my few belongings. I fold my tweed skirt, silk shirt. How ridiculous to think I can stay with no clothes, for goodness sake.

And those girls aren't Bertie, and I would be utterly stupid to join them. The youths with their backpacks and tattoos and laughter and tiny vest tops and tight skin. And I am?

A silly old fool.

I sit on the bed.

'But you've only just got here.' Miriam's large camera bobs, sticking out against her rather ample bosom. 'You can't go home.'

David will be somewhere in luxury. There would be no 'shabby' in his chic surrounds, no matter how tongue-in-cheek the presentation. Everyone well presented - him in his shirt. Even when David does manage to relax, you can tell he is A Man In A Suit. He relishes it.

And didn't I, too? He was slimmer when we first met. A full head of hair. Clean shaven. I had been hesitant; he'd had to woo me.

In the end, I enjoyed his assertive nature. A delightful contradiction to my indecision, my *flighty side*, he used to joke. He continued to say that but after a while—

I can still be decisive.

'For goodness sake, Miriam, they are going to bungee jump. Of course, I cannot bungee.'

I roll my tights into a ball.

'What about your daughter?'

My eyes dart to Miriam's mouth.

'Won't she wonder why you gave up?'

There is a flower print on the wall - framed wallpaper, no doubt an ironic nod to what was here before. Renoir's roses, I believe.

'I'm different to them.'

'It's just age. Just a number. They'll be like us one day.'

Ugh. Look at my clothes, the pathetic few items aligned in neat piles across the bedspread.

'You don't have to do any of the activities if you don't want to.'

Bertie. She won't believe it. She said I need independence.

'This is my first time travelling alone.'

Out of the window, a slither of a gap between the curtains exposes the street outside. A camper van rumbles past.

'The trick is always to have a book,' Miriam says. 'Have a book, and you don't need friends. But do push yourself to speak to others. It's amazing, at home I surround myself in the same bubble of people, and I rarely talk to anyone new, yet I come away, and I have instant friends. Every time.'

I think of Patricia and Hugo. Our 'circle'.

'Have you done much travelling, then?'

'Oh, the usual - India, Bali, Thailand, you know . . .'

I nod. But I don't know. I can't even begin to imagine.

'You know the thing I love best about it?' Miriam says. 'You can be whoever you want to be. Travel is reinvention.'

Reinvention. I play the word over in my mind. 'My aim was to keep a low profile. Just get through the days. Prepare to meet my husband.'

'Prepare?'

'Oh, I mean to say enjoy the quiet, the sunshine. Just relax.'

'I suppose if you want that sort of holiday . . .'

I look up to the challenge in Miriam's voice. Her face shifts, as though all of her features are growing, being used as they are intended - eyes lighting, cheeks lifting.

She clasps both hands over her camera. 'Australia is a playground. There's adventure out there.'

'Perhaps.'

'You said your daughter had a great time here. Don't you want to find out why?'

My breath is in my chest.

'You don't want to miss out, do you?'

Goodness. Is this woman telling me what it is that I need?

Miriam paces the small space. 'I understand that maybe it's not typical in your group.' She wafts her hand as though the group are here with me. Gosh. How would Patricia set her face if I suggested surfing instead of sewing this week? I can't help but give a little grin. 'But to try a new sport, especially one that involves an element of the extreme, is exciting. I want you to question whether deep down you feel you *should* say no because it's not something you would not normally do, or if you genuinely don't want to do it.' Miriam has stopped in front of me, standing in a manner not dissimilar from David - as though she has every right to be in the room, even when uninvited - wide feet, hips thrust forward. 'Come on, Dee. Don't miss out.'

My head jerks.

'Oh, I'm sorry,' Miriam says. 'I heard you tell Sofia. Do you mind if I call you Dee? It's just I had an aunt called Diane and she . . . well. Hey, you could use the name in your reinvention - think of it as a character you're playing, you know?' Miriam hops, throwing her arms out to the sides: '*Hi, I'm Dee Dee. I wear thongs, and I like to surf.*' Miriam ends her impression with a honk of laughter, clapping her hands.

Dee Dee.

I look at the floor. A gnarled bit of wood has come loose from the floorboard, and a dusty hole remains. 'Only one other person has ever called me Dee Dee.'

The desk creaks under the weight of Miriam's rear. 'Ah. A special someone?'

I exhale a silent response. He used to whisper it, his thumb brushing my cheek.

Miriam's eyes are on me in that way Francis does - surreptitiously *sussing me out*, as Bertie would say.

'I was always Dee to my friends, and then I met David, and he preferred Diane, so—' I offer a shrug.

I try to fixate on a pink flower embroidered on the bedspread, but I can't seem to make it stay still.

'So, this David,' Miriam says. 'I assume he's your ex-husband?'

'Oh, no. Current.' Hm. Perhaps this sounds unlikely, given my travel status. 'He's on business,' I manage. 'We're meeting up at the wedding - his nephew's wedding, the one in Southport.'

'How very modern.'

'And you? Do you have a husband?'

'Yes. He's at home. I like to travel alone.'

I sense Miriam doesn't want me to pry and—

Well. I'm not Francis. 'How long are you travelling for?' Goodness, I hadn't thought to inquire whether Miriam would be here the whole time. How stupid of me. What if she—

'Four weeks.'

Oh, thank goodness.

'Look,' Miriam is crouching at my feet, extending a hand onto my arm. 'I'll look after you.'

I think of telling Francis I'm going home. Patricia at the next Sewing Bee. If I stay here, I'll miss that.

'And the bungee?'

'Absolutely not. Just the activities you want to do. Or, if you really must, just sun-seeking and sight-seeing.'

The brown of Miriam's eyes are so dark the iris is almost indistinguishable from the pupil. For some reason, I find myself trusting. *A gentle aura*, Bertie would say.

'When I'm travelling, I have a motto.'

I raise my eyebrows in question.

'Just say yes.'

'Just say yes?'

'What have we got to lose?' Miriam takes my hands in hers. A frightfully intimate gesture. Normally, I would find this awkward. 'Just say yes?'

'You sound like one of them,' I laugh. But ... my chin lifts a fraction, despite myself.

Bertie's parting smile at the airport.

Brave.

'Okay,' I whisper. 'Let's go surfing.'

DAY THREE

Surfing. Goodness. Am I really about to embark on such an act? Or am I in one of those terrible movies where it turns out I was dreaming?

But, alas, one cannot deny the chafing of this wetsuit. That is most certainly real. My limbs constricted by the thick rubber, as though I've fallen into freshly laid tarmac. At home, I have to wrap my arms around myself when I walk past such roadworks, physically restricting my movements in case I lose control and my urge to jump overwhelms. I'm the same at the railway station, wondering what would happen if I stepped into the path of an oncoming train.

Miriam. She has also been very real this morning - proffering coffee, an unassuming smile, leading the way. This is how it feels to have company, and I can't deny its positive after-taste. A distraction from the darkness, if nothing else. I was rather glad to be persuaded against returning to bed. That sort of thing is not always so easy.

And David? He is not a man given to languor. Up early and dressed in formal clothes, regardless of the day. Always a shirt, possibly a polo shirt if he's trying to play golf. I say 'try' because, bless him, he is not a gifted player. Golf is one of those sports he

associates with *men of his type*. Elitist? Possibly. Invariably a
point or two behind the rest, *below par*, unfortunately.

My father is another man given to formality, 'proper'
behaviour. Perhaps that's why I feel the need to rebel against it
now. Is my father still holding down those laws with his pre-
teen sons ('tweens')?

Goodness. The ridiculousness of all that. Even here, on the
other side of the world, I remain embarrassed on his behalf.

Or maybe the embarrassment is my attempt to divert away
from this moment, standing in this group of lithe youngsters,
like a huddle of baby seals. I'm not sure where to place myself -
the out-of-place whale? No. I am the runt of the litter - the mite
that gets left behind and ravaged by polar bears.

We stand in a semicircle on the beach - Miriam to my left,
the *gap-yar* girls to my right, two blond males on either end
who I can't help but notice exemplify the unequal appropria-
tion of the human gene. The younger English one, Jake, I think
is his name, is spindly with translucent white skin, while the
German - Hans? - is a super-sized version of a man with a
healthy tan. Both of them have overgrown sandy hair but Jake's
falls rather limp and sad, hanging down either side of his face
('curtains?'), while Hans's bounces back like that of a film star.
The English boy looks scared. Mr German looks bored. I
expect he is keen to skip this safety chat and get straight into
the sea.

Goodness. The sea - a reassuring good few metres in front
of us, providing a constant soundtrack of calming relief. Funny,
really, when you consider it's fortitude. How dangerous an
ocean can be. Not that the colour of this water looks anything
other than tranquil. One would use broken colours to depict
water in a painting but this seascape is a stunning vision of
pure turquoise, turning to the brightest blue at the horizon; the
sun's rays bouncing off the surface in acute silver triangles.

The board sits at my feet. Massive, cumbersome. How will I

even carry that thing down the beach, let alone manoeuvre it in water? Perhaps I'll rebel and use the board as a Lilo . . .

'So, how are we all feeling today? Everyone ready to get warmed up?' This is Michael - the young lad from the surf shop, the one in charge of supplying this 'fun'. Michael seems to be having his own rebellion. He is bony and well-curated. He sports a 'top knot', I think they're called, a catalogue of tattoos run the length of his skinny arms (a 'sleeve'?), and he has one of those neat little slug-like moustaches. It is appearances like these that confirm how out of touch I have become, because the word that comes to mind when I observe such a character as Michael is: *odd*. It recently came to my attention that there are more and more odd people inhabiting the world.

Although, Michael is really rather affable. Gentle of voice, a contradiction to the tough exterior he seems keen to convey. And not at all *judgey* (thank you, Bertie), but, in fact, reassuring and encouraging, even. While everyone else in the group had grappled for a wetsuit in the wooden shack at the top of the beach, he took me aside and asked if I would like him to assist with my fitting. Then he did the same with my board.

And now he is here, *bantering* (again, thank you, Bertie), while we warm up (star jumps, for goodness sake . . .) and wait for someone called Tom.

I concentrate on my breath.

Apparently, the German man, Hans, thinks he'll be able to *hang ten* (?) on his first run, but my money is on Jake, who possesses a quiet confidence. I think the fear I sensed may result from his wanting to talk to Indie.

Or is that Lola?

'He was so hot. I pulled a great one there.' Yes, this one is Lola. Evidently, she deems it acceptable behaviour to discuss her love life when we are all within earshot.

Indie tactfully changes the subject.

I raise an eyebrow at Miriam.

'That's nothing,' Miriam says, opting to cease the ridiculous star jumps. 'The girls I teach in secondary school are far more out there. You'd be disgusted at the topics they're happy to discuss.'

'Well . . .' This is all I can say on the matter. As always, I maintain the position that a little decorum is not anti-feminist, but polite. Still, Bertie thinks I blur the line between *polite* and *insular*. She tells me it's better to state my feelings, lest they eat me up.

I tell my daughter that on this, we must agree to disagree. Although, of course, there was that one time, when I built myself up to say exactly how I felt, to finally make a change and then—

Well.

'Tom' has arrived. I'm relieved to see he is not as I'd expected. In fact, the boy is not what I expected at all. More of a man, really. You can tell he is a person of the sea; sea folk have a way about them. Relaxed, mostly. They possess a certain comfort of being in their bodies, aware and content with the physical space they inhabit. I can't help but contrast this to David, whose unease with his own physique puts one ever-so-slightly on edge. I'm not sure it's obvious to all – apparent only in the minutiae of his movements. Shoulders never quite released of tension, his continual need to occupy his hands - a wine glass, a cigar, a pocket, a pen. You don't notice these things as things, really, until you meet someone so contrasting. I expect Tom has no idea what a *bottom line* is (one of David's most exhausted sayings), and I expect he doesn't care to know.

I have often felt the same.

Tom moves along the line, asking people about their experience of the sea, surf, their swimming ability. It's all very thorough. Lola and Indie giggle like girls half their age as he passes.

No doubt Tom is used to this. A person in this line of work. And, well, it would be strange not to mention his looks.

Because he is somewhat striking. Tanned skin, that I would imagine has roots in Europe, and a strong jaw. It's interesting - the jaw - I've always thought it can give someone an air of self-assurance. A certain confidence. David is the only one of his school friends to have a rather weak jaw, I noticed recently.

'Hi there.'

'Hello,' I say.

Tom has paused. His gaze flickers across my face, his brow spasms a fraction.

'I'm Dee,' I offer.

He clears his face and his throat. 'Have you surfed before, Dee?'

Oh, goodness. I have just released an impromptu laugh, as I imagined myself at the book club, telling the women I went surfing. No doubt they'll think I'm fibbing. They'll share that look they all seem to have perfected of late, thinking they are being discreet when, of course, I can see. 'No,' I reply, once I've composed my face back to neutral.

And suddenly I'm frowning. I mean, really, can I expect to do this? Francis will think I'm mad and, this time, perhaps she would be right.

'It's a silly idea, isn't it?' I keep my voice low, leaning a little into Tom's space. He smells of manliness. Sweat, I suppose, which is understandable, given it is warm today, but it's not a repugnant smell, it's actually rather . . . pleasant.

I draw back and look at my toes. Neatly trimmed and painted nude for this, my anniversary trip. When I sat watching the dear girl give me a pedicure, I can say with absolute certainty I would not expect to see my feet sticking out of a wetsuit beside a surfboard. I am rather glad I held my ground on the nude colour, and not that ghastly red she had tried to force on me. *Be a little wild*, she'd said. What I refrained from telling her is that these days, 'wild' is switching the filling of

David's sandwich. If it's not egg mayonnaise, he is not a happy man.

Gosh. Egg mayonnaise. How lovely it's been to not think of that for a few days.

'Last year we had an eighty-year-old join us surfing. If he can do it, you most certainly can.' The depth of Tom's voice matches his dark looks, and it sends waves of purple through my mind. The sort of voice that, if it were raised, would reverberate through your chest. Like the bass at a rock concert.

'Eighty? Wow.'

'Can you swim?'

'Yes.' Although, when was the last time I swam in the sea? The time that springs to mind is— Goodness. Not *that*. That was years ago - a lifetime ago. I had been nude. *Skinny dipping*.

Heat creeps up my neck and I am forced to swallow.

'You'll be fine,' Tom says. 'But I'll be there to keep an eye on you.'

It's only as he moves onto Miriam that I realise I'm smiling.

I have made it to the shore. My toes are in the water. I have the board under my arm and I was advancing quite merrily, really, but—

I can't go in. Of course I can't.

'Dee?'

Tom. I nod, emit a rather odd noise, like something being strangled . . . I try to lift my quivering lips into a smile.

Goodness. What must I look like?

Everyone else has trotted into the water, excitable chat, Miriam included, but I am rooted to the sand. The last piece of land before . . .

That.

'You don't like the sea?'

'No, I love the sea, I—' *For God's sake, Diane.* 'It's been a while.'

Tom lowers his board on the sand and stands beside me, arms folded, staring out at the vista. What seemed like a tranquil Impressionist depiction from afar has transformed into the Japanese art of Hokusai. *Under the Great Wave Off—*

Somewhere.

A wave laps over my feet and as it pulls away, my feet sink deeper into the sand; every wave an attack, my feet retreating, hiding. I swallow again, my mouth dry, my shoulder pinching with the weight of the board.

'It's probably harder to stand still, you know? All you have to do is get over the break, and then you can chill out.'

'*Over the break?*' My voice is timid, testing. How does Tom know—?

'I'll help you.'

'I…'

'See where your friend is now?' Tom points to Miriam, who is bobbing up over a wave, her arms paddling in a way reminiscent of a bath toy Bertie used to have - a duck you could wind up and then watch its little red legs circling it round and round, and Bertie would giggle her cheeky little laugh, the best comedy she'd ever seen.

'That's where the waves are breaking. That's *the break.*'

'Right.' Yes, I feel a fool.

'I'll help you get past that point, and then I can push you in. Easy.'

'Easy?'

Tom smiles with only one half of his mouth. 'Easy.' Tom's manner is what I would describe as 'easy'; affable, relaxed.

I close my eyes. The sun is high, and there's a possibility my body might boil in this black material. From further out come screams of joy, cheering amongst the waves.

Be a part of it, Mum, I hear Bertie teasing.

Miriam is waving. I lift a finger in response, but I doubt she sees.

'Come on, Dee!' she adds, her arm now beckoning.

Oh, goodness.

My lungs empty every morsel of air as my head gives the briefest of nods, but it's enough for Tom to see. He places a hand on my elbow, and leads me in.

'Wow, now that's a smile,' Tom says, as I pass Michael my board and thank him for his assistance. Tom sits behind a desk at the far end of the surf shack, his hair still damp, a display of leaflets advertising his surf school face out. The place is full of boards down one side, and hanging clothes scatter the space between the door and the desk.

I laugh and turn. How marvellous the boards look racked up along the wall - their bright colours and shiny edges like a merry art installation.

The others in our group enter and exit, chattering loudly about their experiences in the waves. Their conversations wash in and out, not unlike waves themselves. A low bubbling blue ripples in my mind, but I return focus to Tom. He has been looking at me, I notice, but he returns his gaze to his laptop as I turn.

'Thank you again,' I say. 'For helping me out there. I know it was only one wave but . . .' My voice trails off. I did it. Tom took me 'out back' and I caught a wave. Okay, so I only stood up for a second, but I did it.

I did it.

'Hey, it's a start. And starting is often the hardest part.'

'Have you worked here for long?' I am aiming for casual. For younger?

Goodness.

'Er, yeah, every summer as a kid. It was my uncle's place, and I took it over about seven years ago.'

Seven years.

We make eye contact, me and Tom, and I nod, the world in slow motion . . . Or is it fast forward? My mind plummeting into the here and now, just as the surfboard had crashed beneath the wave.

But I hadn't been scared. I let the wave take me, noticing the roar of rushing water in my ears, and I just ... was.

Tom sits back in his chair, looks at Michael, returns his gaze to me. 'I'm considering maybe . . . I don't know.' He leans forward, elbows on the table, shaking his head.

I step closer.

'This is great - the surf school, you know - but I'd like my own—' He pauses, pushing back on the desk. 'I don't know. It's stupid.'

I tilt my head.

'I don't know why I'm telling you.' A false laugh. I should think these apparent nerves, this second guessing, is uncharacteristic.

I find I don't know how to respond. Because I don't know, either.

'Here she is, Queen of the Waves,' Miriam's voice singsongs into the lofty space.

Before turning, I select a leaflet from the display stand. I fold it into a small square and then turn to my friend. Miriam and Tom are exchanging more 'banter'. This is seemingly the way we communicate with strangers here. A change from the down-turned face of ignorance I perfected in England. Not that I felt unhappy doing that, I rather prefer being discreet, but here . . .

I need not hide. Here, I am unknown.

'I'm not sure about Queen,' I say, as I step next to Miriam. The sound of this woman cheering me on the wave will stay with me forever.

She hangs a casual arm around my shoulder. 'Impressive,' she says, squeezing before she lets go. She runs her hand along the boards. 'These are beautiful.' Not for the first time, I notice how easily Miriam moves in the world. How, like Tom, she has a certain comfort in her skin. I imagine bad things just roll off her, not penetrating. Like the water droplets sitting on the wax of these boards. 'Do you make your own?'

'My own boards?' Tom has left his desk and we stand in a line of three.

'Actually,' he says, dipping his head towards me, 'that's what I'd love to do - to make my own. More of them, anyway. Maybe have my own brand one day.'

'You should,' Miriam says, without pause. 'You're in the right place. It appears you have the perfect setup to start.'

Tom nods, but it's not convincing. On this topic, he speaks differently.

Goodness. I sound as bad as Miriam. Poor lad, what do I know?

'It's not that easy, you know - start-up costs, bank loans ...' He crosses his arms, clutching his armpits so his thumbs rest on his chest.

'All doable, I should think,' Miriam answers, breezy. I deduce she is ready to go.

A laugh. 'Well, we all have dreams, right?'

I look at Tom then - hope in his gaze but, for some reason, defeat creeps in. He looks down.

Miriam is at the door, laughing with Michael now.

I step closer. 'Hold on to it,' I hear myself saying. 'The dream, I mean.'

And I nod at Tom, and I follow Miriam out of the shack.

To: LibertyBridges@icloud.com
Subject: I made it . . .
From: MrsDBridges@outlook.com

Dear Bertie

Well, you'll be amazed to know I have made it
to Australia. I can't quite believe I'm
writing those words but, yes, I am here. Bit
of a mix up with your father but it appears
I'll be here alone . . . Long story, but I'm
fine. Although I have to admit I had
initially been quite put out. Auntie Francis
insisted I return home, and I almost followed
her instruction, but I thought of you and
what a lovely time you had here so I wanted
to come and see for myself. I know I should
have come sooner, I always said I wanted to
travel and, well, I guess these things get
put on the back burner.

Oh, and I met a friendly lady - a little
forward, I must say, but I think of you
telling me to be more outgoing - so I am
trying to be friends.

'Up the East Coast,' I can hear you saying,
and now I am here, I realise what a tremen-
dously brave thing that was of you to have
done by yourself. I'm not sure I ever
expressed how proud I am of you, Bertie. You
told me the easier option was to stay in your
London job and although at the time I agreed

with Dad, now I'm here, I can see why the
harder choice was to go. Better for your
soul, you said. And it was at that point I
realised you were doing the right thing. This
is something I can understand because I was
the person who wasn't brave . . .

But, as I said, I'm here, and I realise I
want you to be proud of me, too. I hope
you are.

All my love,
Mum x

―――――

I am in - oh, my - a bar. I cannot quite believe it, but a bar it is. The last time I frequented a place serving alcohol, which was not the local pub at the end of a country walk, was—

Goodness. Two years ago? Not a pub, but that wine bar Patricia dragged us along to in town. The opening night and it used plastic glasses. I *mean* - can you imagine? Gosh. David's face - the contortion of his mouth as he'd realised this was not a joke he didn't get. This was not modern irony in action; he really was expected to drink from plastic and perch on a 'bar stool'.

Suffice to say, the place soon shut down. I don't live in a town for bars and 'clubs'. Rather, we have country pubs frequented by people in big cars, wellington boots, and wax jackets. There are often as many dogs as there are humans.

This bar I'm in now - just a few doors down from the hostel - is furnished with as much wood as my local country pub, though it doesn't evoke the same upmarket vibe. My skin sticks to the table whenever I move my arm, so I opt for tucking my elbows into my sides. Consume as little space as possible. Perhaps then I'll go unnoticed, which would be a blessing as we're meeting here for an *initiation*. Some godawful meeting where we no doubt have to go around the table and *tell our stories*, recalling the anecdotes nobody has yet heard - a morsel of information to cement ourselves in the memories of others. *Oh, yes, the girl who dated Prince Harry*, or *the man who was an extra on the latest Star Wars movie*. Goodness. And what on earth is my morsel? *The woman who lost her love?*

Gosh. Could said husband be enjoying his own initiation somewhere? No doubt a five-star experience: Champagne, a complimentary massage. No, he doesn't like to be touched, he'd pass on that, but it could be anywhere in the world, I suppose.

I tried to duck out of this situation but Miriam insisted it was vital to my *settling in*. And I saw Sofia, the professional Swiss receptionist, and Eric - one of the owners of the hostel - exchanging rather stern words outside earlier and they didn't seem like the sort of people you would want to disagree with. Sofia with her slick hair and the posture of someone in control, a yogi, no doubt (everyone is nowadays, aren't they?), and Eric, by contrast, smaller, diminished in some way.

Tired of fighting? Perhaps.

I can understand.

In the end, I concluded it was better to observe the local custom.

Besides, who am I kidding? I'm hardly one to break the rules.

Bertie would vouch for that.

'Dee, a glass for you?' Hm. Why is Jake reaching an empty glass toward me? His look of fear is back - his eyes only ever darting up to meet mine momentarily, the pronounced Adam's apple in his long neck bobbing on repeat.

'A glass?' Ah. I've just spotted the jug of beer in the centre of the table. 'Oh, no. I'd rather white wine, thank you. Dry.'

Jake looks at the glass in his hand, bewildered, as though he thought he was holding a wine all along. 'Of course,' he says, finally, scurrying his skinny frame over to the bar. No doubt Jake had a growth spurt in his late teens and soon enough his body will realise and fill out. Not that he can be much older than a teenager. He certainly dresses like a teenager in that pink t-shirt and rather lurid green board shorts. *Boardies*, I remember Bertie saying once. If he wants to spend an evening with Indie or Lola, I suspect he'll need to rethink his outfit choice.

Goodness. Listen to me. My tweed skirt is hardly inspiring, is it? Didn't I too used to love fashion? I liked *whacky clothes*, as David named them. I enjoyed making a statement. But after we married, David said my sartorial choices no longer seemed *appropriate*.

Jake and I were the first ones to arrive, and I took my place in the most covert position in the booth. But I realise my error as people are moving in alongside me and I will soon be blocked, unable to escape. Not without causing a fuss, anyway. The light is dim in here - as, I suppose, these places are designed to be. A low acoustic track plays in the background, the pleasant voice of a male singer: flowery, chirpy, but it's difficult to distinguish any lyrics above the cacophony of chatter. The sounds create a wash of colours in my mind that brings to mind a tie-dye t-shirt I so used to love. Did I pass that on to Bertie?

Ah. Miriam has just arrived - late, I notice - and I'd like to catch her eye but she is laughing at the bar with the other hostel owner - the bigger one, Shaun, was it? I too met Shaun on arrival – he gave me a name badge, for goodness sake - but I did not engage at length. I had only a minute to spare until the advertised start time and—

Well. I shouldn't have bothered rushing as we're now ten minutes past that.

Miriam and Shaun are joined by the other owner, Eric. A funny pair of men - Eric and Shaun. Like the characters from a Roald Dahl novel - what was that one Bertie used to enjoy? *Fantastic Mr Fox*, yes. *The Bogey Man*, she used to say, although I'm not entirely confident that was one of the character names. When David was out, I would draw her their pictures - exaggerated features, characters easy to delineate between good and bad. Not so simple in real life, unfortunately.

And then, of course, all the crayons were confiscated, and it was not so simple to do anything of the sort ...

Finally, the members of our group are together, Lola and Indie squeezing in beside Miriam, who I waved over so as not to be alone with Hans. An amenable enough chap, though I can't help but liken him to one of those army action figures Francis's boys used to play with: hard and unmalleable, bashing into each other with startling force.

'Welcome, everyone.' This is Shaun. He has a jaunty voice, up and down it goes, like one of those playground things that used to make me quite sick, but I would persevere just to hear Bertie's dear little giggle.

Something beginning with S . . .

Not the slide . . . Or swing . . . Or . . .

See-saw!

Of course.

Goodness.

Oh, everyone has turned their gaze this way. Ah, it's okay, Hans is talking: 'I want to understand whether I have a purpose aside from propping up the capitalist grind.' Goodness. *A bit deep*, Bertie would say.

Although, never to David or I. We were never *deep enough*, she once said. But, I mean, I think I have a point here. These 'millennials' could make 'dossing' sound profound.

Or is 'millennial' an outdated term now?

'Dee?'

'Excuse me?'

'Do you want to tell the group why you're here?' Shaun flares out his hands. Jazz hands? 'What I didn't say is that if you're interesting, I may put you in my memoir.' (Oh, good grief. A memoir?)

'Dee?'

'Oh, erm . . .' Picture the box.

Rise and fall.

'Didn't you say you wanted to do some sight-seeing, Dee?' Miriam's voice. She is nodding. Encouraging.

'Er . . . Yes. That sounds good. Sight-seeing, thank you.' I place my hands back in my lap, resting them on the itchy fabric.

I am rather looking forward to getting back into my new leggings. Something soft, plain.

Discreet.

Miriam's turn: 'Well, I . . . I suppose I wanted time away to better myself . . . You know.' The sentence ends with a smile, a shrug, a self-conscious sip of beer.

Hm. A peculiar statement. Miriam seems perfectly *better* already.

But, what do I know? And, goodness, what do these gap year girls know? *I'm looking for fun before my serious studies start*, Lola has just said, a flick of long hair over one shoulder.

That's if she doesn't ruin all her brain cells with cheap alcohol first . . .

'Indie?'

'Oh, er . . .' Indie. The blonde one of the two. A face to be admired. Not unlike Botticelli's *Venus,* in fact. Or is the resemblance closer to Vermeer's *Girl With a Pearl Earring*?

Yes. Vermeer could do a wonderful portrait of Indie's wide-eyes, the slightly parting mouth. There's an innocence to her face. I find myself wanting to tell the dear girl that everything will be okay.

'Same as Lola, really,' Indie adds, her voice purring.

'And last but most definitely not least, Jake.' Shaun's jazz hands reach to Jake who is quick to answer. No doubt the lad's been planning his retort since we started the godawful game.

'I'm with Dee. I just want to see the sights.' Jake casts a brief look toward Indie, then 'downs' the rest of his drink.

'Well,' Shaun says, 'an interesting group. Eric and I are very grateful you have chosen to stay in our hostel—' I glance at Eric. I don't know the man, granted, but I can say with a lot of confidence he is not very grateful. '—and we hope you'll enjoy all Byron offers. There's several excursions we can book for you, and I have some information here . . .'

I tune out. I know, I'm sorry, Bertie. It's just—

Organised fun? For goodness sake. Isn't the best kind of fun spontaneous?

Look at surfing. I hadn't planned on doing that, had I?

'And ladies, what's the first port of call for you? Will you be doing a bungee during your stay?' Hans has left the table, and Shaun shuffles around in his place.

He laughs at my expression, which I should think makes clear my thoughts about the bungee.

'Oh, that's right, Miriam, darling, you told me already. You two doing are doing the art—'

'The art course,' Miriam interjects, somewhat rudely. I give her *the eyes,* as Bertie would say, but Miriam just smiles and asks Shaun if he knows the venue.

'Yes, darling. Madison Gallery. The talk of the town, lately.' Shaun ends the sentence with a flap of his hand. It's a surprising move from a man of such stature.

'Really?' Miriam leans forward.

'Oh, just some silly falling-out between the owners. I heard Vinnie stormed off one day and left Alexandra in the lurch, and now that dear girl must run the entire place alone.'

'Oh, goodness, doesn't sound like a very professional way to run a business?' I say. Imagine David storming off from his place of work and, well— David would not. He would ensure the other person did the walking, I'm sure.

Shaun casts a conspiratorial look around the bar. 'I have a feeling they based the relationship on more than just business, if you understand my meaning.'

'Ah. Somewhat trickier to navigate, then.'

'Yeeees,' he says. 'The poor things have all my sympathies, of course. It's not easy.'

I offer what I hope is an understanding sigh, but I'm distracted by the looseness of this man. Shaun is of the same height and build as David, but I feel it would suit him better to be short.

'Did you and Eric buy the hostel together?' Miriam says.

'Well, strictly speaking, it's Eric's place, darling, but he'd be ruined without me!' At this point, Shaun lets out a sort of jolly evil laugh, if such a thing can exist. Like a villain in one of those dreadful pantomimes Bertie used to enjoy. And, gosh, didn't Patricia tell me they were having a revival? Pantomime becoming *cool* again, apparently.

Well. The mind boggles.

'I pulled that man up from the graveside and bought him back to life and back to business. You know he wanted to make this place into one of those ghastly nightclubs? No natural light and a heavy bass. I shudder at the thought.' Shaun flaps his hand again. 'The hours we'd be keeping! Can you imagine?'

Miriam laughs. 'How long have you worked together?'

At this, Shaun reshapes his mouth, as though trying to suppress a smile: 'Thirty years, darling. Can you believe it?'

'Wonderful!' Miriam says.

I nod, my lips pursed. I can't not purse them. Yes, I can imagine thirty years but—

Well. My thirty don't seem to resemble theirs.

'Do you miss England?' Miriam says.

I lean forward, intrigued to know Shaun's answer, but there's the unsavoury feel of the table on my skin. I recoil into myself. Like one of those yo-yos Bertie used to play with, the string winding back in just as quickly as it had unfurled.

'Oh darling, you know, I do. I would love Eric to visit my family, but he insists he can't leave the bloody place. All my fault, I suppose, as I was the one who pushed him to take it on.' I hadn't registered Shaun's English accent. It's there, but it's been afflicted with that rather annoying habit of Australian intonation in which every sentence must end on a high note, thus transforming all normal sentences into questions.

'You have no one to cover?'

'Well, yes, we have Sofia now who is marvellous. But,

between me and you,' he scans the bar again, before leaning back toward us, 'I suspect Sofia and Eric are a little too similar. It's why she runs the place so well, but it's also why he is reluctant to let go. Twisted logic, but I'm not sure he trusts her yet. Something we're working on. Hey, perhaps I should send him along to the art course with you!' He belts out another hurrah of unselfconscious laughter and excuses himself.

'Why would the art course be good for someone lacking trust, Miriam?' I know I can be a little dimwitted with jokes, slow to *get with the times*, as Bertie says, but I feel I'm missing something here.

Miriam gulps too much beer, then returns her glass to the table, empty. The beat of the music is making itself known, the acoustic becoming more 'rock', the volume increased. 'Art is therapeutic, I suppose.'

'Yes. I suppose it is.'

Was. Once.

Shaun joins Eric, full and large beside small and scrawny. Shaun appears to be telling a story I should think he has told many times previous. Shaun's entire performance tonight seems well-rehearsed.

'Do you think they're—' I nod toward Eric and Shaun.

'Gay?' Miriam says.

My eyes dart. I'm not sure what they're looking for.

'Yes, Dee, those men are gay. Is that okay?'

'Of course . . . I went to art school. Most of my friends were gay.'

'You went to art school?'

'Don't look so shocked, Miriam. Anyway. Nowadays . . . in my circle—'

'I can imagine.'

'What?'

'You'd be surprised, Dee. It's not always obvious.'

I sit with this comment for a moment. Would I be

surprised? Now, possibly. Though my life used to be diverse. *Colourful*, was David's description of the friends I had when we met.

Once upon a time.

But the fairytale plays out, and the protagonist must adjust to make room for other characters. Like that movie . . ?

The Wizard of Oz. Yes. Bertie loved that story. Doesn't the film begin in black and white?

Indeed. Dorothy is caught up in a tornado, and once she arrives in the Land of Oz, everything turns to colour.

The Land of Oz.

Well. I won't draw any parallels.

Although, I can't help but wonder, what will happen if I tap my heels together?

DAY FOUR

I've been giving so much energy to wondering how I'll cope, I have given little thought to how David might be managing. He's good at being alone; he doesn't have the same 'needs' as I, but—

Still. We've shared a life for thirty years . . .

David is not like my other friends' husbands. Some of them sound as though they can't even boil a kettle, the nitwits.

Not that I'm coping overly well here in the hostel kitchen. I've never known a kitchen so large. The white walls and steel surfaces give it a school or hospital vibe. *Institutional* is the word that comes to mind. I take a moment to work out how to flick the tap on the perma-boil cylinder thing and, eventually, water splutters into the cup. I search the cupboards for a tea bag.

Oh, thank goodness. *Tetley.*

Something familiar. Although—

It doesn't taste as it should. Different water, I suppose. Not hot enough. And this mug does not sit in my hand the way my favourite mug at home does. I can't cradle it. It's not bone china with a gentle bottom, but tin and angular. Odd. At least I have a view of a garden through the window. Not that this is anything like my usual view of a long, green lawn. The hostel 'garden' comprises a small wooden deck, a picnic bench and here, on the windowsill, sits a window box full of small flowers, their petals white with yellow insides that look almost fake. Maybe they are fake. Despite the sunny skies, it is still winter, after all.

My stomach groans. I'll have some grapefruit from the 'buffet breakfast' while I wait for the bread to finish in the oven. I'd got chatting to the receptionist Sofia on my return from the bar last night - she had been laying up the breakfast selection in advance - and when I'd mentioned I was missing my English toast she insisted I make bread myself. She said Eric and Shaun love people to feel at home and that people would appreciate my baking. The tools and ingredients were dug out there and then.

And so, at dawn, awaking before anyone else, I got to it. There's something about the slamming of the dough, having to get a bit rough and tough with the kneading . . . It's therapeutic. I built up quite a sweat, in fact.

I've stopped cooking much at home. David leaves before I get up in the mornings and I've often lost my appetite come evening time. I might pick at some toast, but David will eat out with clients, or both of us wait to be fed at our regular meet-ups with Patricia and Hugo, snacks at book club . . . Of course, we always return the hosting duties. But mostly we make do with takeaways in the winter and barbecues in the summer. Not that I mind cooking, but I suppose it just . . . ended up that way. Things took a turn one year and we never got back on track. David made adjustments and those adjustments have stuck.

I wonder what David is eating. Gosh. I feel sorry for the staff of whatever hotel he's staying at. He needs somebody's ear to bend. Someone to hear his complaint about the *state of the eggs.* Or - yes, this is more likely - the *state of the market* or the *morons running our political system.*

That's if he's staying in a hotel, of course. Perhaps he's taken himself to some bespoke campsite ('off-the-grid glamping'?)

pitching itself as one of 'Nature's Most Authentic Health Resorts'. Will David wear the swim shorts I retrieved from the back of the wardrobe? I hold little hope of them fitting as they've been hiding in the cupboard since we went to that four-star hotel in the Cotswolds last year, and even then he didn't go in the pool. Gosh, yes, he'd gone on the biking excursion and I've never had to stifle laughter like it - a middle-aged man with a ballooned stomach should not be seen in Lyrca. He looked like one of those bright-coloured water balloons Bertie used to enjoy filling. If you compressed the thing in your fist, it would protrude out at odd angles, threatening to burst under pressure. I'd prayed David didn't reach his arms up and risk exposing that slither of white skin, the scattering of red pimples from the rash we've never fathomed visible to all. I've maintained my position that the irritation must be down to stress, but he insists it's nothing. *Just an allergy, Diane.*

Could this departure be further evidence of his being overstressed? What if he's not even in Australia, but has taken himself on some extreme mountaineering excursion or some such? I read recently that you can pay a person to push you to the limits to discover your 'real self' (one for you, Bertie), like that irritating man on the TV who miraculously got commissioned to take Barack Obama trekking. Patricia had insisted it was all for tele, that Obama and the other celebrities were sure to be staying in a five-star hotel nearby, but I like to believe.

Or is it that I suspend disbelief?

'Wow, good morning. It smells fantastic in here. Are you baking bread?' I smile at Hans. *Bwead.* A chink in the armour of what otherwise appears to be one of God's examples of How To Create Man. Not that I believe in God.

Well, not now . . .

'I hope people don't mind,' I say. It does smell superb in here - the air is thick with the scent.

Hans fills a bowl with every fruit on offer, tops it up with yoghurt and nuts, takes another bowl with cold oats, and a further bowl with three rolls and six packets of butter. 'They have nothing cooked, no?'

'It seems not.' I rinse out my cup as the timer pings on the oven, glad of the job I must finish. It's these 'small talk' situations I find uncomfortable in institutions such as this. (Miriam had laughed out loud at my use of the word *institution* when I'd expressed this concern yesterday. She had insisted that *some anonymous, soul-less hotel would not deliver the experience we need*, to which I offered no retort.)

As I open the oven door, the waft of heat is startling in both temperature and voracity. *Ha, see David? I can put myself in extreme situations, too.*

'Is that for everyone?' Hans dabs his mouth with a napkin, having already demolished the contents of his bowls.

'Yes, but it will need a minute or two to cool.' I use a tea towel to lift the bread from the tin and close my eyes to concentrate on the scent. I am reminded of Bertie at, what? Three years old? No, she must have been two. My mother was still with us. But it was near the end, a task of distraction, a break from keeping vigil. My mother even tried a small piece of the loaf. But goodness, no matter how sick one is, it would be hard to resist a two-year-old Bertie. She was such a cute toddler. One of those children you know beyond doubt will be bright, like she was lit from the inside and her light shone out of her large, innocent eyes, not yet touched by disappointment or fear. Such a blessing, our baby. No wonder David had been saddened not to have had more.

'Dee?'

'Yes?' I look up too quickly; my vision dapples. 'Oh, Miriam, good morning.'

Miriam places a hand on my shoulder. 'You okay?'

'Yes, of course, I—' I look at Hans. He must have helped himself to the still hot bread.

He murmurs appreciative noises, and something unfurls in my chest. Pride, perhaps? I can't help but compare David and his . . . indifference. A slow creeping. He used to like my food, didn't he? Not that I'm a decent chef, goodness no. Patricia will vouch for that.

But, well, how lovely to feel appreciated.

'You ready to go?' Miriam says.

I look at the tea towel, still in my hand, and I place it carefully on the side.

'Yes,' I say. 'Yes.'

Miriam and I walk away from the hostel in companionable silence. Thinking of Bertie here, I'd picture her in a Cubist painting. A Picasso mish-mash of straight streets, squares and buildings – all geometric, angular and obtuse. But the view is more pleasing to the eye. An Impressionist's piece. Short strokes, bright colours. There is movement in this scene. Life.

I'm torn between wanting to know all about this place, what drew Bertie toward it, but . . . I am reluctant. It's been easier, of late, to not look. To not pay attention to anything.

I haven't needed to. To observe is for the curious. But me? I can drive to a place at home and find I have no recollection of getting there. I couldn't tell you what I saw en route, how the traffic was, the weather . . .

Auto pilot.

Too comfortable, Bertie says.

We reach the town. I force my eyes up. Look. Take it in.

We pass an array of shops, their wooden frontages bringing to mind those western movies David enjoys watching on a Sunday afternoon. They are of no interest to me, of course, all that gunfire and horse noise. Just grown-up boy stuff; adult cartoons. He insists on turning the volume so loud I can hear the nonsense all the way into my bedroom. Galloping torrents of brown in my mind.

But these wooden frontages hide more than simple saloon bars. There is an eclectic mix of offerings here. From the tat of the souvenir shop to upmarket boutiques, health food stores to this garish establishment - *Byron Pies*. It's the same in the UK what with those awful chain pastry shops everywhere . . . And we wonder why we're a nation headed toward obesity?

Oh. There's a cat in the doorway. A stray? Funny creatures, these. I'm a dog person. Cats possess a restless curiosity, with no fear about going anywhere. Although - oh - something has riled this beast. Its spine is arching, hair bristling, eyes wide.

I hurry past to catch up with Miriam and—

Goodness. The gallery is all white and glass and raw concrete. A clean frontage that juxtaposes the wash of the high street. I breathe into that strange feeling. No distractions left. I suppose this is anticipation; a stirring sense of wrongdoing. A nest of bees someone has told me not to poke. But I'm about to pick up a stick, aren't I?

And yet? Byron provides the safety net. A safe enclosure in which, perhaps, poking the stick is okay. Like a laboratory test. A controlled environment.

Control? My, oh my. In reality, there is nothing controlled about this entire experience.

I follow Miriam into the main entrance and down to the studio. Might I find some order here? This *place*. A space dissimilar from the studios of my time. It's so . . . bright. White. Clean. I remember basement rooms, dim lighting, scores of unfinished canvasses aligning the worktops, mess . . .

But - wow - this studio is beautiful. My shoulders settle and I drift into the room. There are hard floors, rough walls, a large, solid wood table. My home in England is also very ordered - David likes it that way - but it doesn't make me feel calm as I am experiencing now, here. We have thick carpets, heavy curtains,

scatter cushions placed with precision. But our home is more . .
. oppressive, I suppose.

Personally, I like the Scandinavian style. I once showed
David a magazine feature in one of the Sunday broadsheets - an
'inside the home of so-and-so' - displaying photos of the most
incredible Scandi home. It was raw and bright and striking.

Of course, David shunned it. Said it was *stark, lacking personality.* I'd looked at our own home and wondered what personality he could possibly find in the beige.

'Shall we take a seat?' Miriam says. She pats down her hair
and pulls at her top for not the first time this morning. If I
didn't know better, I'd say she's nervous.

And I have to admit, my anticipation has morphed into
nerves. Nothing cataclysmic, especially now we're in the studio
and I feel a sense of inner serenity I've not experienced for a
while, but there is that undercurrent of excitement that goes
alongside putting yourself in a new situation.

Although art is not new. Certainly not to me . . .

A young couple are already sitting at the far end of the
table, wearing the same overalls we find hanging on the back of
our own high stools. Perhaps it's because these two are wearing
matching clothing, but they look very similar. They're very -
what's that word Bertie uses? *Androgynous*, yes. Bertie once said
I suited androgynous clothing, but there's no way David would
agree.

The couple here could almost be interchangeable. Both
sporting short, spikey cropped hairstyles which I can't help but
notice match their pointy features. They are very . . . 'Cool'. The
sort who can rise above a trend, I should think. They smile, but
continue to speak in their blunt language - German, perhaps?
Dutch? - with an intimidating intensity. I need not tell Miriam
that we shouldn't interrupt. I can't tell if they are having an
argument or declaring their love for each other, but it all
sounds very passionate.

Or perhaps it's just the English language that rings rather dull. It recently came to my attention that David no longer bothers to vary the intonation of his speech. Quite the opposite to these spirited youngsters. Perhaps it is simply too much effort for him to converse with me at all. Sometimes I take myself to bed when I'm not yet tired, just to save him the hassle.

'Well, these are quite becoming,' Miriam says, as she steps into the blue boiler suit. They are paint covered and have evidently been worn before but they don't—

Oh, my. The smell of dried paint. The feel of the heavy fabric on my skin, the way the suit hangs from my shoulders . . .

'Dee?'

Goodness. *Dee Dee.*

'Are you okay?'

'Oh. Yes. I . . . hot flush, I suspect. This material is not very . . . Breathable.'

Rise and fall.

Hm.

I join Miriam, who sits at the large workbench. Flyers scatter the surface, and she is reading one. *Welcome to Art Therapy.*

'Er, Miriam?' I lift up a flyer.

'Yes?'

'Art *therapy*?'

She gives a pleasant nod, as though I've merely commented on the weather.

'Therapy,' I repeat, elongating the pronunciation of the 'th'. Isn't that what David used to do with Bertie who, as a toddler, struggled with her 'th' sound? Despite what he said, I know he was paranoid she'd end up with an *immature tongue*. (I'd heard someone utter this phrase at dinner once and I'd glanced at David, but he'd moved the conversation on. Seamless. Best not attach to upsetting details.)

I turn the flyer over - photos of people, faux smiles over kilns and canvases. 'Are you telling me I need therapy?'

Miriam opens her mouth, but decides against answering.

The main door shuts with a heavy thud and a woman who, I assume, given the confidence of her walk, is the teacher, approaches.

'Why do *you* need therapy?' I whisper, rushing.

'It's art therapy. It doesn't count. Oh, hello.' Miriam is all uplifted features and handshakes. I am still staring at her when I realise the teacher is awaiting a response.

'I'm Diane, Dee, hello, sorry.'

The teacher greets us all. She is a smart-looking woman, early forties, I would guess. Not much like an art teacher at all, in fact. The combination of smooth cotton shirt, cropped black trousers and low heels lends itself more to the look of someone I imagine working in corporate marketing. Not that I'm sure what corporate marketing entails. David mentioned the term once. I suspect that was the point in the conversation when he lost me. He keeps telling me that happens. What I refrain from telling him is that perhaps if his conversation were not peppered with such terms as 'corporate marketing', I wouldn't get lost.

The woman introduces herself as Alexandra. Perhaps she is the therapy part of this situation.

'I'm the gallery owner,' Alexandra adds, nodding, smiling, hands clasped at her front. The shine of her black bob is so slick it gives the impression of not being formed of individual hair strands, but rather one solid mass, as though I could pop her entire hair off as Bertie used to do with those Lego figurines.

The neat presentation of the studio makes sense now I know it belongs to this woman. I imagine her sock drawer is just as orderly.

Like David. He likes his briefs aligned by colour, neatly folded. My shoulders rise at the thought.

'Some of you may know that we often use art in the treatment of mental health issues. The purpose of this course is to take a light look into the world of art therapy. We won't be doing any deep psychoanalysis, but I find the course helps uncover issues which people sometimes don't even know need addressing.'

I glance at Miriam, but she keeps her gaze fixed on Alexandra.

I close my eyes. I see the overall bunched up on the floor.

Dee Dee.

I open my eyes and focus back on Alexandra.

'We have several materials at your disposal. There is painting, collage, and photography. You need no prior art experience, but we hope that these sessions will release creativity and perhaps help increase awareness of your state of mind, and then we can address issues as they arise.'

State of mind. Another phrase David would mutter. More often, lately. And definitely after I'd stopped listening.

Alexandra walks over to a table under the back window of the studio; its glass covered in an opaque film which blocks the view but not the light. On the table is an array of art materials: paints, brushes, scissors, glue, and magazines.

'Feel free to familiarise yourself with the materials, get a feel for the items, maybe try them out, and decide what form you would like to explore further.'

Miriam and the cool couple rise from their seats and head over to the table.

Hm. I don't seem able to move.

'Dee, do you have any experience in art?' Alexandra says.

'Oh, a little, in painting . . . Yes.'

'Great, so will you be choosing paint today or would you prefer another medium?'

'I . . .' I search Alexandra's face. Goodness. As if she has the answer. But . . . I don't even know how to frame the question. Is there a question? 'I'd better stick with something else, I think.'

'Okay, perfect. Well, if you have any questions, I'm happy to help.'

At that, I can't help but laugh. I remember the push/pull of the artist's mind - one minute feeling you're creating a master-piece, the next moment happily throwing it away, cussing at your stupidity, your audacity to think you could do it.

Dee Dee, please don't throw us away. Not now.

'Dee?' Miriam's voice.

'Yes?'

'Are you coming?'

I nod, feeling like a teenage Bertie in a strop.

'This is nonsensical,' I say, once I'm close enough for no one else to hear.

Miriam tuts. She is flicking through a portfolio. 'Has anyone ever told you that you get out what you put in?'

'I . . . No.'

Miriam looks at a large black and white painting of what I can only guess is a woman's nether region. Oh goodness, we won't be expected to partake in life drawing here, will we?

Miriam closes the portfolio suddenly, and the page slaps into the silence. She turns to me. 'Perhaps it's time to consider that.'

'I, er . . .' And for once, there is nobody telling me not to.

We've been getting stuck into the collage. Choosing images, cutting, slicing, changing old into something new. Reforming, reworking. I suppose it is therapeutic. My mind is empty as I cut. Although I'm not sure what the end goal is here. To discover something about ourselves through the slicing? Alexandra is offering no guidance beyond *familiarise yourself with the material* and I feel quite familiar now, thank you very much. She has popped in to check on us several times, looking increasingly anxious with every visit, as though we are an unruly group of school kids she doesn't trust to be left alone.

And perhaps that is true of the couple opposite. They have been giggling at length for some time, and have just left the studio, making noises in broken English about 'getting coffee'.

I look up from my mess of a creation and turn to Miriam, who is engrossed in neatly trimming a tiny image of a poodle.

'So.' My voice lands small in the vast space. 'Is this course part of what you were referring to last night? About *bettering yourself*?'

'Ha, are you trying to get personal on me, Dee?' She flashes me a look then, as if she knows, well, everything. 'There's room for everyone to better themselves, right?'

I pick up a pair of scissors. 'Yes. I suppose there is.'

'I wanted to do this course because I thought I might . . . I don't know . . . Be able to lose control? We're so ordered in our lives. My life, anyway.'

I think of my life. *Ordered*. That's the perfect word, isn't it? Even my linen cupboard is labelled.

Goodness. When did I become a person to label their linen?

Miriam puts down her scissors and looks toward the window. 'I just wanted to cut the fuck loose, you know?'

'Oh—'

'Sorry. But—' She exhales, turns back. 'Do you know what I mean?'

I think of what Miriam said yesterday - the hint of marital dispute. 'Sharing a life with someone is hard.'

'Ha . . . Yes.'

'Maybe it's healthy to have a break.' Do I believe that? Goodness. Who am I to give advice?

'Mm, drop the pretence for a while.' I don't want to lift my gaze, but when I do, I realise Miriam is nodding, talking about herself.

I let out a sigh, and I can't continue with the questions. We continue to cut and stick.

Cut and stick.

Cut and stick.

Eventually, Alexandra comes back in. She stops as she sees the empty seats in which the androgynous couple once sat.

'Coffee,' Miriam says, smiling in sympathy. I think we all know they're not coming back.

Alexandra lowers her shoulders, shakes her head, sits on a stool opposite us. 'Ladies, I'm sorry, but it looks as though there has been a mix up with the art therapist. She can't come.' Alexandra is talking to Miriam and me but her gaze keeps flickering down to the table, the only rift on her otherwise calm, centered air. She is the opposite to me, I imagine. David says I have a tendency to twitch.

I sit on my hands and listen to Alexandra and Miriam talking about the teacher not giving any notice before she cancelled.

'This is Vinnie's doing,' Alexandra says, shaking her head. 'Gosh, I'm sorry. This is so unprofessional of me, I—'

'It's okay,' I offer.

She looks up then, from me to Miriam. 'I can get her to send me the lesson plans and do it myself, I know what's involved so . . . whatever you think—'

'That would be great, right?' Miriam nods at me.

'Of course. I'm just happy to be here.' I look at the space. The art. The feeling it evokes . . .

I shrug.

'It's a beautiful space,' Miriam says. 'It's so orderly. I thought artists were messy?'

Alexandra smiles as she shifts her weight on the seat.

'Believe me, my house is. I practically sleep with the art material.'

'Do you do a lot of painting?' I say.

'Not much, now, no. The running of this place is intense and recently it . . .' Alexandra drops her gaze. I recall what Shaun had said about her breakup. If I didn't know this, I wouldn't read anything into the hand clasping, but I wonder if she needs it to occupy her hands. 'It's been busier. I suppose I feel at least if the paints are out and ready for use, I'm not giving up yet.'

I think of my art: the canvasses, easel, brushes, oils . . . We moved into David's house after we married and he didn't like to have my painting everywhere and, of course, I couldn't go back to the studio . . .

Bertie was born and David was going back to work, and I said that perhaps I could take out my art materials, make room for it somewhere, maybe do something while the baby napped . . . But David thought it best we throw all that out. He didn't want a toddler tearing through paint, trudging it over the new shagpile. *A fresh start*, he added. I remember the flush of his cheeks. Like Bertie's when we'd go to the coast for the day, making castles on a blowy winter beach.

David would ask where we'd been. He didn't like to come home and have us not there. He values family, David. I'd show him Bertie's cheeks to compare, and he'd smile but—

He wouldn't put her to bed that night. Sometimes he wouldn't come to bed himself.

Not on those nights.

'Listen, I haven't paid for my place,' I say, 'but I think we'd both love to complete the course, whichever way you run it. Miriam booked me on this last minute and—'

'Of course, Vinnie sorts—' She stops. A sudden rise of her chest. 'Let me handle it, Dee. Come into my office.'

. . .

'I'm so sorry for this,' Alexandra says, leading me into the office. Her room is next door to the studio and I can see that further down the hall is the gallery entrance, but I'm not sure what's on at the moment. Perhaps I'll find time to stop in.

We walk into another bright white but compact space, huge canvasses aligning each wall, a sideboard covered in artefacts. 'I'm so embarrassed about everything.' Alexandra drifts her hand away from herself, then seems to let her mind drift with it. After a moment she comes to and steps behind her desk. 'We're going through some changes at the moment, so—'

'It's okay. As I said, I like just being here. You've got a great setup.'

Alexandra is frowning at something on her screen, but she's paused, as though forgotten what she was looking for. She sits down. 'You said you've done some art before?'

I inhale. Nod.

'And you stopped?'

'Yes, er . . . It didn't seem to fit anymore, I suppose.'

'I understand. It requires a large investment of time. Not always easy to navigate around family, work . . .'

'I worked in art for a short while. I taught children, briefly. Just the odd workshop. Nothing, really.' I think of David: *Those little classes*, he'd said. But to me, they were everything. 'A long time ago now, of course.'

There is a paperweight on the desk that appears to have captured a wave - rushes of blue and white, crystallised bubbles. I recall the feeling of my face under water yesterday.

'Maybe this is the place to reignite that love.'

I look up with a start, but Alexandra is looking at a painting on the wall. Of course she's talking about the art.

'Oh, I . . . I don't know if I could dig all that up now. I doubt I have any talent left. Part of an old me, I suspect.'

Alexandra has me in her sights, her expression clear. 'Maybe you need not hark back to the old.'

I frown a question into my features.

'Australia, so far from home, is the place to begin again, isn't it? And everyone wants the chance to begin again.'

She smiles, turns to her computer, and I look back to the paperweight. I pick up the bulbous object, its density in my hand, and I close my eyes and feel that wave crash over me all over again.

———

'You're in Byron? Diane, why would you go there? Look, just stay put, wait there. What if you— You know . . .'- a tut, as though Francis is being forced to say what's next and I imagine her shaking her head in irritation at Roy - *'make a scene.'*

I am sitting on my bed, a wall of lilac ahead of me.

'I'm okay.' I let my voice yield to the sudden sense of affection I feel toward my sister. Her intentions are in the right place, but sometimes I wish she'd try to see past the obvious. It occurs to me that people only know David's version of me.

And wasn't that one of his favourite lines? *Don't make a scene, Diane.*

The last time I heard this had been at that dinner party with Patricia and Hugo - I found myself in the garden at dusk, watching the carp in their pond. David berated me, snapped. *You'll get cold*, he said, though it was obvious to all that was not his real reason for annoyance. He'd been doing that more often, the snapping. Followed by an inevitable reconciliation, of course. Usually in the car on the way home. The sigh, trying to catch my eye as I stared out of the window - looking for something? Francis would call first thing the next day, and I'd know. Their little conspiracies. Wonderings. *Caring*, apparently.

But now?

I look around the single room, and I can't say I feel very cared for in this moment.

'It's not long.' Am I telling this to myself or my sister?

'Diane, please. I'm worried about you.'

I step toward the window and push the curtain aside. 'I know, I—'

'Roy has been trying to reach David.'

There is a window box of flowers perched on the outside sill. It's winter and yet there blooms the most extraordinary flower. A type of Australian Eucalyptus, I should think. It has the oddest form - like an exposed pink jelly fish that's dried out in the sun, it's useless shrunken tentacles quivering in the breeze, the pollen stem alert and ready.

Francis continues: 'David's in Australia.'

My fingers grip the curtain. 'I suppose he must be, you know. We have an agreement to meet up. The wedding. He has to come here at some point.' I have a vision of David waiting for my flight to have landed, for time to pass, for there to be no risk of me waiting for him at the airport.

For me to have given up?

'But if he knew you were in Byron, perhaps he would come to you? He can't expect you to cope there—'

'Please, Francis. David must do whatever he has to do.'

I close my eyes, picture him walking out into the sunshine, his skin immediately reddening in the heat, sweat dappling his receding hairline. The huff and puff of him.

Goodness. The constancy. For all his faults.

Now gone.

There's a knock at the door.

'Oh, Miriam. Hello.' Miriam stands the other side, bright eyes, big hair, camera round the neck. Kindness, I think.

'Who?' My sister says.

Ah. I have the phone to my ear. I step back to let Miriam in, indicating that I won't be long.

'I'll call you when I can, okay?' Hm. I've accidentally matched my sister's tone. Perhaps I need a break from her, as David clearly needs from me.

'But, Diane? Are you really going to stay there? Are you going to go to—'

'I can't talk now. I'll call you soon. Take care.' And as I press the button to end the call, I feel light-headed. Cut off.

Free?

Miriam is smiling at me.

'I'm sorry,' I say. 'My sister. You know, she worries.'

'Older or younger?'

'Younger. So, really, I suppose it should be my job to worry about her but . . . It's in her nature.'

'Do you give her cause to worry?'

'I . . . Erm . . .'

'I was just joking,' Miriam says.

I look to the window. Goodness. If David and I were a flower, this eucalyptus would be us. The plant is a beautiful creation of nature but looking at that unrelenting pollen stick - obtuse, alert, ever-ready - aside the reticence of the retreating petals, makes my mouth dry.

'I just came to tell you that a group of us are going climbing tomorrow morning. I know you were resistant to the surfing but perhaps, now you're in therapy, you know . . .'

I can't help but laugh. 'Oh, my . . . I'm not sure.'

'Just say yes, remember?'

'Ha, not this time. I can't lift *this*.' I wave my hands over my body. Goodness. What am I wearing? Leggings and, begrudgingly, one of Miriam's shapeless t-shirts.

I need to go shopping.

'It's important to work out, Dee. Especially as we age. You should be able to lift your body weight.'

'I do work out. I do aerobics and Pilates videos twice a week. Tuesday and Thursday at nine.'

'Videos? You don't go to a gym?'

'Goodness, no. Nobody wants to see me flinging this old thing around. *Especially* as I age.'

Miriam tilts her head. 'Dee, have you ever considered that perhaps no one cares?'

'Well, I care.' My chin has retracted into my neck.

'Exactly. Most people are self-obsessed so they wouldn't bat an eyelid at what you're up to.'

'Well, I . . . No.' Hm. I find I can't summon a counter argument.

'Will you come along as the photographer, at least? I'd love to send my sons some photos of me climbing. They'll be so impressed.' She steps forward a little. I am aware of the space. Conscious of the small room.

'Just as the photographer?'

Miriam smiles. 'Just as the photographer, I promise. I don't trust Indie or Lola to keep their eyes off the men long enough to concentrate on me.'

I'm surprised to find I'm laughing.

'Great. So, it's a done deal. I'll add your name to the list.'

Then Miriam leaves me here in this little lilac room. And, somehow, the space feels even smaller.

DAY FIVE

Rock climbing. I can't quite believe I say that but, yes, rock climbing it is. Although these sheer faces would be more accurately described as cliffs. Dali's *Penya-segats*. However, I believe Dali's woman on the rocks is naked. So ... there's something.

As I stand at the base of the ravine, sandwiched by these vast walls either side, I watch the others take turns putting on a harness and I wonder if the daredevil nature gets eroded as we age. But then you read about these octogenarians who scale Everest and all other sorts of scary nonsense ...

But. The minority, I should think.

I scan our little huddle of travellers, most of whom are inappropriately dressed in 'thongs' and board shorts. I'm not sure when ghastly colours came into fashion but I have to bite my tongue from telling them that it's not always advisable to follow Vogue. Most of the girls seem nervous with their fiddling and forced laughter, while the boys puff their chests and imitate confidence, I imagine. I know everyone is about gender equality these days, but I just can't see the male bravado dropping in the immediate future. It's like an innate mating call: *must look macho in front of potential mate.*

'Dee?'

Oh, goodness. I think I was talking to myself. Okay, I don't think anybody heard. One of the climbing guides is checking Miriam's harness and the adjacent bearded one is looking at me, with what I would describe as a look of expectation on his face. I can't imagine why.

'Dee? You ready?' Ah. Tom. When did he arrive?

And, oh my. I let out a laugh because I sense the lunacy of what Tom is about to say as his mouth twitches into a smile.

And, yes, here is his hand - extending toward the empty harness.

'I don't think so,' I say. 'But thank you for the offer. I'm just here to take photos of Miriam.'

Miriam looks up from the man who is fiddling with a strap a little too close to her womanly region for my liking and gives me that smile I'm starting to understand means she's a step ahead of me.

'You lured me along as the photographer because you thought once here I'd want a go? Ha!' I make a point of thrusting her camera into my bag and I cross my arms. The rock ahead looms large and overbearing, us mere mortals at its base, specks of nothing against the absolute vastness of this natural formation. Clouds pass at speed across the opening of blue sky above.

'I can take photos of the both of you.' Hm. Tom again. What a shame, I had been warming to the man.

My eye moves to the young lad from the climbing team, waiting to help his next victim into the harness. He bites his lip, eyes unsettling. Impatience? I'm not surprised. He's no doubt not used to old fuddy duddys like me holding up his afternoon. He probably wants to get moving so he can finish up and return to being a beach bum.

Or to his beard trimming.

Don't judge, I hear Bertie saying.

Well. I must remember to email Bertie about this. *Why didn't you give it a go?* she will say.

I'm still looking at the irritated lad. He's altered his expression now. A forced smile, pretending to find me amusing.

I think of David. The smile of late never quite convincing and always an underlying current of irritation. He denies it, of course, but I see it - glimpses of another emotion he fails to keep at bay when he thinks nobody is looking.

Tom takes the harness off the irritable bearded man. 'I'll be your belayer,' he says. 'You trusted me with the surfing, so I'm sure you can trust me here.'

Miriam, I notice, is shrugging, the original belayer lad looks ... Sceptical?

'Okay,' I hear myself saying. *Okay?* This seems to be an agreement...

Oh, goodness. I have officially lost my marbles.

'You know I'm blaming you for this?' I turn to Miriam, who has climbed up beside me on the rock face. We're ready to ascend adjacent tracks but I seem to be stuck. People are barking directions from below, but all I can do is cling to this little precipice. Apparently, I'm to launch myself backwards and hope the person on the bottom has my weight. Silly, really, that I managed to climb to the top, and now can't get back down.

'You're doing really well,' Miriam says, short of breath. She hoists herself up another level, so she is just above me. I look up at her, but she throws her face back to the wall. 'Oh, gosh. Don't look down.'

'No,' I say. I am focusing on the wall. I am not looking up or down or right or left.

Rise and fall.

'You seem calm.' Miriam's voice has become a little shrill.

'Hm.'

'I was half expecting you to freak out up here, goodness knows I am.'

I nod, but I have no capacity for speech.

'You don't reveal much, do you, Dee?'

'Well, best not to get hysterical.'

Hysterical. That's how the security guard described me to David. One of those words assigned only to women, by men. Although hadn't Francis used it too? Ha! If anyone acted hysterical it was her the morning she married Roy. Still, I wonder now if it is healthier to feel the emotions, whereas the morning of my wedding I was a little . . . Resigned, I suppose.

Or was it removed?

'I'd like to get down now, Miriam.' My palms are sweating and the harness is digging in uncomfortably.

I glance up. I can hear her breathing, see her shoulders lift and lower.

'It's okay,' she says. 'Let's do it together.'

I wet my lips. I find I am nodding.

'If we can conquer this, we can conquer anything.'

'I'm not so sure about that.' My voice is quiet, breathy, staccato.

'Brené Brown says there is no courage in comfort.'

'Well, I am most certainly uncomfortable.'

'I'll be courageous. I'll go first.' Miriam's voice is plunging into my mind in streaks of yellow. It is still up here on this rock face. The odd call of a bird, the rustle of the trees. If my limbs could speak, my arms would be screaming.

'Ready when you are,' Tom calls. As belayer, he has my life in his hands.

Hm. I won't give the idea too much consideration.

Miriam checks that her belayer, the impatient kid, is in place for her descent, and then she pushes herself gently away from the rock. What was an audible breath is now silence.

When I regain the ability to speak, perhaps I should remind her to breathe.

Just breathe.

I understand why people say that, to give a person a focus point, to remind them to concentrate on that simple yet vital task, but I always found it condescending. Still, I suppose it's better than, *It's alright.* Because, obviously, it's not alright, is it? If it was alright I would not be hyperventilating into a brown paper bag.

But. Such moments are rarely the time for arguments.

And now I draw my breath in, as Miriam pulls herself back to the wall, pressing her face up against the rock so her mouth turns into a squished pout.

'I can't do it,' she says, apparently trying to become one with the rock. Her arms are spread, fingers like claws drawing herself into the cliff face, legs spread and harness giving her a rather unsightly rear.

And then my mind is pierced with shards of pink. That noise is—?

Oh, goodness. That noise is me - giggling. Giggling like those gap year girls. I don't recognise it coming from myself.

And I can't seem to stop. The more I try, the more it bursts forth. And it's a feat to keep the strength in my arms, as my limbs are suddenly weak and shaky and no longer wanting to scream, but to sigh.

'It's okay, Dee,' I hear Tom shout. 'You can let go now. I've got you.'

I've got you. Aren't those the words I have been longing to hear? And I've had to travel to the other side of the world and climb up a cliff face to hear them from a stranger.

For some reason, this is even more hilarious.

'Dee, what is so goddamn funny?'

Miriam has inched her chin away from the wall, and I can see from my lowered position that her face is oddly contorted.

A misshapen starfish, which pushes me even further. I am now howling.

'I'm sorry,' I manage. 'It's just—' Oh, goodness. I can't hold on. I can't. My *arms*.

I look at the line I'm attached to, and I take a deep, steadying breath, and I ease one hand away from the wall slowly, and I hold the rope.

'Are you doing it?' Miriam asks.

I'm too focused to answer. I feel weirdly light. Ethereal. Because, I suppose, what do I possibly have to lose? Perhaps David wanted me to get into this situation. Maybe this was his plan, all along. He couldn't bear to give me a dignified exit, so he just abandoned me.

And now, what do I have to lose?

Nothing. Because I have nothing.

And so? I let go of the wall.

———

'Cheers to us!' We cry, our little gaggle of victorious rock climbers, having conquered the *wall of fear*, as Lola branded it, all thrilled to have survived and made it to 'après' here in the bar. Tom bought us a celebratory jug of beer, and it would be rude to decline. After all, he was the one who talked me through the descent, calmly guiding me through the abseil as he instructed me where to place my feet and hands. I wouldn't have managed without him.

'Thank you for not dropping me,' I say, raising my voice so Tom can hear me above the music and chatter of our group, and I nod in acceptance at the beer refill he is offering.

'My pleasure.'

I look at my hands, which I find are tugging at my top.

I force my fingers to interlace in my lap and look up directly into Tom's eye line. After a moment, he lifts his glass, and, slowly; I mirror the gesture, my mouth forming a rather genuine grin. He seems like a good boy. Well . . . A good man, I suppose.

Unlike Miriam's spotter - the juvenile del—

Sorry, Bertie. I must not judge. He may not be a delinquent, but he was not what Lola here would call 'egalitarian.' He seemed fine to push the strong lads, spitting words of what I assume were encouragement - his language and accent foreign to my ears - but for women, especially us older women, I feel he wrote of us off before we had even begun.

Still, Miriam managed. We abseiled down together and I think I might even have been an aide to her.

'Thank you, Dee,' she says now, sliding closer along the bench and clinking her glass against mine.

Hans has enticed Tom into conversation, and I turn my full focus to my new friend. 'Anytime.'

'So, do you think you found a new sport?'

'Ha!' Evidently, Miriam has a lot to learn of me yet. If she knew me, she would understand I have never been one for sports. Of any kind. 'It was your *conquer anything* speech that spurred me on.'

'And you conquered.'

The music switches tempo and the atmosphere in the bar suddenly seems energised, lifted. Some of our group, including Tom, stand to dance.

A hint of pleasure teases across my face. 'I showed him, didn't I?'

Miriam reflects my look, but her brow flickers a question.

'Surfing and now climbing,' I clarify. 'David won't recognise me.' I feel strange, all of a sudden. His name seems so far removed from this situation. Odd, really. I mean, *rock climbing with strangers?* Shouldn't this be the thing that is odd?

'Is that a good thing? That he won't recognise you?'

I consider this. 'Yes. I should think so. He could barely believe I was prepared to eat the plane food, although, of course, he wouldn't have let me have the wine.'

'He was with you on the first flight?'

'No, he—' Ah. I realise my mistake.

Miriam eyes me, assessing. Oh, thank goodness, I'm blessed with the interlude that is Lola, approaching the table. She makes a remark about a guy hitting on her at the bar - a tall blond who, on inspection, actually looks rather presentable, but she is insisting he is a *bit of a douche but maybe worth a shot*. She finishes her drink in one undignified gulp and then retreats.

I sip my own drink, cradling it between my hands.

Finally, Miriam speaks: 'The empty seat on our row. Your husband left you on the flight, didn't he?'

I watch Lola whisper something in the blond guy's ear, and whatever she said seems to have made his day. I scan the room for Lola's sidekick, Indie, and locate her at the other end of the bar in conversation with Jake.

'I'm sure he had his reasons,' I manage.

Miriam's gaze stays on me, further assessment.

'We've agreed to meet up at the end of the trip. At the wedding.'

Agreed? Well. I look up, nodding.

But Miriam is still. Unreadable. 'How long have you been together?'

'Thirty years. Our anniversary is later this month. This trip was . . .' Hm. I find I'm no longer sure how to define this trip.

Miriam's hand is on my arm. 'I'm sorry,' she says.

I feel my face contort into a frown. Is this event worthy of an apology? 'I'm sure it was all my doing,' I say.

'I doubt that.'

I laugh at Miriam's confidence. She always seems so . . . Sure.

'So, this trip is now a chance for you to prove yourself. Hence the rock climbing, right?'

'I guess so,' I say, because, really, what other choice do I have?

'Well, nothing changes unless you change it.'

I smile and nod as per conversation etiquette but—

Well.

Rise and fall.

Sometimes things change beyond our control, don't they?

As the evening progresses our group interchanges between the bar, dance floor and our table here in the corner, and it's pleasing that all I have to do is sit in this one position and have people bring me drinks.

Hm. Too many, I suspect. I appear to have lost count of the exact amount, in fact. It's difficult to keep track without

David here to whisper in my ear or cast me one of 'those looks'.

Goodness. Am I destined to be a 'loose cannon' without him?

Ah, now this is a loose cannon. Lola, closely followed by Indie, squeeze into the booth opposite Miriam and me.

A funny friendship, this one. Indie is consistently behind Lola, her reserved nature juxtaposing Lola who is full everything - big eyes, big lips, masses of dark hair, character. When I first met Lola, I have to admit to feeling meek by contrast, but - goodness, perhaps it's the beer (Dutch courage?) - but tonight I feel energised by her. If I can park whatever that distasteful feeling is aside, her enthusiasm is infectious. I liken myself to one of those plants . . . Let my brain work a moment . . . Erm . . . Oh! Venus Fly Trap!

Yes, and there was that movie that Bertie enjoyed as a teenager - a retro film most likely inappropriate but . . .

Little Shop of Horrors. Thank you, mind. Yes, I recall Bertie dancing to the soundtrack. Her little head and that crazy mess of hair bopping as though not appropriately attached to her body.

Goodness. Where has this memory been hiding?

'What's funny?' Lola asks me now.

Oh. I am smiling. Laughing, actually. Bertie was such a warm teenager. Yes, I can remember some large upsets, but I always admired her ability to wear her heart on her sleeve; to be boundlessly . . . Open. If something upset her, we knew. Whereas I—

Well. I tuck my heart firmly away.

And Bertie settles our grievances as fast as they emerge. She is not one to hold a grudge; can't bear an argument to fester. But at least she is brave enough to have them.

'You agree, don't you?' Lola is asking me.

'Oh, I'm sorry,' I say, pulling myself up straight. 'I didn't catch what you were saying.'

Miriam intervenes, with what I suspect is a look she reserves for her more unsettling students. 'Lola here is being rather pushy toward Indie—'

'No no no,' Lola laughs. 'I'm telling it like it is.'

Miriam and Lola exchange words in jest but I can't follow. I catch Indie's eye across the table and offer what I hope is an encouraging smile.

'I guess he wanted to start university single,' Indie says with a shrug. I piece together the snippets of chat I can catch and deduce that Indie was 'dumped' recently. Lola thinks this is awful and she should - *goodness me* - have a . . . No. I can't repeat—

'A revenge fuck is the perfect payback.'

Well. Not the sort of language I expect from a lady and yet I am—

Laughing?

I put down my beer.

'Well, Jake is cute,' Miriam says.

'What happened?' I manage, despite myself. It is vastly inappropriate to be discussing Indie's love life in such overt terms, but I also really want to know.

Goodness. Am I turning into my sister?

Lola slaps a hand on the table between us. 'No no no, we're not getting back into it. It's like the land of the broken hearted in here. This should be a *fun* adventure. If we waste it pondering, then we'll look back and regret it, I know it.'

Indie is wearing a half smile. She does not look as sure of this mission as her friend.

'Indie's ex-boyfriend was clearly punching with my gorgeous friend.' Lola places a hand around Indie as she says this and, well, it is a reminder that you can't tell much about someone just from their facade, regardless of how confident they may appear. I mean, *punching*? 'And now he has grand delusions about his ability with women and wants to go to university and test the theory. So you, Indie, sweetie, should get in before him and spread it about while you can. Jake over there is keen, even if he won't last much more than a minute.' She cackles out a laugh and I find I have to cover my mouth.

My eyes have darted to the crowd at the bar, but instead of finding dear little Jake, I find Tom.

I lower my hands and cradle my now warm beer.

And then I have another swig.

Goodness.

'We're not all heartbroken,' Miriam says.

'Oh, yes. Okay for you, missus, in your safe marriage,' Lola says, amiably mocking.

But Miriam no longer sounds so cheery. 'Actually, I'm here alone because I couldn't face another summer pretending to be one big happy family.'

Oh! Well ...

Miriam fixates on the table. Indie and Lola are still.

'It's me,' she says eventually, nodding. 'I want out but—'

'He doesn't want you to leave.' I am surprised to realise this is Indie speaking. Lola, for once, is silent.

Miriam looks up. She shakes her head. 'He doesn't want to tell the children. He thinks I'll change my mind ...'

I should put a hand on Miriam's shoulder but—

She has a family. Yet she wants to break it up?

'The children probably already know,' Indie says, her voice tender, quiet. Her voice suits her face. It's the face of a child on a very womanly body. It's almost ... Disconcerting.

Miriam sighs, her breath shuddering.

'And Dee, what's your marital status?' This is Lola again. I suppose sensing Miriam's reticence.

'Oh, erm ...' Goodness. How did I get here? Am I really going to discuss my love life with an eighteen-year-old in some crummy bar instead of being in that love life, in the comfort of my home? 'Confused,' I manage.

'Well, if there's one thing we can take from today's climb, it's that the brave survive. If you didn't take hold of that rope and step off the cliff, you'd still be dangling at the top right now. Know what I'm saying?' And she swigs from her drink and plants a kiss on Indie's cheek.

'Well,' I say, after a moment. 'I suppose it's not always that simple.' But I don't think Lola hears.

I return my glass to the table, suddenly feeling rather sober.

I leave the others to their party. Binge drinking is not becoming for a person of my age. Tom asked me if I was *still here* and I sensed he was joking, he didn't seem to *have a problem*, as Bertie would say, quite the opposite, I think, as he'd infused it with a kind expression, but—

I took it as my cue to leave.

Miriam, however, stayed. But I have at least ten years on her ...

A time and place for everything. I can't help but notice what a shame it is to feel as if I missed mine, however.

But, of course, thoughts like this won't do. I had Bertie. My blessing. *Our* blessing, obviously. I wouldn't change that for anything.

Or anyone.

'Oh, hello.' Eric, the scrawnier hostel owner, is standing in the empty street outside the hostel, staring at the wall. His hair, in this dim light, seems luminous. It spikes up and I suspect it would hurt my finger to touch it. In fact, his whole demeanour is very jagged. Pointy. He has that sort of papery skin that falls from his prominent cheekbones, shoulders as visible balls beneath his t-shirt.

'Are you okay?' I should feel fearful, being here in the dark with a man, but—

Perhaps it's the alcohol. And, good grief, if Eric were to attack me, I shouldn't think it would be difficult to fend him off. I suspect a flick of the finger would suffice.

His breath sighs, craggy, his hair moving atop of his shaking head. 'Those bleedin' kids,' he says. His voice is raspy, it seems a voice better suited to the dark. He himself, I should think, would prefer a nocturnal existence.

He walks over to the wall and kicks at a spot. Graffiti.

'Ah.' The graffiti is not what Bertie would call *street art*, but it appears to be someone's initials, spread in large print across the wall.

It was Bertie who drew my attention to that street artist who sold their graffiti work for millions. Banksy? Yes. Goodness. Art really is subjective if someone will pay that much. Although, people will pay for anything, I suppose.

How did the Banksy person have the courage to charge so much? How did they manage to switch off negative self-talk? Courage, I suppose. Something I often struggled with. I heard it phrased once . . . How was it? Oh, *imposter syndrome*. Yes. The term resonates.

At least, it did. Once upon a time . . .

Eric grunts in anger and, although it is obvious he is not best pleased with this defacement, it would not surprise me if he lived his life in a permanent state of anger. Some people have a knack for finding the problem, I feel.

Goodness. Less judgey, please, Diane.

Dee Dee.

I shake my head.

Creativity takes courage. A quote from someone else, I'm sure.

'I know I sound like an old man,' Eric says, 'but I'm sure kids had more respect when I was younger.'

'You know? I'm prone to agree.' (The least I can do is to be sympathetic to the poor guy. Besides, I don't *dis*agree.)

We stand in companionable silence for a moment (definitely the beer. A beer jacket?), before Eric's lighter sparks, and the orange glow of a cigarette moves through the dark. Evidently, his old habits are not so stuck in the past.

I pull my cardigan tighter around my chest.

'I wonder if you made a feature of this wall,' I say, 'if it had a purpose, people wouldn't feel entitled to deface it?'

'How do you mean? Like, selling it as advertising space?'

'Perhaps. Or . . . a mural.'

Eric draws a long inhale of his cigarette. 'I don't suppose it could look any worse,' he says, blowing out a balloon of grey above our heads.

I try not to inch back; I don't want to be rude but—

No. I'm afraid I cannot be privy to second-hand smoke.

I make my excuses and leave Eric to grimace alone.

To: Liberty.Bridges@icloud.com
Subject: Still here . . .
From: MrsDBridges@outlook.com

Dear Bertie,

So I'm still here, in Byron. And, wow, what
an adventure. I am scared to stop in case my
conscious mind takes too much notice of what
is happening and backs me away. So far, we've
been on the go non-stop and Miriam told me to
try saying yes to everything and I am, but I
often wonder if these things are better
suited to the young . . . I must look like
some blethering old fool, but it helps that I
can imagine you doing all these things -
surfing, climbing, exploring. And I smile as
now I have a real sense of what it is you
loved about this place. That is enough to
outweigh my nerves.

Okay, time to go as there is a queue for the
computer.

All my love,
Mum x

P.S. Have you heard from Dad? Nothing to
worry about. I just hope he's okay. I'll see
him at the wedding and catch up then. Silly
old man, I can hear you saying.

DAY SIX

I am sitting in the gallery cafe - in my favourite armchair, which is just like one my grannie had with a high back and regal arm rests - enjoying the temperature-controlled calm. Out of the window lays a familiar scene. Familiar because of Bertie's photos, I suppose. I've already seen it through her eyes and I have a vague sense of living in a memory. As though I'm already looking back on this experience. The cute boutiques, the beach, there was a waterfall she went to, I'm sure. I must find time to see that.

She didn't mention the gallery.

I had a stroll around the exhibits and, afterwards, I purchased a butter-soft leather-bound notebook from the gallery shop. The item smells like one Mum gave me and the feel in my hand - the soft heaviness - transports me to the moment she gave it to me. A wedding present, or a pre-wedding present, I suppose, intended solely for me. A strange gift, now I think of it. *A keepsake*, Mum said, clasping her hands over mine with more force than necessary, her attention lingering.

That beautiful notebook was never used. Instead, it now resides in a box of keepsakes in the loft. Buried in a memory box. The past.

'You like this spot,' comes Miriam's voice, a soft startling.

I gesture for her to join.

'There's something reassuring about the art. Being near to it, within a space solely dedicated to painting.' I look at my lap, neaten a hangnail. 'I'd forgotten how much I love it. And, you know, there are no rocks to climb here. Plus, I must admit, I find my head to be a little sore today.'

Miriam laughs. 'I've seen you doodling.'

'Oh.' I touch a hand over my open notebook. Scrawls exposed. This keepsake will be used. 'Silly, really.'

'Not silly at all.' Miriam leans back, tilts her head. 'If you could be any painting, which would you be?'

'Oh gosh, there's so much choice.' The Impressionist scene of Byron moves beyond the window. Would I be this? 'I'm not sure. What would you be?'

'I don't know much about art but I've enjoyed the collage we've done on the course. Or perhaps I'd be something modernist?'

'A synthetic collage, fusing the bright with the simple. Yes, I can see why you'd choose that.'

'Hey!' Miriam throws a sugar cube at me playfully. 'Come on. You have to choose one. Say the first thing that comes to mind.'

The first thing that comes to mind. 'Would it be too cliché to say Munch's *The Scream*?'

Miriam considers this a moment. Then she seems to come to, a smile. No judgement, I feel. 'Well. I should have guessed. Good job I got you into therapy.'

'Did you know the original painting was stolen?'

'Oh?'

'Yes, it's been locked away from light ever since.'

'Funny you should choose that one, don't you think, Dee?'

'The Munch Museum will display it again. They just need to get the control system working.'

Miriam observes me for a second, before leaving to order her coffee at the counter. When she returns, she is laughing.

'What?'

'There's something about you, Dee. Something . . . unsaid. I can't decide if you used to speak it, or if you've been—' she pauses, her hand extending as though physically reaching for the desired word, 'silenced.'

My breath leaves me unintentionally as a sigh. I close the pad. 'We can't continue these nonsensical things as adults, can we?' I say, when I realise Miriam is awaiting an answer. I think of Lola. Will her enthusiasm wane with age?

The waitress - the sweet Irish girl with the red lipstick - brings Miriam's coffee to the table. We exchange pleasantries.

The Irish girl leaves, but Miriam's scrutinising stare remains. I can't help but laugh. 'Why does everything have to mean so much to you?'

She shrugs then, as if to say, *It doesn't.*

And as Miriam moves the conversation on to other, less meaningful topics, I notice a reluctance in myself.

Byron, this space, will also soon be a memory, and I won't be able to recall what I fabricated and what was real. Those things not captured, slowly fading, and all of this could never have happened.

Memory has a way of reforming itself, realigning to what you wish it to be, or what you've been told, or what has become evidenced in photos. Our wedding, for example. Could I have seen in a look, or read deeper into a comment, a foreshadowing of what was to come? To see that David would have the guile to leave me in another country ahead of our thirtieth anniversary?

And I . . . I was smiling on my wedding day. Wearing that beautiful headdress I'd made and— David remarked, years later, attempting joviality about *that ridiculous adornment*, but—

Now the memory of the day, that comment, what I see in

photos, is all intertwined like the distorted landscape of *The Scream* and I cannot sift through to reality. Not really.

It's worrying that we can be so sure of our actions in the moment and then hindsight—

Well.

I was smiling.

In the pictures, I smiled.

'So, ladies - do you mind if I call you ladies? I know it can be offensive for some but—'

'Hey, if you think we're ladies,' Miriam replies to Alexandra, 'then we'll be ladies. Right, Dee?'

I shift the high stool so I'm sitting closer to the workbench in the centre of the studio. We are the only people here and I like the way our voices land in the cavity of space. A reverberating noise. 'Absolutely,' I say, noticing that when Alexandra calls me a lady, it's very much tongue-in-cheek but when David refers to me and my friends with this term in that satirical tone he uses it stirs a mild rage. A struck match flaring in my gut.

Hm. Might I be too harsh on the poor man?

'Well, ladies, the task today for our art therapy class is to make a list of the things that make you happy,' Alexandra says, passing us each a piece of white paper and a pen. This can be as abstract or exact as you like. Try not to overthink it, just write whatever comes to mind. Maximum of nine things, please.'

Miriam is already scrawling.

I look at the blank page.

B-E-R-T-I-E

Okay, that's one.

Oh, and, of course: D-A-V-I-D

I look to Alexandra, but she is across the room, fixing something to the wall.

'Sorry, how long did you say it should be?' I say.

'Maximum nine.'

Nine?

I tap my pen on the pad. I suppose I could write 'friends' but—

No, I should add it: F-R-I-E-N-D-S

So, six more . . .

I scan the room, the canvasses on the wall, the smell of the suits we're wearing, the quiet of the studio. Once upon a time, art was the only thing that made me happy.

Gosh, how can it be that I don't know what to put here? I am content, but I suppose I'm not materialistic . . .

What would David put?

Hm. Definitely his bike. Gosh. It's insane to think a person could be jealous of a bike. However, would I really rather trump the bike? David has an ability to fix that machine with a dexterity I myself never experienced. His never quite understanding what I needed and the male ego such a fragile thing that to give anything veering toward criticism would be to bestow unrectifiable damage. The bike didn't flinch. The bike didn't have to fake anything.

Goodness. Thirty years.

'How are you getting on?' Miriam says.

I make a face and show her my list.

'Ah.'

'Indeed.'

'Alexandra said it could be abstract, remember? Look, I have 'joy' on mine.'

'Joy? I'm not sure that is something you choose. Rather, life chooses for you, don't you think?'

Miriam puts her list down. 'But when you have it, you're happy, right?'

'Well—' I pause and then write it down anyway: J-O-Y

'What about baking?' Miriam says.

I shake my head. I can't help but laugh.

'What? You sure look pretty happy after you've baked.'

'I . . . Yes, I suppose I am.' I suppose, baking in the mornings has made me feel happy. 'But I don't do it at home. Not anymore.'

'Why? If it makes you feel good?'

I open my mouth but . . .

Rise and fall.

'I was advised not to partake in baking.'

'What? By whom?' Miriam shifts on the stool.

I pick at my fingernail.

'Right. Of course. And his reason?'

'Oh, well, I suppose he had a point. He didn't want to clear up more soufflé.' I try to force a laugh.

Miriam widens her dark eyes.

'I may have thrown a soufflé across the kitchen.'

'Er . . ?'

'They're very hard to make.' Gosh. David's reaction. A look somewhere between bewilderment, hatred and concern. Sometimes he scolded me on these sorts of occasions, other times he chose not to draw attention to the matter. As if this were just normal for us. He'd sigh, and untuck his shirt in that way he did, long fingernails scratching across the rash on his expansive white tummy, snaking red trails that would wind across the flowery patches, flaky skin peeling off under his nails, catching in the black wiry hair or falling like dandruff— Where? I would try to spot it snowing down but I could never hold my gaze for long, instead feigning some toilet need so I could scoot away before I said something I couldn't retract.

Or maybe it was this gesture that caused me to throw the dessert in the first place.

'Okay, so a soufflé is hard to make. I can believe that,' Miriam says. 'And?'

'Since then, I've . . . I forgot. When it goes right, it's enjoyable.'

'But does it matter if it doesn't go right?'

I turn back to my list.

'Could you put drawing? You know - your doodles . . ? Or sex?'

'Miriam!'

'Love? I'm putting love.'

Goodness. Doodles, sex and love. Once upon a time . . .

And happiness?

Yes. But happiness that immense cannot last.

'Okay, ladies, are we ready?' Alexandra strolls over, hands clutched at her front.

I look at my list and quickly add: L-O-V-E

'Now I want you to assign a colour to each item. You have the paints here, so just dab a dot of colour you feel best represents the word, and mark it on the paper.'

I pick up a paintbrush and—

Goodness. A rush overwhelms me. Anticipation. Elation? A world of could-have-been.

I breathe.

I dab at my list:

Bertie. Definitely a bright sunny yellow.

David. Blue? Yes, blue. A dark blue. I smudge in some brown as well.

Friends? Grey. Because we're all going grey. Although Delilah from the book club had blonde and pink put in her hair which I rather liked. David maintains the opinion she is *inappropriate for her age*, but I thought it was fun. But he doesn't like it if my hair grows a single millimetre beyond my neat bob. And it always grows so fast, it means I'm in the blimmin' hairdresser every four weeks.

Joy? A light pink.

Goodness. I recall my hair when it was past my waist. I had been very young then. Early twenties, at the most. There was that photo. Me, standing at the easel in the dappled sunlight.

I'd tucked the photo away, of course. *He* had taken it. David would know and—

Well.

Love? A deep pink. The type of pink that connotes pain. Bloody. The deepest shade of—

'Dee?'

'Sorry, yes, I'm ready.' I nod at my list before I catch sight of Miriam's, which looks like a glorious rainbow. Hm. Miriam follows Alexandra over to the far side to where two pieces of white paper, larger than our bodies, have been stuck to the wall.

'The second task is to draw an outline of our bodies.' Alexandra says. 'Miriam, I'd like you to stand here.' Alexandra gestures for Miriam to stand in front of one piece of paper before she gently shuffles her back into position, so she is backed up against the wall. Alexandra's expression keeps flicking back to what I can only describe as constricted. Tight.

Perhaps she is nervous, having to cover this class, but there is no need to be. I must tell her later. I could write a review. Somewhere. Trip Advisor?

Goodness. I too am suddenly nervous. *Art therapy.* Gosh. What will David say? And Francis?

Well . . .

At Alexandra's request, I have stepped in front of Miriam and am drawing an outline of her body on the paper. I would like the outline to be smooth but it turns out rather jagged as I have to allow for all of her pockets. I've never known a woman to wear clothes with so many pockets. Even her pockets have pockets.

Then it's Miriam's turn to draw my outline and there's a little excitement bubbling amongst my nerves, but then I register Alexandra's worried expression and I remember this is supposed to be therapy and nausea washes over me from head to toe. What is that Picasso quote? Ah, yes: *Art washes away from the soul the dust of everyday life.*

All very well. But what if you need the dust?

'Can you put your arms a little wider, Dee?' Alexandra and Miriam are exchanging fast, jovial whispers. I find my arms reluctant to leave my sides. To let someone touch your ribs, inner thighs, is—

I close my eyes and hope she can be quick.

'Great, now let's pin your lists here.' At last, I can step away and Alexandra pins our lists next to our chalk outlines. 'Now, I want you to go through your list, and paint onto your body the things that make you happy, using the colour you have assigned. The colour should reflect how you feel about that thing, where it sits on the body and so forth. Is that clear?'

'Okay, so *love*, for example, would be in the heart?' Miriam asks.

'If you feel it that way. But maybe love in this moment is not centred there for you.'

Miriam turns away. 'No. A bad example, perhaps.'

'Not at all. There are no wrong answers. But as you think of each word, I want you to close your eyes and really *feel* it. Visualise how that thing makes you react, how it affects you, *feel* it affecting you. And then? Paint.' Alexandra throws out her arms to stress this final word, gives a little nod, and steps away.

My eyes remain on my outline. This is a simple task. I must not overthink it. All I need to do is dab some blobs of paint on the cut out. *No big deal*, as Bertie would say.

No big deal.

I look at my list:

B-E-R-T-I-E

D-A-V-I-D

F-R-I-E-N-D-S

J-O-Y

L-O-V-E

Let's start happy - yellow - for Bertie. My glorious little sunshine. She is going in my heart. Right in the middle.

David.

My breath leaves my chest with a noise.

Miriam already has three colours that circle each other in rings out of the centre.

Friends. I'll paint them on the periphery. The edges. They're there, but perhaps not making me ecstatic right now. The pretense is—

Well. Pretending is not conducive to happiness, is it?

I look at the paintbrush in my hand. I still have the divot in my finger. It feels like . . . Home, I suppose. Where everything makes sense.

Or maybe nothing makes sense, but it doesn't matter anyway.

I go through the motion of wetting the brush, cleaning off the colour, wiping dry. The process is meditative. Robotic. Years unwind in that motion alone, as though all of this might never have been.

Would it never have been if—?

Hm.

That line of thinking does not serve.

Joy: Light pink. I dab at the edges, little dots in the ether. Sometimes I grasp moments but they're fleeting. Already passed, perhaps.

And love?

Miriam has five colours. A circular rainbow.

I look at my own pathetic, garbled—

'I can't do it.' Oh. This is my voice. It sounds odd in the studio's silence. Leaving me involuntarily.

And my body - now moving.

Dee Dee.

Don't go.

'Dee?' This is Miriam.

Alexandra has returned to the studio. Her face forms a smile at me, before altering, miniscule. 'Everything okay?'

I nod but—

I have to leave.

I have to—

I have to go.

———

I close my eyes, hold my face up to the wind, breathe.

Isn't this what I used to wish for? Those times when I would lie in bed and try to imagine - a guttural need to be standing barefoot in sand, the wind thrust in my face in this way and—

The day I got up I was a diminished version of myself. My clothes no longer fit. My face sagged. I felt like . . .

Half a human.

To be an artist is to believe in life, says Henry Moore.

I have not been an artist.

But now?

I am standing on two feet, and I am steady. The wind blows with a whistle and the trees at the back of the beach rustle.

'Dee?'

I start at the deep voice. I thought I was alone on this stretch. I'm not entirely sure how I got this far down the sand, away from town but, alas, here I am. Evidently, not alone.

Tom has appeared from—?

Hm.

'Are you okay?' He is out of breath. Screwed up expression. He raises his voice above the wind. 'You passed the shop, and you looked upset but then I had to take a call and . . . You must have run.' He shakes his head. Steps closer. 'Are you okay?'

'Oh, erm, yes.' I lower my chin. My cheeks are wet, I notice. I rub at my nose. Dripping.

Goodness. *Don't cause a scene.*

I can see the lighthouse up on the hill, but Tom is in my way. I look to him and—

I need to sit down.

'Do you want to talk about it?' Tom is slow to lower himself beside me.

I'm looking at the sea through a tunnel, a scene I am

observing from afar, not part of. Like when Bertie and I used to hold up toilet rolls, pretending they were telescopes, us the pirates. The view ahead is somehow focused, pertinent. The perspective sharpened. Isn't this how Van Gogh's *Bedroom* was described? Yes. A sharpened perspective gives the view a nervousness, an instability to which I can sympathise.

The surf is doing that energetic wish-washing thing - the waves tumbling and jumping and the white water iridescent. The noise of it washes in my mind in the same tone. I close my eyes and concentrate on the salt springing onto my face. It's almost imperceptible, but if you focus, you can register every iota of sea spray as it tickles onto the skin.

Goodness. When did I stop feeling? *This* - feeling in my body. *Of* my body.

'The ocean is a good remedy, hey?' Tom squints out to the expanse beyond, his hair blowing up straight, the late afternoon light illuminating him like a model in a photographer's studio.

I manage a noise of agreement.

We sit like this - companionable, no expectation, easy.

When did I last sit with David easily?

I did a lot of sitting when Mum was dying, I suppose. In the aftermath.

And David? My life saver. He'd been so caring; considering the things I could not. A man who picks up when others are unable. He rallies, makes himself useful. Practical. Francis is similar. Although I don't want to be resentful, for all his helping, all I'd wanted was for David to listen. I'd wanted, no, I'd needed, to cry. Unabated. Unjudged. I often wonder if Francis ever cried.

I suppose the practicalities help some people - avoidance, perhaps, something to occupy. David is a man who likes to be busy; it didn't serve him to wallow with me. And he had to get back to work. I suppose he needed to know I could cope, know I could look after Bertie.

And I did, didn't I?

Although - *coped*? Do we ever really cope? Or do we just divert our attention? Box it up and carry on.

'I'd like to go surfing again.' I close my eyes, smile, imagine driving my head into that crashing wave. In the sea, everything else is insignificant. 'Have you always surfed?'

'In the summers, when I'd visit here, but . . . Not as much as I'd like. And now the business . . . Excuses, I suppose.'

Tom looks at his hands, clasped loosely as they hang between his knees.

'Did your parents get you into it?'

'Ha, no. I think they're the straightest couple in Australia. I bonded with my errant uncle - the waif of the family. I waifed with him, I suppose, despite their protestations.'

'That takes courage.' I think of Bertie. *Breaking free*, she'd said. *Dad is not always right.* 'Do your parents see how well you do now?'

Tom laughs, then. 'I don't do well.'

'What do you mean? Taking over the shop can't be easy. And the boards?'

'I'm not doing the boards. I took over the shop with all these grand ideas and they said it would be hard and . . . I don't know. My folks are right, I suppose.'

'What happened to the grand ideas?' I ask but my voice, I notice, is lost in the crush of the sea. The two of us lost in the expanse of the unfurling beach. If we weren't here, the sea would still move, the waves still crash.

'Life doesn't always turn out as you hoped, right?' Tom says.

I try to smile. I should ask his story but—

The box.

Isn't it easier to hide?

'Here you are,' Miriam startles me from my reverie, placing a gentle hand on my shoulder. I'm in the bakery eyeing up the selection, trying to steady myself as though the wind might still blow me off balance, despite my being inside.

'I looked for you in the gallery cafe. I didn't think to come here.'

I reach a steadying hand to the counter. 'I'd forgotten how much I love these places. All this selection . . . it's like an adult sweet shop.'

Miriam turns to the display. Glazed fruit covers tiny tarts on one side, cakes in the middle and beautiful loafs of varying colours and sizes on the far side.

'I'm sorry,' I say, though to speak is a struggle. 'I lost the plot.'

Miriam doesn't flinch. 'It's understandable.'

I look at her.

'David?' she says.

I pause, then nod.

A scream from outside. A joyous scream. A child.

'And other things?' she adds.

But to this, I give no reply.

There is a clatter from the kitchen out back and a smell of fresh bread wafts into the eatery.

'Alexandra had to go out so I have the key to the studio if you want to finish?'

'I'm not so sure that's a good idea.'

I hear Miriam exhale. 'Therapy was never going to be easy.'

'For you it is.' I peer closer to inspect a slice of pumpkin cake.

'For me? No.'

'You're one of those people - one of the lucky ones - everything works out.' I stand back upright.

Miriam shakes her head. 'Dee Dee, my dear, you couldn't be more wrong.'

Dee Dee.

Gosh. Did life work out for *him*?

The baker - the owner, I suspect - comes out of the back room to attend the counter. A small man with a shiny bald bonce, prickled with sweat, and I'm relieved to see a hair net pulled down around his neck. He has more hair on his face than he does on his head, and I have the sudden image of him wearing the net around his close-cut beard.

'How can I help?'

'Jolly' is the word that comes to mind. I point to the display. 'Two of the French custard tarts, please.'

'Two?' Miriam says.

'You're not going to let me indulge alone, are you?'

Miriam smiles. 'And two glasses of Prosecco.'

I raise an eyebrow.

'You're not going to let me indulge alone, are you?' Miriam winks, before seizing upon a just-vacated table for two in the window. The café is scattered with ornate features; shiny, delicate. Would I have *hung out* in places such as this if I'd gone to Paris? Drawing, painting, mooching around patisseries in my spare time.

He told me about Paris.

'Did you make these?' I ask the man behind the counter.

'Yes, I trained in France. Many years ago. Long before you were born, I suspect.'

'I doubt that.' I laugh, because I'd put this man at a similar age to myself. 'They look fantastic. I had some olive bread yesterday and . . . Wow.'

'Thank you.' He pauses in his rejig of the display. 'Are you in Byron for long?'

'A few weeks. I'll need to work myself through everything you have here.' And then, before I can talk myself out of it, 'I'm Dee.'

'Derrick. Nice to meet you.'

I smile at Derrick and retreat to join Miriam at the table. She takes the plate from me, holding the cake up close to her face, waving it from side to side as she inhales the scent.

Finally, she puts the plate down and unfolds her napkin. 'Is this your favourite?'

'Oh, my goodness, I've forgotten what's my favourite.' Oh, look at this perfect little pudding, its custard glistening, the spattering of icing sugar like a dusting of snow . . . I am salivating.

'Don't tell me, David didn't let you have treats, either.'

I put the tart down.

Miriam sips from the flute. She eyes me. Tilts her wild head. 'Do you ever wonder whether it might be a blessing that he left you on the plane?'

The window frames the Byron high street. A Monday afternoon, people back to work. Others moan of a Monday but for me, it was a break from David's schedule. The enforced fun of a Sunday. When he went back to work, I could be quiet. The house was still again. Nobody there to interrupt so I could talk in peace . . .

'No.' I pick at a flake of pastry. It is buttery and light and—

Would I have liked Paris? Or would I have felt lost?

'You're within your right to be angry. Do you do anger, Dee?'

My eyes flick to my friend. 'Of course.'

But she says nothing more.

Outside, Alexandra hurries past the window, talking in her phone, her spare hand gesticulating as though miming wood chopping.

'She doesn't look okay,' Miriam whispers, her head turning so she can keep watch.

But Derrick is at our table and he is topping up our glasses and somehow, I have already drunk most of mine.

'Goodness, a Monday afternoon. You must think us utter winos.' I touch a hand to my cheek, which feels hot.

'Not at all. We only get one chance to enjoy ourselves.' And he nods and sort of bows away from the table.

I fork a piece of tart and—

I close my eyes. My oh my oh my. Is it possible for food to be transcendent?

Goodness. Why have I been eating only bland food of late?

'Should I see if she is okay?'

I take a moment to realise Miriam is talking about Alexandra, who has stopped across the street. She's holding a hand to her head and still talking into the phone.

'She looks somewhat occupied, don't you think? We shouldn't intervene.'

'It's not intervening. It's checking she's okay.'

'You don't think it's nosy?' I think of Francis. Persistent 'checking'.

Miriam turns back to me. 'No, I think it's care. I want to help her.'

'But we don't know her.'

'So, let's get to know her.'

'But—'

'I can't see that caring about people - forming relationships and listening - is nosy. Surely that's just . . . life?'

'I . . . I don't know.'

After a pause, Miriam speaks. 'No. I'm beginning to realise that.' And she waves at Alexandra, managing to catch her attention, and beckons her over.

'Dee,' Alexandra says. I'm surprised to find her embracing me. 'Are you okay?'

Don't make a scene.

'Oh, yes, I'm . . . Yes. Sorry for leaving class.'

Alexandra bats my comment away and takes the seat Miriam has pulled over.

'Are *you* okay?' Miriam says to Alexandra.

Alexandra emits a groan. 'Ex's, hey?' She holds up her phone and then places it on the table.

'You're preaching to the converted,' Miriam says.

'Well—' I offer. But my breath catches in my throat.

'Miss Alex, a drink on the house?' Derrick appears at our table, proffering a glass of bubbles for Alexandra.

'Oh, Derrick. You're a kind man. I forget what a small place this is. No doubt you've heard . . .'

'No need to explain, dear. You just make sure that place keeps running.'

Alexandra reaches out and holds Derrick's hand for a moment. They exchange gentle smiles, and then he departs.

'A lovely guy,' Alexandra says, turning back to us. 'I should take lessons from him in how to do life alone.' She lifts her glass in salute, then takes a large sip. 'I'm sorry you two have met me in this state. I was so involved with the gallery and Vinnie and—' She laughs, fiddling with the stem of her glass. 'You've come at a time of change.'

'Break-ups are hard,' Miriam says, and I find myself nodding. Although I've not broken up with David . . .

'Never do business with your partner unless you're married and plan on staying married.'

'The gallery is fabulous, though. Did you run it together?' I say.

Alexandra puts her drink down and her expression brightens. 'It was always my project, but Vinnie helped me with finance and business advice and now—' A sigh. 'I want to sort it out. I want to continue the gallery alone and I'll pay the money back. I will, but . . . Vinnie is impatient.'

'Can't you formulate a plan? A repayment thing?' Miriam says. Her face, I notice, is full of a darkness I've not seen before. 'I'm sorry,' she says, sitting back in her chair. 'It's not my place.'

'No, it's fine. And yes, I have a plan but that doesn't prevent Vinnie from giving me crap about it. I have this exhibition I'm putting on at the end of the month and now I'm . . . Ugh. It will be okay.'

I remember I'd had a plan to continue running my art classes.

'You can do it,' I surprise myself by saying. And, really, who am I to say this, for goodness sake? What do I know? Although Alexandra is a woman who, right now, yes, might doubt herself, I can tell there is a strength there. A formidability I suspect is hard to dent.

Me? Perhaps I broke too easily. Although, unlike Alexandra, I didn't need to run a gallery; I didn't need to do anything.

Maybe that was the problem.

'The artist is amazing,' Alexandra says, sitting upright. 'Vinnie found him on Instagram and his stuff is—' She nods, then looks at Miriam, laughs and shrugs.

'I'd love to come,' I say. 'What's the date?'

'Twenty-ninth.'

The wedding date. 'Oh, that's a shame,' I say. 'I'll have already left.'

'I'll still be here. And I'd love to come,' Miriam says, the warmth back in her face in full force, and I notice my own warmth seems to have simmered away somewhat.

Miriam and I stroll back from the cafe in the lowering light of the late afternoon, the sky a Turner canvas of dusty blue, wisps of white and I feel—

Goodness. Emotionally spent. A wilting azalea. Yet . . . there is hope there. Deep down. An archaeologist whose been digging for years, and the spade's hit an obscure solid mass, but the sunlight has faded before they uncover the form. The archaeologists are tired but excited for the days to follow.

We walk in amiable silence. I long not to overthink the emotion but just . . . Be.

I just want to be. Here in this image. The background of Turner, the foreground classic Monet. His animated brush-strokes would capture this scene – the light bouncing from glass shopfronts, the wet road as the cafe owner washes down his terrace, a depiction of one element to exemplify the scene . . . There. *Woman with a Parasol.* Yes.

The formality of the typical portrait is released. My formality released.

Fancy free. *Woman with a Parasol.*

'Oh, my. Look at that beautiful scarf.' Miriam reaches a hand to my arm, and we look at the window display of this cute boutique. The scarf is soft and floaty but the print is bright and bold. 'I think it would look fabulous on you.'

'David would hate it,' I laugh.

David prefers me in muted colours, but perhaps I could wear it to the book club? Patricia, I'm sure, would have an opinion but—

Perhaps I could shrug her opinion off.

'It's very . . . Yellow,' I add.

'Your colour for Bertie, was it not? It could remind you of her.'

Gosh. Look at the gorgeous garment. I lift a hand to rest on the glass. Once upon a time, I would have paraded right into the shop and bought the item with no second thought.

Once upon a time . . .

'Oh, hello girls,' Miriam says behind me. Dragging myself from the window, I join Miriam greeting Indie and Lola. 'Where are you off to?'

'Indie here is off for a date with Jake,' Lola says.

'It's not a date, it's—'

'A meaningless sunset surf?' Lola has a mocking tone that gives me cause to think of a teenage Francis. *She's just jealous of your friends,* Mum had said, soothing. I didn't believe it, of course, Francis always had far more friends than I.

'Why don't you guys come too?' Indie says. 'And then you'll see it's not exclusive.'

'Hey, we can't crash your date.'

'It's not a . . . I don't want it to be a date.' Indie's bright expression flickers. Her own hidden gems, briefly illuminated.

'Does he know that?' Miriam asks.

Indie opens her mouth, and then shrugs.

'You really don't want it to be anything romantic?'

'No.'

'Really?' This is Lola. Incredulous. The strength and power of her, as always, so . . . present. I wonder if Lola struggles to comprehend anyone who is not as gung ho as her.

'Would you prefer it if we were there?' I say. Indie gives the impression of a Woman Needing Help. Hopefully this is something she'll grow out of.

'Well, I mean, if you don't mind. If you think it would stop him from assuming this is something it's not? I don't want to lead him on.'

Our huddle moves aside to let a woman with a pram power-walk past, her high ponytail bouncing as much as her breasts. I hear myself tut.

Hm. What was I saying about jealousy?

'Why did you agree to go, Indie? The poor dude.' At this, Lola kicks at a stone on the ground. It brings to mind a four-year-old Bertie - she didn't have many tantrums but occasionally she would strop and throw her limbs around uncontrollably. I always found it rather endearing but David struggled. Especially in public, I seem to remember. Not one given to embarrassment is David.

Although, is anyone?

'You were there,' Indie says. 'It was casual. Jake asked us both.'

Lola looks up the street. 'Well, I'm going to check out the tattoo place. I'm not keen for a surf today.'

'You're getting a tattoo?' Miriam asks.

Lola makes herself even taller. 'Ohmygod, yes. There's this one I have seen online and I just love it. But I want to scout the place out first, check its creds, you know? I've not had one before.'

'No, me neither,' Miriam says. 'But I reckon I might want one. Dee, what do you think?'

Me? A tattoo? Ha! 'No, thank you.' And I mean, really, a tattoo on Miriam? She's younger than me but she's no spring chicken, for goodness sake.

'I'd love to come with you, Lola, but—' Miriam looks at Indie, the darling girl with the expression of a cartoon bunny about to be eaten by a big bad wolf. Not that Jake is wolf-like . . .

'I'll go surfing with Indie,' I offer. I mean, I feel bad for the poor girl.

'Okay, great,' Lola says. 'We'll come down to the beach once we've finished.'

'I'll bring my camera.' Miriam winks. For some reason, she's keen on capturing all of my experiences here. Bertie is the same, living as though unless there's digital footage, the event didn't exist.

We leave Lola and Miriam chatting and gesticulating with equal fervour, and Indie and I head down to the beach.

'You know, I really don't want this to be a date,' Indie says, as we cross through town and wind our way along the main street. We pass the gallery, the lights switched off, the cafe closed, and I wonder whether Alexandra is sad about her breakup, whether she was the one who instigated it. I see her worrying about the financial side of things but—

Gosh. It's none of my business, is it? Despite what Miriam says.

'Well, there are usually other people in the sea, so you won't be alone together.'

Lola nods. 'And I saw Tom earlier, and he said he was going out, so that's someone else we know.'

'Oh, yes, that's good.'

'Lola thinks I should forget Jake and ask Tom out, but . . .'

I swallow. 'You don't like him?' I manage.

'I guess I'm hesitant about all men right now. He's probably just another surfer dude. Working in a place like this.' We leave the town and start upon the last part of the road that leads to the beach. 'He must meet lots of tourists, you know? Play around?'

The sea has come into view ahead. The wind has dropped; it is calm. Expansive, broken only by the occasional line of waves (a 'set') which glide in small and clean. 'I don't know. I think there is more there. I think he has high aspirations, actually.'

'Mm, maybe. Lola says he probably lives in a van and can you imagine if I told my father that's who I was dating?' Indie gives a little giggle like an elongated hiccup.

'Oh, well . . .'

'I'm just kidding.' Indie lifts her feet to slip off her flip-flops. 'Apparently he doesn't even have a van.'

'The only person in Byron who doesn't,' I say, as we move back to allow a camper to pass us into the car park.

'Yeah, but Lola said don't tease him about it, because she did and he went all weird. Said he used to, but . . . Hey, there he is.'

We reach the sand path crossing down to the beach. In the distance, Tom is outside his shack, talking to Jake.

'You okay?' Indie asks. She has continued to walk and talk while I am—

Hm. I seem to have stopped.

'I'm . . . Fine. A little queasy, perhaps. It's nothing.'

And, really, Diane? It probably is nothing.

I tell Indie I need a minute on the sand. I watch her skip to the boys and I wave, then move further down the beach. Even from this far away, however, I can deduct from Jake's body language that Lola is right: Indie will need to be straight with him. My being here will not change that boy's expectations. My being here will not change—

It won't change anything.

Goodness.

The sea. Still battling with itself, despite the drop of wind. Another Impressionist piece. Short strokes, movement, the changing passage of time. The sea is an apt symbol of life, isn't it? Consistently altering, changing. Pushing forward, quickly receding.

Is my tide coming in? Or going out?

I look back to the shack. Indie and Jake are heading down to the surf and Tom has gone and—

That building. From this angle. Didn't Bertie send me a photo from here? I should come back with Miriam - ask her to take the same so I can email it and—

I need to go in that water. I—

I am under the sea. A weird phrase, when you consider it. I am actually *in* the sea. Underneath the surface. Hidden. I am 'wiping out', but I must stay calm. Water roars in my ears and I'm no longer sure which way is up and oh—

Ouch! That's sand. That will hurt when I come up - it was my face. I'm tumbling, turning, bubbling, and . . . Where is the—

Here! I'm here! I gasp for breath as my head pops up to air, staggering as my knees locate ground. Another wash overhead before I haul myself back up the shoreline where I collapse on the sand. All I can focus on is my breath, heaving in and out of me, my body slack, my head settling.

And - goodness - tears.

But it's okay. I'm okay. I'm on land.

You're okay. I've got you, Dee Dee.

Jeez. Why is my filter not weaning him out? I'd buried him, forgotten, entombed because what choice did I have?

I roll onto my back. It must be late as the blue of the sky is deepening and it won't be long before the first star can be spotted.

Star gazing. A thing we no longer have time for, but—

Am I really too busy? David would think I was Having An Episode. Maybe I am. I'm not sure I know anymore.

What am I doing here? Without David?

I can't do this.

'Hey, are you okay? Dee, you have your clothes on. Goodness, Dee. Did you hurt yourself? I came to take photos, but all I got was you dragging yourself back up the beach. What were you thinking? Oh, your face looks sore.' Miriam peers over me, inspecting.

I sit myself up. 'Do you still have the key for the studio?'

Her head tilts, awkward. 'Er . . .Yeah. Why? Don't you think—'

'I need it.'

———

If it weren't for Miriam, I would still be in my wet clothes, but she forced me to change. Goodness knows what Michael thought of my speedy exit from Tom's shop wearing a t-shirt and shorts from the lost property but I was thankful not to bump into Tom. My body is pulsing with an energy I can't name. Like I've had too much coffee, I suppose. I sense my veins pumping. Widening, constricting. Worked up. *On one*, as Bertie would say.

I can't speak. I can't explain. Miriam let me into the studio and now I am here, frozen still as I study the sketch outline of my body – only yellow and a touch of pink dabbed on.

Jesus. This cannot be all I have to show for my happiness.

This is not all I have.

Veins pump more. Faster. I pick up the paintbrush, dip it into the dark blue and I streak it over the paper. Thick, gloopy lines, navy diagonal crossings, left to right and right to left and back and forth all over again.

Something hiccups involuntarily from my gut. I hear myself stammer, breath shuddering, a relic of a steam train, out for a trial run after a long restoration.

'For God's sake, I don't know how to do this without him. I don't know what to feel without him. I can't—'

I bang the heel of my hand against my head.

Miriam is beside me. She takes my hand. Lowers it.

'Or maybe you haven't been feeling anything, and now you're exposed.'

My expression clears. I want to argue but—

'*Goddamit*, Miriam.' I shake my head. Look away.

Miriam is still. 'It's not a bad thing.'

'Of course it is. I know what I'm doing at home. I . . . I can do that. For God's sake, I can do that.'

'Dee, he left you.' Her voice is calming. A daisy white in my mind - edging towards pink, just as a petal.

I look at my friend, and I want to say it all. To tell her this happiness isn't—

I would be exposed. Different. People avoiding happy around me. Or doing so with that follow-up look of regret. Pity.

'David keeps this—' I throw my hands over my body – 'in check. Secure. I'm freewheeling without him. I . . . I . . .' I look down at the ridiculousness of my outfit. 'I need my luggage. I can't believe I'm here without . . . *anything*. It's lunacy. If you'd told me this is what I would do in Australia, I'd feel—'

'Stripped back? Honest?'

The box. A physical need to hold it. Cradle it. I make a fist, press it into my gut.

'You're surviving, Dee. You're doing this. And you're doing it without him.'

'I . . .' I drop my head. Something comes out of me - a noise. Nonsensical. Black in my mind.

Veins full to bursting. I am going to burst. I pummel my fist and I—

'I can't do this.'

Because? I can't.

I just can't do it.

———

It's eight in the evening and if it were my choice, I'd be in bed, hiding in shame at my outburst earlier. But Miriam insisted I join everyone for a drink. At least, I suppose, an outing will provide a distraction for my brain. A chance to keep it busy and not revert to—

Well. My body is also reluctant. The effort of having dragged myself out of the sea is taking its toll. I pull my bedroom door shut behind me. What would I usually be doing at home right now? Certainly not going out, not during the week, anyway. David would probably just be getting in from work, regaling me with the latest gossip from his office or perhaps he'd be in one of his quiet moods and I'd know to go to bed then. Best leave him to catch up on the news alone.

In fact, Sofia's mutterings are not far off how David would act at this exact hour. She's shaking her head, sputtering to herself as she takes her place behind the reception.

'Everything okay?' I venture. I've agreed to meet Miriam here before she drags me off to this 'dance'. *A barn dance,* apparently. I look at my sandaled feet and sigh. Inappropriate footwear for a dance, of course, but my heels are in my lost luggage. When I packed them to match my wedding outfit, I can say with a lot of certainty I would not expect to need them for a barn dance. I doubted I would even get to dance at the wedding reception, but I let myself daydream about David asking me, anyway. For a brief interlude, in the relaxed setting of the wedding, perhaps he'd want to have fun, I thought. Maybe he'd feel like he could. There.

'I just caught another kid trying to tag the wall,' Sofia says. 'I mean, what the—? I won't tell Eric because he will berate the boy, just a teen, you know? So, I confiscated his stuff.'

I'm about to ask what 'tag' means when I spot the bag of spray cans and recall my conversation with Eric the other night.

'I'm not sure how to dispose of these.' Sofia's voice spits balls of red in my mind. Staccato, rapid. 'Can I recycle them?'

'Oh, I'm not sure,' I say, and she shrugs and drops the plastic bag under the desk. I offer a smile but Sofia is abrasive, absorbed in her own world. She must be the only person in the hostel not desperate to make friends. Nobody stays for long. (Although they certainly hang around the kitchen when they smell my bread. This morning it was all gobbled up before I had chance to sample a piece.)

'Wow, a woman in a skirt. I like it.' As Miriam approaches,

she holds out her hand and I take it, letting her spin me round. After seeing me in the clothes from the surf shack's lost property earlier, Indie insisted I borrow one of her skirts. It's a plain black sixties number that flares out when I spin. I feel rather glamorous, actually. 'You look great.'

'As do you,' I offer, happy to see Miriam looking a little more feminine than usual in a linen dress. It's khaki, but at least it's a dress. With pockets, of course.

'I'm glad to see you put your dancing clothes on.' Miriam links her arm through mine and we bid Sofia goodbye. 'Along with a smile.'

'Yes, I'm—'

'Don't apologise,' Miriam interrupts. She stops, places her hands on my shoulders, warm and firm, then plants a kiss on my cheek before opening the hostel door. Goodness. What's the correct reaction here? Well, I needn't worry, as she is now gabbling on about the tattoo place and I find myself looking up. As I suspected, the stars are fabulous. Like bright seeds of hope sprinkled wide.

'I hope she's okay,' Miriam says.

Goodness. I appear to have tuned out for a moment. 'I'm sorry?'

'Alexandra. I wonder if she'll have the class tomorrow.' Miriam steps aside to let me walk on the inside of the curb. The tarmac is still warm, although dampness simmers on the night air, nature preparing a fresh morning.

'Is something wrong?'

'She just said she needed to confirm some things and—'

'But we saw her earlier. She said *see you tomorrow*?' I'm not sure how I feel about the possibility of the class not running. I suppose I dislike the idea of not completing the course because, well, it would be a waste of effort. You know, to start something and not see it through.

Then again, the thought of seeing whatever atrocity I created earlier makes me want to recoil inside myself. Turn my skin inside out like some weird horror movie from the seventies.

'I messaged her.' Miriam stops outside the bar. The music thumps on the other side of the door, pulsating grey in my mind.

'Oh. Right. I didn't know you had her number.'

'Yeah. You know, with the key and everything. It's no big deal.' *No big deal.*

Miriam opens the door before I can see her face, and she walks into the bar with the same ease as if she were walking into her own home.

I've never been one to *go clubbing*, as Bertie would say, but I do love dancing. As with so many things, the chance to dance seems to diminish as we age. Patricia took Hugo to those dance classes that time and I have to admit to having felt somewhat envious. David would never agree to such a thing.

And this thing is beyond anything I could have imagined. The noise, for a start, is unnecessarily loud, the crowd thick and sweaty, like a large being - an entity all of its own as it sways and leans and, goodness, let's hope it doesn't buckle.

I tighten my grip on the sticky bar, my nose wrinkling at the smell of sweat and spilt beer. Gosh. What will this place look like in the morning?

'So how did the non-date date work out with Jake?' Miriam asks Indie, who we stand beside in a huddle alongside Lola. Well, Lola is physically here, but her focus is elsewhere, her eyes flitting along the patrons at the bar.

'Oh, he's sweet,' Indie says, dipping her head to suck from her straw.

'*Sweet*?' Lola pulls a face, but keeps her focus wayward. 'Indie, my dear, you need a rebound shag. Someone tough, passionate . . . Someone who'll blow your ex right out of your brain. Him!' Lola points at a tall square man at the far end of the bar.

'Oh,' I say, but thankfully the music drowns me out. I don't want to rain on Indie's parade but—

'Lola! He looks like an assassin.' Thank goodness, Indie agrees.

'Maybe Indie should get there in her own time,' Miriam suggests.

'He's hot. And he looks keen.'

'Or desperate,' Indie says.

'Not desperate. He just looks like a man who knows what he wants,' Lola retorts, turning her full attention to our little group. 'Life would be far simpler if we all knew what we wanted and acted on it.'

'Yes, but sometimes that's easier to say,' Miriam says.

'And it can be scary,' I venture. 'Don't you get scared?'

Lola lifts her chin. 'My father taught me to be bold. Actually, he taught my brothers that. I listened to everything he told them and I took it as gospel for me. Why shouldn't I follow the same rules? So, no, I don't get scared. Feel the fear and do it anyway, right?'

'Until people laugh at you,' Miriam says, looking at me. 'Like when you're petrified up a cliff and your so-called-helper giggles hysterically?'

I cradle my drink to my chest. 'Yes. I'm sorry about that.'

'Ohmygod, I'm just the same in situations where I should be calm,' Lola says, flapping a hand in the middle of the circle. 'My father is a very serious surgeon and often loses people on the table and when he tells me I just want to scream with laughter, like there's something wrong with me. I remember when his mother died, and I had to leave the room because I just had to laugh. Like a freak.'

Freak. I suppose this is one of those words that's had its meaning altered amongst the younger generations.

'You're just like the girls in my class,' Miriam says. 'You're all so fearless. Do you really not find anything scary? Nothing makes you freeze up like I did trying to conquer the climbing wall?'

Lola considers the question before she shakes her hair out and presents her palms. 'Once, yes. And maybe that's why I love acting - the one thing I feel I need to, as you say, *conquer*. I had the lead in Annie at school - singing and dancing and . . . I loved it. But every night, I would freeze side of stage.'

'Annie?' Indie asks. 'How do I not know this?'

'Yep,' Lola says, lifting her chin. 'I made the local papers. Sold out run at the local town hall, I'll have you know.'

'Ha, first stop Bishops Stortford, next stop—'

'Hollywood!' she cries, hands flaring to the side as though she has just launched herself onto a stage.

'Really?' I say, before I can catch it.

Thankfully, Lola laughs. 'No. The reality for most actresses is a permanent out-of-work job status, right? I couldn't do that. I wouldn't handle failing.'

'You only do the things you know you'll be best at,' Indie says.

'And what's wrong with that?' Lola swishes her hair, and none of us have a reply for her.

'So, what are you going to do?' I say, after a moment, taking my chance to speak at a normal level as the music pauses between tracks.

'Brain surgeon.'

'Right. Of course.'

'You might fear climbing but you're not scared of getting a tattoo, are you? Did you choose one?' Indie asks Miriam.

'I can't decide between a symbol or a phrase.' Miriam's voice strains above the new, heavier beat. 'I prefer how a symbol looks, but what if they tell me it means one thing, but really it says *Chicken fried rice*?'

'Hm. Maybe check on Google first, do some research.'

'Do you know what you'd have, Dee?' Miriam says. 'If you were to get a tattoo?'

'A bird.' Ah, I have answered before my brain has engaged.

Miriam narrows her eyes. 'Your doodle?'

I look down, clink the ice cubes in my glass. 'Silly, really,' I say, eventually.

And I can feel Miriam regarding me long after I turn back to Lola telling us about her 'inking' idea.

I shuffle away from the dance floor, through the dense crowd, arms tucked into my sides, focus on the bar. Heat builds through the throng, like I'm wading through waist-deep mud towards a hot spring. Finally, I make it, breathing in the space, the reprieve of alcohol laden-breath and sweat a relief to my lungs. I pull my waist up to the bar and lean on it.

Goodness. It's insane here tonight.

Ah. I have slid in beside Eric and Shaun. Eric is nodding, gaze fixed on the ceiling as Shaun gesticulates. Grandiose is the word that comes to mind when I look at Shaun. His cheeks wobble in a similar manner to David's, though Shaun has a deep tan. I've always thought a tan can hide a thousand sins. On Shaun, I expect it does.

'Look, we should ask a fellow English woman.'

Oh! Shaun is talking to me. My cheeks blanch as Eric moves one of his boney little shoulders to allow me into their huddle. I step into the space, unsure what to do with my hands. I had been returning to the bar, wanting to hold the wooden edge like a crutch. I'm reminded of that little wooden train

Bertie had as a girl. She took it everywhere with her until, one day, it got left behind on a bus. Goodness, how distraught she'd been.

Right. Smile, Dee. I'm on unfamiliar territory here - alone with two men. I don't have many of the species in my life. Only partners of friends, and I only see those men through the lens constructed by said friend. Patricia's husband is the thoughtful one, but careless with his clothes and a terrible cook. Mary from the library's husband is clumsy and useless with a hammer. Delilah's husband is far too soppy for his own good. I've never spared the time to form an opinion of my own, have I? Yet if any of those men were my friend, it wouldn't matter to me if they were useless with clothes or rotten with a hammer. I suspect a kind heart would suffice.

How rare it is to find a kind heart nowadays.

Goodness. I sound old.

'I'm trying to convince darling Eric here to visit the mother-land, my dear. But he's being awfully stubborn, aren't you?' Shaun says, dipping his chin to create a roll of neck skin that reminds me of Bertie's pink swimming ring she used to play with in the leisure centre pool. My, she loved to swim. Or, rather, splash. She splashed so much there was never any chance I would keep my bob in check, and on those occasions, I felt so buoyed up in Bertie's joy, I didn't care. I could walk past David's disapproving glance, brushing it off as though it were a speck of lint on my shoulder.

My hair is already tickling at my neck now. Goodness, I thought I'd miss my curlers but— Perhaps I've had no time to care here, either.

'Have you been to England?' I ask Eric, who is screwing up his face and puckering his lips as though he's taking a long drag of one of his disgusting cigarettes.

'No, Dee. I like it here.'

'But, darling. We've been here for years. I need to see my

family. I want you to see my family, to meet my relatives, to see where I'm from.'

'It's cold,' Eric says, like some old miser in one of those black and white movies David would make us all watch on Christmas day. 'Isn't it cold?' Eric asks me.

'Well, the weather is not as reliable as here, but autumn is beautiful. I love the seasons.' There's a large oak tree at the end of our garden. Recently, I've been wondering whether I could stay in bed for an entire year and simply watch the leaves change colour. They were a marvellous zingy green before we left, and I suspect the edges will already be tickling toward orange upon our return. Then, once they turn brown, they wave their goodbye, before falling, maybe offering a twirl in their descent, lowering back down to earth with grace. It's a dance of nature and I find it, in some way, inspiring.

Are you watching that pointless tree again? David would say, unable to keep the annoyance from his voice. He didn't like me sitting on the bed looking out of the window. I wasn't harming anyone, but he insisted it was odd.

But David was never one to see the appeal of the tree. Recently, he mentioned applying for planning permission to have a house built down there. Apparently, Steve from his office sold part of his garden as a plot and got *money for nothing*.

But. I like the tree.

'Oh, we could go in autumn and the dales would be just splendid. Have you been to Yorkshire, Dee? Tell Eric how splendid it is, darling.' Shaun places a large hand on my forearm, and a dampness remains long after he removes it.

I clasp my own hands together. 'Yorkshire? Yes, glorious. I've only been once, a long time ago, but I have fond memories.' I think of my father. Francis. They had backpacks, a compass, sturdy walking boots. Mother had taken my hand, and we swung along as though sauntering into town, watching the other two clamber ahead on a private mission of their own. Did

Mother know then what her husband was up to? 'What's your hesitation?' I ask Eric. Shaun mimes another drink and I nod. Gosh. I've drunk more in the last week than I have the entire year.

At what point should I consider it a problem?

Eric downs his dregs and passes the empty glass to Shaun, who presses his stomach against the bar. 'The hostel doesn't run itself. Shaun thinks Sofia can run it, and she probably can, but with those youths around I'm unsure.'

'The ones tagging it?' Goodness, I am ridiculous. When did I become a person to say *tagging*?

Eric's barely-there eyebrows arch. 'I don't know what they'll do next.'

'I should think it's harmless fun to them, though,' I say. 'Don't you think? Why would it be anything sinister? Perhaps it's just their expression, their art needing a release.'

Eric looks at me as though I'm insane, and, with comments like this, it's understandable.

Gosh. I've been spending too much time with Miriam. *Art therapy*, for goodness sake.

'Time to get the party started!' Shaun has three grim-looking green shots in his hands.

'Oh, darling. Really? Again?' Eric draws his bony hands into his chest, and I only now notice he's wearing a thick, grey knitted jumper. I rather like it, but it seems inappropriate for the setting. I, myself, am insufferably hot.

And now, on seeing this offering from Shaun, another wave of heat surges over me. Shaun places one of those damp paws on my shoulder and hands me the drink.

He lifts his own glass into the middle, Eric, with reluctance, lifting his to meet it. They both look at me and— Oh. I'm expected to do the same. To *down it*, as Bertie would say.

The moisture of Shaun's hand seeps deeper into my shoulder and— Well. What else can I do to escape the grasp?

And so, I lift my glass, I say cheers, and I down the drink.

Somehow, I find myself stuck in the middle of a barn dance. A
heave of people, a small dance floor, and loud music. My mind
is a kaleidoscope of colours, unable to fixate on one thing.
Perhaps I should try not to fixate. Veer away from connection to
reality; an abstract piece. To let go?

Rise and fall.

It's surprisingly freeing. Like being in the sea and, as I found
with the surfing, not as scary as I imagined. Maybe that's what's
working for me here - I can't overthink and talk myself out of
things because I can in no way anticipate what's to come. I
couldn't have imagined I'd be in a barn dance, alone in
Australia, a little drunk. Any of those facts taken alone, given it's
a Monday night, would be unusual for me. Goodness, regardless of the day, in fact.

And, actually, a barn dance is an easy way to move. The
caller tells us what to do, and we follow. There's no panic about
form or partner, because it's all I can do to concentrate on the
steps.

One-two-three-step. One-two-three-step.

Move it to the right.

I meet Miriam's eye across the circle and I shrug, and she
tips her head back and opens her mouth. I can imagine the
honk of her laugh - I'm surprised I can't hear it above the music.

Ah! Shaun has linked my arm.

'That's not the steps!' I say as he spins me round, the crowd
a mess of colours in my sights.

'Let's show these Aussies how it's done, Dee!'

'But I—' Oh, goodness. I'm skipping faster and faster and
any faster and I will lift off the floor, I swear. This must be how
a young Bertie felt when I would swing her in circles by her
arms. David disapproved of the move, not 'lady-like' enough for

his tastes (unladylike behaviour for both me and Bertie, in his eyes) but I did it anyway and we would laugh until our eyes watered and bellies ached, collapsing on the grass in a messy heap. In those moments, I didn't care what David thought. I didn't care at all.

'Oh, Shaun, no!' And now I'm flying because Shaun has lifted me into the air and— 'I'm too heavy for you! Shaun, you'll hurt your back!'

'You're a waif, Dee. A twig, my darling.' And he jigs us around and his sweat is beading in diagonal lines along his receding hairline and I put my hands on his shoulders and the surrounding people are reaching up and cheering and now they've parted into two lines and we are jigging up the middle, Shaun somehow still lifting me up and—

Tom. I see him by the door. He is watching us, smiling, a bottle of beer in his hand. I tip my head for him to join us, but he throws up a hand. I mouth *help*, but he just shakes in decline.

'Please, Shaun,' I say, laughing. 'I can't take anymore!'

Finally, Shaun drops me down so we're face to face. 'Thank you for the dance, fair lady.' And he gently touches my feet to the floor and plants a sweaty kiss on my cheek, before he grabs Lola's hand and skips her up the centre. His next victim.

Well. Two kisses in one night. I'm not sure what signal I am sending out here but—

'Having a good time?' Tom.

I put both hands on the bar, having squeezed back to my steadying crutch. I'm panting. Goodness knows what my hair must look like. More of a slob than a bob, I suspect. Gosh. What would David say if he found me now?

Oh! I am laughing at the thought.

'You sure have a great energy,' Tom adds. He leans back against the bar, arms folded. The beer bottle, I notice, is empty.

'Oh, I don't know,' I say. The bartender hands me a glass of water.

'Hey, I saw you again this afternoon at the beach. Were you okay?'

I glug down half the glass in one go. Goodness. I have become a woman who glugs.

I dab at my mouth. 'Oh, yes, I'm fine. Really.' Although I do feel somewhat flustered all of a sudden. Had I been scared in the sea earlier?

'It's tough when you get stuck in the break,' Tom says, as someone shoves him from behind and he lurches forward, thankfully catching himself on the bar before he falls into me. 'Sorry.'

I lower my gaze, brush myself down. 'Embarrassing, but yes. I'll get there.' I feel overcome, the heat filling my face and mind, a teapot full of boiling water. Goodness. All this conversing with strangers . . . How does Bertie manage so easily? She always has - perhaps out of necessity as an only child. Ingratiating herself on other families with toys at the beach, smiling at strangers. *A free spirit*, Mum had said.

'You know, Dee? I believe you will get there. Surfing suits you.'

I think of going to aqua aerobics that time. I actually enjoyed the class - the water acting as a barrier, a protection against onlookers and a shield to hide wayward limbs which undoubtedly moved not as one intended. But David had voiced his concern over my dishevelled bob. After that, I kept up with my videos in the privacy of my home instead.

'Besides,' Tom adds, 'you shouldn't worry about what others think.'

You shouldn't worry about what others think. That's what Mum had said. I thought she had been referring to my outfit that day - one of her last days when I'd worn something purple, her favourite colour, which of course David despised, but now - it strikes me that she may have been talking of something greater. Not just the clothing but—

Did she know?

I look out to the dance floor. Jigging people, laughter . . . A picture of fun. Carelessness, in a good way.

Freedom. Our basic human right . .

Isn't it?

———

'Wooo.' I exhale a happy sigh of relief - my feet light and floaty as I collapse onto the sofa in the hostel lounge.

'Tea?' Miriam asks, as she heads into the kitchen. We appear to be the only people back already. I was thankful Miriam was ready to go home as exhaustion had crept up, although I was reluctant to leave Tom. He's amenable, easy to chat to, friendly. Without ulterior motive. Hans and Jake, other men of Tom's generation, barely glance at me. The Invisible Woman.

Oh, goodness. I don't like Tom because he's the only one who doesn't ignore me, do I? How . . . *Desperate*, as Bertie would say.

Or - oh, wow - do I like him because I want to flirt with him? No. No no no. I just like to talk. But— Does that classify as coyote behaviour? No, the wrong word . . .

Cougar.

Yes. Cougar was the word David used about Delilah and her new pink hair. She can't be a cougar if she's married, I said, but he grumbled some incomprehensible reply. Some people are adept at grumbling . . .

I clear some magazines from the coffee table as Miriam brings in a tray laden with the tea and a pile of Digestives. I can't imagine Miriam grumbling. She's so stout; she'd shake off any inclination to grumble the same way she shakes out those masses of curls from her hairband.

The battered leather squeaks as she sits next to me. We sip our tea. Dunk our biscuits. It feels naughty, at this hour. A Monday night, goodness. Or is it Tuesday morning already?

'When was the last time you danced?' Miriam says, catching the biscuit in her mouth the moment before it breaks.

'Well, you know, weddings, anniversary parties.' I watched dancing, anyway. 'I like to salsa,' I say out of nowhere.

'Oh, David dances salsa?'

Breathe, Dee. 'Not David, no.'

Dee Dee.

Inhale. Exhale.

Rise and fall.

'Ah. The *Dee Dee* man.' Miriam's voice is slow, the edges of words wobbling a little like one of those jelly desserts Bertie used to like, shivering almost imperceptibly in the summer breeze.

'At the time, he was probably not much more than a boy. Goodness knows, I was young.'

Am I really saying this? It's the dance, I suppose. I feel ethereal, untethered and—

Here? Here, I can release.

God, I need to release.

'Oh gosh, do I need to call a lawyer?' Miriam shifts in her seat to face me, cradling the mug to her chest.

'Not like that. I mean we were young, inexperienced, reckless.' I'm saying this. I am speaking these words.

'The best type of passion,' Miriam sighs.

'It was certainly passionate.' Because, back then, hadn't I been passionate all by myself? I was also willful. With painting, anyway. He unleashed that in me. I'd seen an advert for his classes at the local community centre where I went to Keep Fit. I went along and—

Well. I found the thing I hadn't realised was missing.

'Love?'

I look at my hands. Eventually, I nod. 'The all-consuming type.' My voice is like this Digestive dipped in tea: softening, crumbling, having to catch it before it breaks.

I remember his gaze. Being in it. I haven't been looked at the same way since. Like I was his muse, him in awe of me.

And it was mutual. *A meeting of souls,* we used to say. He had a purity about him, but also something broken. Fragile. We made each other whole. Of course we did - it was transcendent.

We often couldn't wait. One time, even, in the store cupboard. Catching moments as though we only had that moment. That was all there was. That was all there ever would be.

As though, somehow, we knew.

'I see,' Miriam says. 'And this is your problem.'

'What do you mean?'

She lowers her chin. 'David is not all-consuming.'

'Well, marriage is something else, isn't it?'

Miriam shrugs. 'I suppose it depends what matters to you.'

'David is my pillar. I need him.'

'But now you're on your own.'

I make a face. I have been holding onto the image of David and me sailing off on a cruise together like some of our friends, looking forward to reinventing themselves as people with grown-up children.

I had been looking forward to that. This was that trip. This *is* that trip. Us, as new.

And yet—

'The Dee Dee Man - he was before David?'

A nod. Then, 'Mostly.'

Goodness. The guilt still simmers. I hadn't meant for it to go anywhere. I can't imagine many people who cheat do so intentionally. But when something like that takes over . . . well. It felt more wrong *not* to give in. And I had considered it, weighed it up, I chose Him.

But then - Mum. The sickness. She deteriorated, and I discovered I was pregnant and a shotgun wedding seemed the only resolution. I was devastated about Mum, and David provided stability. I wanted her to know I was happy. After what my father did, I needed her to know I had picked a steady man who supported me and that I would be okay.

And, for a long time, I thought I was.

I thought I was okay.

'Ah.' Miriam is nodding.

'What?'

'Look, I don't know David, but he seems to have a good . . . handle on you.'

'I suppose he has to be, with me as I am and—' Miriam has pursed her lips. 'We've been through a lot. And I wouldn't have managed without him.'

'You're managing now, and he put you in this situation.'

'Well—' I'm not comfortable. This talk. It's me who is in the wrong, not David.

'Was Soufflé Gate an out-of-character act, or is that a common event in your house?'

I laugh at Miriam's use of *Soufflé Gate*. Something Bertie would say. 'Gosh, no. Usually I manage to hold it in.'

'Hold it in?'

'You know . . .'

Another look. Miriam opens her mouth to speak, rethinks.

The room is momentarily illuminated as a car rumbles past, the vibration shuddering through the floor.

And then all is still again.

I sip my tea. I have a sudden feeling of being on a boat that has come away from its mooring. I can see the land but as the swell increases, I move out to sea. I am alone.

And I don't know how to sail.

'Tell me about you,' I say. I need to focus on something else. Some*one* else. A life raft - a buoyancy aid to keep me from falling into my own murky mind. 'I want to know about Miriam.'

At this, the footing of Miriam's statue seems to falter. Like the smallest earthquake nudging at the foundations. 'There's not much to tell.'

I tilt my head.

'We all struggle, don't we?' Miriam says, in a way that makes me wonder whether she is questioning me or herself. 'But my struggles are micro. Others have such catastrophes to deal with and I'm fortunate to have a family and—'

'It doesn't mean you're automatically happy.'

'I *should* be happy. I have it all. I chose this all.'

A frown tickles at her brow, the small shake of her head, sending it away.

'But it hasn't worked out as you'd hoped?' I venture.

'I should try harder.'

'Is that what you really think?'

She lifts her gaze and her eyes, I notice, have misted over. 'I miss my boys. I don't want to lose them.'

I reach a hand along the sofa toward her. 'Plenty of people get divorced. You think your boys would want to live with their father? Is that why you're hesitant to split?'

'I suppose.'

'But didn't Indie think your children would already know? Do you think there's a chance they might?'

'I— I'm sorry, Dee.' And she shakes her head and turns her shoulders away from me, just as the door bursts open and a rowdy ball of partygoers rolls into the space.

'No. I'm sorry,' I say, but I don't think Miriam hears.

DAY SEVEN

Miriam and I enter the studio. Our movements today are slow, cautious. There was no baking this morning. I popped in for a takeaway coffee and a croissant from Derrick but it sits in its white paper bag, untouched. I must return later, give him a more generous smile, a lengthier exchange.

But perhaps no more Prosecco.

Goodness. The coffee is sitting in my stomach. A murky bathwater, unable to drain through a blocked plughole.

I force myself to walk to my 'creation'. The body outline is hardly visible, instead a mess of dark blue. The pink overridden. And the yellow?

Gone.

I stand very still. I stare.

After a time, I feel Miriam beside me.

'Do you want to talk about what happened here?'

The chalk outline seems like that of a real murder, the gloopy blue so ... *brutal*.

I force my eyes away. 'Do you?'

In the silence of the studio, Miriam breathes - slow, steady. 'I know. I'm hiding too.' She's being kind, offering me this gift, but—

'I don't see what the problem is. I've been doing just fine as I am.' I'm a spider, fallen from the web, drawing in my legs. Ball-like. Tight.

Closed.

'Soufflé?'

My head is shaking. A lorry rolls past the window and a grey wall builds in my brain. 'I'm so fed up with people reading so much into their actions. What happened to the days of just feeling sad? Maybe I don't want to be my 'best self'. Maybe I can just *be*.' My anger is a clenched fist in my gut, flinching every time a knuckle moves. Twitching. Trying.

To get out?

No. I've done so well.

'Yes, I suppose. But for many people, being sad can become something more. If we're mindful of our feelings we know if we're unhappy for a prolonged state and then we can fix it.'

'But why do we always need to fix it? Maybe some people are just meant to be sad. Life deals them shitters and that's it. Sad.' *Shitters*. Is this a word I want to allow into my vocabulary?

'But what we teach in school is that to be aware of our mental health is to be healthy. It's vital. Youngsters need this knowledge.' She looks at me. 'Adults too.'

'And you? Do you take your own advice?'

A steady look. Nostrils flare. 'This isn't about me.'

'How convenient.'

Miriam looks as though I've slapped her. I suppose, in a way, I have. 'I'm sorry,' I say. 'I'm sorry.'

I take a step back - physically removing myself from this conversation and no doubt Miriam will think I'm hiding from—

'Ladies, I'm sorry, I'm late. I'm glad you let yourself in already and—' Alexandra has entered at speed - a woman on a mission - placing her bag on the worktop, removing her jacket, scarf. She powers over to where Miriam and I stand and she stops at the sight of my atrocious creation. 'Continued,' she adds, letting the word fall out of her mouth in a mirror of her composure, dropping momentarily, before she gathers herself back to centered.

'I'll take it down,' I say. I put my coffee cup on the side and roll up my sleeves. The only way is to start again. I need to take this painting down, remove the awful mess from sight and begin again. David will be a bright blue. Positive. Because I chose him. I created our life. I was part of that, privy to it, wanting it. And he cared for me. For us. His family.

I was wrong to tell Miriam the other things, bring Him up and—

Goodness.

Alexandra settles a hand on my forearm. 'No,' she says. Firm, but soft. This tone reminds me of someone. A uniform. A memory that teeters on the outer reaches of my mind, another stretch and perhaps I could reach it but—?

'But—'

'It should stay there,' she says. Again, with the tone.

'But it's awful.' I can't keep looking at it. I look at my hands. Alexandra's hand. Pale, neat.

'Art is subjective,' she says.

'It may be subjective but there's not a person on earth who would think that's good.' I turn my back to the wall.

'*Bad art is a great deal worse than no art at all.* Oscar Wilde.' And she nods, a full stop on the conversation, and returns to the workbench in the centre of the space.

Miriam places her hand - larger, sturdier, a working hand - on my shoulder, before she follows Alexandra.

'Today, I want you to choose a discipline, and simply create. Think of those things we've listed that bring us joy, think about where they sit on the outline of the self, and create something. Use our moment of introspection for inspiration and . . . Free yourself.' Alexandra splays her fingers at her sides, her chin knocks up.

My feet have walked me to the workbench. Miriam is picking up paints from the selection on the sideboard, choosing paintbrushes. I see them. I must close my eyes. I know how they will feel, how they will smell . . .

I inhale sharply, the gasp of the breath a surprise. I have to keep it together here. Here, I am a woman in control. That's what David wants. That's why he's trying to help me. I can't unravel without him. I have to show him I have this.

'I'll do pottery,' I say, nodding, convincing.

Trying.

I open my eyes. Alexandra is to the side of the room, frowning at her phone. There's a heave of her chest before she closes her eyes and thrusts the phone in her pocket.

'I'll do the pottery,' I say again, as Alexandra approaches. Her power has wilted. The urgency, lifted head, raised sternum, a fraction diminished. Subtle differences, but differences I understand.

'Great.' She gives a perfunctory nod and settles me with the equipment. Not a potter's wheel, but clay, like Bertie used at school. I remember the flower she made me once. A yellow sunflower. I thought it exemplified her creative potential, perhaps taking after me, but David couldn't see the value in pursuing the arts. *Can't earn a living from paint,* he said. He pushed Bertie to take the academic subjects, getting her a private tutor to help in the lead up to exams. Those things mattered to him.

And to me? As long as she's happy. Perhaps that is a little idyll. Or idle?

Bertie was not idle. She studied, she got the grades; she went to work in an architect's practice.

David was happy about this. Proud.

And me?

As long as she's happy.

But, there? In London? In an office?

Clearly, she was not.

'I'm sorry if I spoke out of turn, earlier,' I say to Miriam. We've been sat quietly in the studio all afternoon, peaceful in our own reverie.

She hovers her brush over the paper. 'You didn't.'

'I did, I—'

'Dee.' She puts the brush down. Looks up. 'You're here, so why not fully embrace it?'

'I—' I pick at a nail.

'Diane, you are doing it. You're here. Live it. That's enough now.'

That's enough now. A woman undone.

Karma, Bertie would say. I imagine Francis laughing.

After a time, Miriam speaks: 'Did you consider finding him?'

I know the Him to whom she refers. My hands settle on the clay, smudging it back down to nothing.

I shake my head.

Of course, I'm lying. Because I can't think of it now. Whenever I do, everything changes. Whenever I try to make an alteration, change happens, but never as I intend.

Look at this trip. We were at last breaking out of our routine, David finally dragging himself away from his work and—

'David?' Miriam asks.

'I can't risk losing him. Not now.'

'You still think David leaving you is a negative thing?'

My head jerks back, my expression no doubt conveying what I think is obvious: Of course.

But Miriam doesn't reply. Her gaze drops to my broken

mound of clay, in seeming consideration, before she meets my eye again. 'That's a shame,' she says at last.

She can't understand. I've been letting myself go. I need to get back on track. Focus on surviving, passing the days, meeting David.

I glance at the picture across the room. The atrocity.

I stand, reach for a paintbrush from Miriam's work station, dip it in the colour, and I cross the room. There, in the centre of the outline, I place the blob. Bright, bold, yellow.

Bertie.

Smiling at the airport. Brave.

Bertie.

It's time to email her again.

To: Liberty.Bridges@icloud.com
Subject: Reflections
From: MrsDBridges@outlook.com

Dear Bertie

I am still here, in Byron, the town you loved
most. I can see why. The place has a unique
energy about it. Was that what drew you in?

Being here, travelling, the whole shebang as
I hear you say, is making me introspective. I
had been enjoying my time, doing what I
should have done a long time ago, but I
wonder if people see me as an old fool. A
couple of people in our group went for
tattoos and I'm sure they were mocking me as
they invited me along and I feel so . . .

Old.

It's Grannie's birthday today and a reminder
that I'm older than she ever will be. It's an
odd feeling, being older. I always thought
she'd be around. I needed her when you were
little and she deteriorated and then I had to
care for her. I know you don't remember, only
being two, but there was a time . . .

I don't know how to say it. But I feel I need
to tell you some truths. About us, our
family, history . . . Is there ever a good

time? I often wonder if I should have told
you sooner. But David—

Your dad is a good man, Bertie. I don't know
what's going on with him right now but I do
know he's a man of morals. I know you didn't
always agree with his outlook but he's
decent. Maybe he's sifting through some
thoughts.

I think I need to do the same. I will sift
and, please, Bertie, bear with me, I will
tell. I know I need to tell.

All my love,
Mum x

DAY EIGHT

Alexandra invites us into her office to look at a sculpture Vinnie commissioned the Instagram artist to produce. It's made of clay and, I have to say, is far beyond anything I could produce from the material. It sits on the sideboard surrounded by hardback books and unhung artwork leaning against the wall. It's bright orange and round and bulbous, but also spiky and unsettling. A juxtaposition. There was a time when I could have delivered a decent analysis, when I could have formed an opinion of my own, but now? I'm not sure what to make of it.

'It's supposed to be a flame. And here—' She points to a small brown triangle, sticking up from the orange. 'The phoenix. Ready to rise.'

I smile and nod. A mute fool.

Miriam makes a joke to which Alexandra laughs and I force myself to partake, tune in.

'I like it, but Vinnie was the one who had it commissioned. It's a relic. A reminder of what we had. Our relationship, burned to the flames after all those years.' Alexandra takes a seat behind her desk, looks out of the window, taking herself elsewhere.

I clear my throat. 'But the phoenix takes on new life from

the ashes, doesn't she? A relevant metaphor for you, I should think.'

'If there are any ashes she's intending to leave,' Alexandra says, indicating for us to take a seat on the small sofa.

'Hm. This is something I worry about if my husband moves out,' Miriam says as she lowers herself next to me. 'Will we have to split all our possessions? Trawl through the reams of arte- facts collected during our time together?'

'Maybe you should begin to hide the things you like most,' Alexandra says. 'Stow them secretly into storage.'

'At least you no longer have to put up with the things you don't like, though,' I offer. I think of David's great grandfather clock. A family heirloom. I know they're antiques and carry history but it's so goddamn heavy and oppressive and I can't help but think of men whenever it chimes. The heavy chime of the patriarchy, ringing their unwelcome noise for far too long.

'One of the worst things? Vinnie went after my clothes too, and took my favourite scarf.'

I look at the current floaty accessory setting off Alexandra's outfit and wonder what the Vinnie of my mind - a bald, tall man in a suit - would look like with a scarf of this style. 'Was he into that, then?' I can't help it, Francis would be proud.

'Ha, no—'

Miriam interjects: 'Vinnie is a woman?'

'Vinisha. She's Jamaican.'

I glance at Miriam to share my surprise but Miriam is staring at Alexandra with a fixed look. It's unreadable and, whatever it is, it's extending a moment too long.

'Much to my father's disgust,' Alexandra adds with a gentle laugh. 'The gender, I mean. Although, probably the heritage too. We weren't just partners in business.'

'Your father struggled to understand?' Miriam says after another beat.

Alexandra shrugs. 'He lives in a small town in rural Australia. I get it.'

Miriam drops her gaze to her hands, clasped in her lap. 'Well, you seem to have this place in order without Vinnie.'

'Yes, it's fantastic,' I add, hoping to imbue a little more confidence in Alexandra than Miriam is managing.

Alexandra gives a curt nod, but she doesn't seem able to force a convincing smile past the tooth biting down on her lip.

I move to the edge of my seat. 'What is it?'

Alexandra stands, paces the room. Finally, she stops at the window and looks out. 'It's the Instagram artist. I don't know . . . I have a feeling he's not going to come through for me.'

Miriam lifts her head. 'What do you mean?'

'I thought this was all a definite? The exhibition is in less than two weeks,' I say.

Alexandra turns to us, her defined eyebrows furrowing, her gaze downcast. 'He was supposed to return the contract three weeks ago, and he said someone sent it but I haven't received it yet and I'm sure he's stalling, avoiding my calls . . . It's the same situation I had with the art therapist. I'm an idiot. I should never have proceeded without the contract. I took him at his word, I trusted and—' She shakes her head, drops into her seat. Finally, she looks from Miriam to me. 'Vinnie wouldn't have let this happen.'

'Hold on, you don't know for sure yet,' I say. 'Maybe the contract did get lost. Maybe he is trustworthy.'

I hear Miriam sigh beside me. I look up, but she's fixated on Alexandra, seemingly, for once, short of words.

'The woman from the arts council is coming. The person in charge of giving out grants. I've applied for this special one and . . . God, I'm so stupid. I can't *not* have an exhibition.'

'Okay, so, worst case he doesn't show. Could you get someone else? Prepare now?'

'At such short notice? I just don't know.'

Gosh, I wish I could help. I wish I could do something but I'm...

Nothing. Useless.

I look to Miriam again for support. 'Why don't you just wait, maybe call him again, ask him for a definite answer, and then you can move on and think of an alternative if needs be. Which you won't. I'm sure it's fine. He's probably just... Gone surfing.'

Alexandra hangs on my every word. Finally, she nods and attempts a smile.

'Often things are worse in our mind than they are in real life, right?' I try to sound like Miriam, seeing as Miriam herself seems to have been rendered speechless, but I don't think it's working. Alexandra is staring at her computer screen, lost in the maze of her mind.

I stand, giving Miriam a little kick to get her to follow.

'Let us know if you need any help,' I say. 'I don't know how, but... Good luck.'

Miriam and I have come to the gallery cafe. The Space of Light, as I call it in my mind. I read recently about an artist who works with light. Turrell? Yes. Not painting light interpretations, but actually using it to form their art. The light *is* his art. Or perhaps it's our interpretation that is the art. Fascinating, really. There's something so captivating about light, I find it transportive.

There's a certain time in the afternoon here for example, when the sun is low, filtering through the glass in wide beams, and it feels as though everything that has gone before and everything that is to come is at one. That ray of light a reminder that we are all of the earth. Money, titles, possessions - all are extraneous, superfluous, because we are born of this light and it is to this light we return.

Goodness. It's just light, Dee. What on earth am I talking about?

I sit down. 'I have an idea,' I say.

'Tell me.' Miriam takes the coffee I hand her and tuts at the carrot cake and two forks I set between us.

'What if we help Alexandra out?'

'How do you mean?'

'The exhibition. It sounds like the artist is not going to produce the goods, right?'

'Right . . .' Miriam forks a piece of cake.

'So, what if we put one on instead?'

'Us? Create an entire art exhibition in less than two weeks? With what?'

Hm. No doubt Miriam is thinking of my art therapy atrocity . . .

'It wouldn't be *our* art. We could collate the work of others. A showcase of what this area offers. Local businesses could contribute and offer samples of what they do, you could take photos of people, places . . .' I put my coffee down, straighten my spine.

Miriam tilts her head. 'Like a trade show of what's on offer in Byron?'

'More like—' I waft a cloud of dust out of its spotlight. 'A love letter to the place.'

'O-*kay* . . .'

'We could write up the stories of the people who've lived here for years, the stories of travellers passing through - what motivated people to come here, what makes them stay . . .'

'It sounds like a lot of work.'

'We could do it.'

'We're supposed to be on holiday.'

'But Alexandra—'

Miriam's expression clears. 'You're right. We should help her.' She shifts forward in her seat.

'So? Is that a yes?'

'That's my motto, isn't it?'

And I laugh and I hug Miriam and I look at the light and I'm sure, if I stretched out my fingers, I could stroke it. A Turrell masterpiece, right here in Byron.

An hour later and we're deep into list-making. What needs to be done, a division of jobs, and, most importantly, who will feature in the exhibit.

'What about Tom?' Miriam says.

Branches of heat tickle up my neck like poison ivy. I pick at a nail. The flyer I took from his surf shack is still folded up in my bedroom drawer, but I've not been brave enough to look at it yet.

'Maybe we could feature one of his boards?' she continues. 'They're pieces of art in their own right.'

'Oh, er . . . Perhaps.' I manage to nod. 'And Derrick?'

'Definitely Derrick.' Miriam holds my gaze, a smile expanding across her face.

'What?'

'Nothing. I like his buns.'

I shake my head, unable to stifle a return smile. 'Shaun and Eric?' I offer.

'Yes. And the yoga instructor.' Miriam has been going to morning yoga classes while I've been baking. She keeps inviting me along but—

Well. The stillness doesn't appeal. All that forced thinking . . . Miriam said the hip opening class made her emotional. So much so she cried on the mat at the end, as did several others. It all sounds very . . . Overt.

Miriam puts her pen down, looks out of the window. 'It's a funny place, this.'

'How do you mean?'

'We've only been here a short time and yet . . . I feel very settled. Connected, I suppose.'

'Yes.' Connection. Is that the appeal? Was that the appeal for Bertie?

'We already know lots of people and it has a vibe, like—'

I smile. 'Home?'

She stops, considers this. Turns back to me. 'Yes,' she says. 'Like home.'

I sip my drink, observe the moving subjects beyond the window.

'You know,' Miriam says, 'I'm really glad you want to do this exhibit. Have you thought about doing a piece of your own? You know, if you get the time . . .'

'Oh, I don't think so. I'm happy just dabbling.'

'Perhaps, during this course, you'll try?'

I offer no comment.

The waitress checks on us, a brief exchange with Miriam. Outside, the sky is beginning to darken.

Miriam continues: 'If you could be anyone, which painter would you be?'

I place my empty cup on the table, look to my friend. 'Picasso. With you as Braque beside me.'

'Braque?'

'He and Picasso created Cubism. They challenged perspective, developed new ways of seeing the world.'

'Well. A lofty aim but I suppose we can try.' Miriam's laugh is sweet, soft. I've never seen Miriam be malicious.

'I think George Braque might have focused on real interpretations, nature, natural light and the like. Similar to your photography, in a way.'

She shrugs. 'I've never heard of him.'

'The sidekicks are always under-rated. He was hugely influential to the Cubist movement.'

Miriam puts the lid on her pen, shifts her weight on the seat. 'I know you said you don't want to paint, Dee, but have you ever thought about teaching art?'

'Me? Well, I taught children once, a long time ago. But, goodness, no, not anymore.' I close my notebook, place my things in my bag.

'But you have so much knowledge and skill. I can't believe you've not done anything with it.'

'No, well. You know how these things are.'

But Miriam does not move. 'Not really, Dee. With you? No, not really.'

DAY NINE

'Oh, Diane. At last. How are you? Why have you not been answering my messages?' My sister's voice is a pendulum, swinging from remorseful to annoyance to regret, unable to decide where to settle, it seems.

I sit on the bed and hold the phone a little way from my ear. I concentrate on the Renoir flower print framed on my wall. I could ask Shaun and Eric about the history of this hostel. I heard Sofia mention in passing it was one of the oldest in the area. Perhaps I could use that framed wallpaper in the exhibit.

'Diane?'

'Yes, sorry.' I am over-enunciating my words. Like that time Bertie was in the school play and she showed us all these obscure vocal warm-ups she'd had to do. What was that one about the actor? Ben someone . . .

'And? Are you okay?'

'I'm fine. How are you?' Not Ben. Colin?

'Why have you not been answering my messages?'

'Oh, you know - phones . . . I've been busy, actually.' Richard?

'Yes, well, apparently too busy to remember Roy's birthday.'

Ah. Of course. Roy's birthday. The same day as our mothers.

But Francis doesn't mention that.

'Did he have a good day?' I hold a hand to my head. B. The name definitely began with a B . . .

'Diane. You didn't used to forget birthdays. You used to be such an organised person.'

'*Used to be*, Francis. Used to be.' Once upon a time I was the person David wanted me to be. The respectable wife. One to diarise events. I forced myself to act that way. I played the part.

And then?

I got tired. Life . . .

I just got tired.

Francis is still talking. 'I know it must be painful for you there but it doesn't serve to carry on without giving any consideration to those who are at home waiting for you.'

'David is not waiting for me. And you're in America.'

'Hypothetical, Diane. I don't want you to make a fool of yourself. You know you've been—'

'What?'

A pause. 'Foolish . . . In the past.'

Benedict! The lovely Benedict. Cumberland?

No. That doesn't sound right.

I'll wait. It will come to me.

I pace the room.

Goodness. I've been waiting for David for years.

Waiting? Or yearning for someone? Passing time until—

No, Diane.

'I'm sorry,' I say. Because I am sorry. 'I didn't mean to worry you. I'm fine. Miriam and I have been busy. We're putting on an art exhibition for—'

'An *art exhibition*? Diane, you've not painted in years.'

'I'm not painting. I'm curating. Other's work and—'

'Shouldn't you be making a plan to leave? To meet David? Don't you want to see him?'

'Of course I want to see him. And I will - at his nephew's wedding. But this exhibition is—'

'Don't get carried away, Diane. You know you need to keep your head. In Byron, I . . . I can't believe you're still there.'

Cumberbatch! Thank you, brain.

Benedict Cumberbatch, Benedict Cumberbatch, Benedict Cumberbatch. Young Bertie, trying to wrap her mouth around those words with such earnest. She was dedicated to that play. I'd tried not to laugh but it was very sweet.

I reach out a steadying hand; my outstretched fingers soften into the bedspread.

'I don't know, Francis. I feel, somehow, that I'm . . . meant to be here.'

I hear her sigh. I imagine the shoulders dropping, the tilt of the head. Her matronly manner. Me, the naughty schoolgirl. Always such a disappointment . . .

'Look,' I add, 'I realise how it sounds. But, here, I'm—'

'What?'

'In touch.'

A drawn-out silence. Finally, 'I understand this must be incredibly hard for you. But I'm worried.'

'I'm fine. Truly, honestly, fine. Yes, it is tough being here. But also, I don't feel as though I could be anywhere else. This place . . . I don't know. It has a . . . pull.'

'Of course it must feel like that after—'

'Nothing to do with . . . anything. It pulls me for me. Something in the air or energy or something I—'

'Diane. Listen to yourself. The *energy*?'

It's my turn to pause. I think of what Miriam said about David leaving me being a blessing. But what I can't help thinking is - Did he want to let me fly for my sake, or could he no longer bear to keep me caged?

I lift my chin. 'It was Mum's birthday too. Did you remember that?'

I hear an exhale. Finally, 'Yes, I remembered, Diane.'

I look back to the wallpaper. If someone hadn't preserved that segment in the frame, the beautiful rose print would have been forgotten. Unknown by future generations.

Goodness. Perhaps some things are inevitable.

———

'You okay?' I find Miriam alone in the hostel lounge. She has a can of beer and as I approach, she pours some into an empty glass and slides it to the other side of the table.

I take a seat and gulp down a little more than is ladylike. I take a tissue from my pocket and dab my mouth. 'My sister,' I say, lifting my phone. I slide it along the table, out of my sight.

'Ah.'

I let my shoulders round and spin the cold glass in circles, the residue creating shapes on the linoleum. 'She's so . . . Judgmental.'

Miriam stops the lift of her glass en route to her mouth and *throws me a brow,* as Bertie would say.

'Okay, yes, I may be prone to *judgey* behaviour myself, but I'm working on it.' I think of my sister, continually casting aspersions on the people in her life. 'She just needs to talk to her own folk and stop casting theories on everyone else.'

'That's what families are best at, aren't they? Creating theories to things they know nothing about?' Miriam lowers her glass.

I rest back in my seat. 'What if she does know?'

'How do you mean?'

I look around the room at the shabby-chic interior. Is it a little *try-hard*, as Bertie would say? 'Am I making a fool of myself here? I mean, at my age . . . All this . . . pretense?' I take a steadying breath. 'Socialising with men, drinking, dancing . . . Who am I?'

'To be honest, you sound like a hoot. The question I think you need to be asking is who were you before?'

I pause.

'Do you even know the answer?'

I trace my finger along a dewy circle, wiping it clean away. 'I did.'

I'm sure I used to be a more relaxed person. As a young mother, I was. It was just Bertie and me. We needed no one. No friends, no family, not even David . . . We were a team. Then as she became a teenager I sensed her desire to move away. A subtle shift. I suppose that's when I became more . . . as I am now. I didn't intend to become this person but—

I was so worried something would happen to her. So . . . anxious.

Always so anxious.

But I couldn't explain that. Not to her, not to David. I suppose it manifested as uppity behaviour, tense, *cranky*, even. But I just wanted her—

Well.

I just wanted her.

Miriam looks to the window, watching as a group of rowdy teenagers walk past. Once silence is restored, she speaks: 'Reclaim the title of the older woman, Dee.'

'What?'

'Rewrite the rhetoric. Be whoever you want to be, regardless of your age.'

I can't help but laugh. 'I'm not sure what my sister would make of that.' Goodness. Francis in her smart clothes, legs neatly crossed, hands folded in her lap. Outwardly she appears to have graduated from finishing school with first class honor's, the type of person perfectly suited to being a quiet and retiring First Lady, but get to know her and you realise she should be president. A big, hardy, republican president.

'You know what I say to the girls in my school?' Miriam leans forward. 'Negative behaviour typically stems from one's own insecurities. It's not usually an affront to the person on the receiving end. Nine times out of ten, it's the giver who has issues.'

'Yes, but we're not in the playground. You'd think my sister and I were above all that.'

Sofia is talking on the phone in the reception. The abrasive tone of voice is clear even from this distance.

'Some issues are deep-rooted.'

I consider this. My sister, living the life of freedom without financial pressure - her as a grandmother. I don't see what issues she could have.

'Maybe confront her,' Miriam says. 'She won't be expecting that. Call her out on it.'

'Call her out on it,' I repeat, remembering something Bertie once said. *Auntie Francis is a little strange*, she joked. I laughed it off at the time, but perhaps I should have asked her for a reason.

Miriam smiles. 'Or, you know, do what the girls in the playground do and just throw her a bitch slap.'

At this, I launch my hand to my mouth for fear I'll spit my beer all over the table.

DAY TEN

Lola saunters into the hostel lounge, looking especially fresh and long-limbed in her short shorts today. At least they cover her bottom. I've seen some young girls around Byron and—

Well. In my day, the problem was with the skirts being too short; I dread to think what my father would make of these things. One has to resist covering them up with a sarong.

'What are you two up to?' she says. 'This all looks very serious.'

Miriam and I are back at the table, going over our list for the exhibition. We have invited Alexandra over and—

Goodness. I do hope she likes it.

Miriam tucks an imaginary fallen hair behind her ear, and I clasp my hands in my lap. I'll have no manicure left at this rate. I dread to think what David will make of these nails. I must remember to have them done before his nephew's wedding.

'We're thinking about helping at the gallery,' Miriam replies. 'Putting on an exhibition about local life. A friend might need help.'

Lola nods, her gaze moving from us to a boy shuffling about in the kitchen. It's a boy I've not seen before. He is very triangular - his body, head, nose - and pointy. Picasso's self-portrait.

'Would you like to help?' I say.

'Oh, no. Thanks.' Lola is slow to drag her attention back to us. It's like watching a mental tug of war. 'This looks far too much like a school project for my liking. But good luck. When is the exhibition?'

'Well it might not happen, so . . . Less than two weeks.'

Goodness. Less than two weeks.

'Ah, shame, we're leaving soon. I'm off to meet Indie at the travel agents now. Hey, we do want to visit the flea market before we leave Byron, though. Apparently, there's a great one near here. Do you guys want to come? We could share a taxi?'

'Oo yes, please,' I say. When I lived in London, I loved the markets. The hustle and bustle and energy. Didn't I secure a stand once at Spitalfields? A chance to sell my art, but—

Well.

We bid goodbye to Lola just as Alexandra appears at the window. Miriam stands with haste, rushing to let her in the door. After a moment, Miriam reappears in the lounge, her expression set and unreadable. Behind her comes a loud 'Oh!' that can only belong to Sofia.

Miriam hears it too, and spins to find Alexandra has not followed. She lowers her head, then returns to her seat next to me and folds her arms. If I didn't know better, I'd say this was Miriam *having a huff*, as Bertie would say.

I raise my eyebrow in question, but Miriam lifts her chin in a most un-Miriam-like manner.

Or perhaps this is Miriam-esque, and I've not encountered this side of her personality. I thought I was the one who didn't like to be kept waiting.

'A bit rude, when we're trying to help her, don't you think?' Miriam whispers, her voice low but the annoyance loud.

'She doesn't know we're trying to help her though, does she? She might not even need help.'

At this, Miriam humphs, and I'm reminded of my father once again.

Eventually, Alexandra bustles in, landing her oversized handbag on the papers we've collated, her cheeks flushed. 'Sorry, I haven't seen Sofia for a while—' She looks from me to Miriam, nods, and then takes a seat. There's another floaty scarf around her neck and I find my fingers creeping up to touch my own bare (boring?) neck in response. 'Anyway. Tell me. What's all this about?'

I look at Miriam, who also seems enamoured with the scarf. She can't seem to take her eyes off it, in fact.

'Oh, goodness,' Alexandra says as she notices me trying to shuffle the papers out from under her tote. 'Sorry.'

'No, it's fine, I—' Goodness. Why do I care so much? It's just Alexandra. I place my hands flat on our list and sit myself up straight. 'Miriam and I want to help you.'

'Right . . . How do you mean?'

Steadying breath. 'The artist. The exhibit. He's not going to come through, is he?'

Alexandra dips her chin. 'No. He sent a message this morning, actually. Didn't even have the courtesy to call, would you believe?'

'Well, yes, I would believe.' Artists not calling? I can understand. Sometimes stereotypes are stereotypes for a reason. Too few people try to defy them, unfortunately.

And me? I forced myself out of the stereotype. As David said, you can't be a good artist and a good mother.

Miriam sits forward on her chair. 'We don't want to see you fail.'

'O-*kay*.'

'We have a proposal,' I say, and Miriam and I explain our idea - the plan pouring out of us in fits and starts.

Alexandra doesn't speak. She doesn't ask questions. She simply listens. It's remarkably refreshing.

When we've finished, we show her our list of intended subjects and photos, trying to form some concrete perspective on the rambling. She is still as she reads them. Miriam's hand reaches over and squeezes my leg under the table. I grin in return, but I can't take my eyes off Alexandra.

Eventually, she meets my gaze. 'Wow.'

'Good wow or bad wow?' Miriam says.

Alexandra shakes her head. 'Good wow. But . . . Do you think this is possible? Given the timeframe?'

'You need this grant, right?' I feel like Bertie suddenly - energised and—

I take a breath.

'We can do this. We want to do this,' Miriam says. And I reach across the table and I take Miriam's hand, and I really hope that what she's saying is true.

For all our sakes.

DAY ELEVEN

'So, darling, I have a plan for you.' This is Shaun. Armed with two bottles of champagne.

I raise an eyebrow at these items. I'm waiting for Miriam in the hostel lounge. It's seven o'five, and we were due to meet at seven.

'It is your birthday, yes?'

'Oh. Yes . . .' I reply. I don't recall telling anyone other than Miriam about this. And that was only because it came up in a conversation about how my family's birthdays all fall within one month of each other.

'So, I think you should get utterly, royally, trolleyed, as we say in England.' Shaun places the bottles on the table and two flutes appear from—

Hm. Apparently, by magic.

'Miriam and I are just going to get dinner, actually. Something low key, you know.' I flick a glance toward a cluster of young people I've not seen before. Two boys and two girls sit on the sofas, the leaflets of local offerings spread amongst them.

I take a small step back, hoping to blend in with the wall.

'What? Don't be ridiculous. It's important to celebrate these things.'

'Don't you find as we age, that you'd rather let the day pass you by?' On my birthday last year, I didn't want to do anything. So we didn't.

Shaun pops the champagne with a flourish of his head, and I can't help but laugh. Hardly inconspicuous, is he?

'My darling girl, if you can't celebrate you on your special day, what can you celebrate, hey? Besides, it's increasingly vital to indulge yourself the older you get. Do you know what I mean?' At this, he performs a stifled sort of guffaw.

I concentrate on the bubbles in the drink and try not to let my mind wander.

'Cheers!' He lifts his glass.

Ugh. What can I do?

'Cheers,' I say, joining Shaun in a smile, feeling a warmth grow toward him. Like a flower, its petals opening up to the sunshine. Shaun is very . . . Full. His large belly protrudes in a way reminiscent of his personality - his body has to be this big to fit all the character in, surely. Full of energy, full of life, full of . . . Pizzazz.

I must ask Bertie where she stayed when she was here. How could I have not thought of this? Maybe she would know Shaun, and—

'Here she is! The birthday girl!' Miriam alerts us to her presence with a honk of that foghorn laughter. Indie and Lola follow closely behind, dressed up in what I can only describe as 'disco clothes'. No doubt that's not the correct term. I'll keep the thought to myself.

'Wow, you look lovely,' I say, kissing Miriam and the girls on each cheek. And they do. Sparkly and shiny and—

I deflate in comparison. Miriam has jazzed up her pocket dress with large earrings and a bold print neck tie, her curls spritzed with something that makes each individual strand glisten.

'I thought this was just dinner?' I swig more champagne

and the fizz descends right down to my gut that groans with responding hunger.

'Darling,' Shaun says, a hand on my shoulder, 'it's never just dinner.'

I look at my new friends as the champagne works on my brain and I take a steadying breath. 'Okay,' I say, the word bubbling out of me like a bubble in this flute. 'But let me stop at a shop on the way.'

Miriam tells me that Ellen is the name of the woman who owns the boutique, the one harbouring The Scarf. I'm not sure when Miriam found the time to befriend another local, especially as Miriam professes to not even enjoy shopping, but I'm glad of the contact. After seeing the others dressed up *in their fancies*, as my mother would have said, I'm inspired to treat myself to a birthday present.

I locate the shop, which is thankfully still open (thank goodness for tourists and their evening shopping habits). My scarf sits pretty on the mannequin in the window.

'Hello.' Hm. My voice has apparently chosen to stay outside. I clear my throat. 'I'd like to try the scarf, if that's okay? The one in the window?'

A woman fitting Miriam's description of Ellen - *short and round like a bubble with a smile* - sits behind the counter near the entrance. I'd frowned when I heard this portrayal but now I can't help but agree. Ellen looks up; the apples of her cheeks shine and her pink lips sparkle with glittery lip gloss. She would look quite fitting in a Beryl Cook painting. David despises Cook's work, but I find it . . . cheerful. Curvy and colourful.

'Oh, yes, most splendid, that one. A local designer. They're all one-offs. Screen printed in a local factory, as a matter of fact.' Ellen's voice sing-songs and I imagine her centre stage of a choir. The fluidity of her tone fills my head with lemon. Or perhaps that's the scent of the shop. One would assume this type of tiny boutique to be musty and stuffed full but it is light and airy and . . . Beautiful, actually. Only a select few items on display but what is here is iridescent and floaty, the shop adorned with several little stands displaying the most gorgeous jewellery . . .

Gosh. I've forgotten how much I love clothes. I must find a reason to wear fancier things when I get home.

'Oh, goodness, thank you,' I say, as Ellen heaves herself out of the window display. Her breath wheezes in the exertion of retrieving my scarf, but still she smiles as she takes it upon herself to wrap the material around my neck, tying with care, before she cradles my arm and leads me to the full-length mirror at the back of the shop.

And, of course, the scarf is fantastic, but—

'What is it? Not quite what you thought? Oh, wait there, dear.' She holds up a finger and puts on the heavy-framed glasses that hang around her neck. I'd opted for similar reading glasses last time David and I went to the optician, but he persuaded me to get the frameless ones. *Timeless*, David said. I felt rather disheartened not to get the trendier shape, but . . . I suppose he was right. Who was I kidding? To suddenly start buying things that would look better on Bertie?

Although seeing the look on Ellen, I have to admire the style. Combined with that bright pink cashmere jumper and a deeper pink trouser, she's a picture of jubilance. Not *inappropriate*, as I imagine David would say. Just . . . merry.

Ellen returns with a pair of trousers and a top and before I can protest, she is shushing and bustling me into the tiny changing room. I hang the selection on the hook and—

I can't help it. This must be what it is to swoon. The fabric is so soft and the colours . . . My perfect outfit.

'I have different sizes, if you need them,' Ellen calls.

I tease back the curtain, its thick loops sticking, and take a steadying breath before presenting myself.

But Ellen is a delight, clapping her hands up to her mouth and sighing dramatically. 'Well,' she says. 'Don't you look a picture.'

I step back, observing the full effect of the look, and as Ellen once again adds the scarf, I—

Oh. I am inexplicably emotional.

'Goodness. I'm sorry.' I wipe at my eyes. 'What a silly fool I am. It's my birthday, you see. Perhaps I'm tired.'

But Ellen says nothing. She has moved into the shop, returning with something in her hand. 'Well, then, let me give you a present.'

'Oh, no. I didn't mean—'

'These would be a fantastic complement to the outfit, don't you think?' Ellen hands me a pair of oversized earrings, not unlike the ones Miriam was wearing, but fancier. They must be in fashion.

'Oh, thank you, but . . . I couldn't. Really, I—'

She presses them into my palm. 'I insist.'

Wow. Really?

I manage a nod. 'Okay, well, thank you.'

'Do you want to try them on?' Ellen brushes the hair off my shoulder (on my shoulder already?) and holds the jewellery up.

The colour clashes with the yellow of the top but in a good way, I think. A *statement*, I would have once said.

But now?

'Perhaps they're too much?' I can't pull this off. Miriam is younger than me and I am—

I don't know. This is the sort of costume jewellery David cannot abide.

'Nonsense. And after tonight, you could wear them at home with all sorts. Look how they alter colour in the light.'

'Oh, I don't really have a call to wear such things in my day-to-day life. My husband and I don't go out so much anymore. Only to friends, the local pub . . . you know.' I fiddle with the scarf; the fabric is comforting, sliding through my fingers.

'My dear, waking up every day is a good enough cause to dress up in my eyes. If it makes you smile, then why not?'

My thumb runs smooth over the earrings. I do love how they change colour as the light hits them - one minute mother-of-pearl, the next a shimmering pink, all the way through to lilac.

'Why don't we put together the whole ensemble, and then you can see.' Ellen leads me back to the changing room. 'Perhaps I could fix your hair, too? It would be a shame to cover the earrings and this low neckline is fabulous on you. You have great skin. Why hide it?' Ellen presses her lips together, humming jovially as she sits me down, and sets about doing something to my hair. Without asking, she also lifts a makeup bag from the back room and adds blusher and lipstick. I should mind. I should feel affronted, but—

I suppose I feel somewhat glamorous.

Besides, it's my birthday; perhaps I should treat myself...

And so, I close my eyes, and I let Ellen work her magic.

'Wowzers,' Miriam says, as I join her, Lola, Indie, Shaun and Eric in the wine bar.

Shaun wolf whistles in jest, then jumps off his seat to spin me round with one hand. 'Fabulous, darling. You look a million dollars.' He kisses me on both cheeks.

I sit on the high stool and accept a glass of fizz from Eric, who nods several times, pout in place.

I touch a hand to my scarf. Goodness. All eyes on me. I am exposed . . . Although, I have the odd sense of feeling more 'me' than I have in a long time. And yes, the colours are bold but—

Perhaps bold is good.

Besides, it's dark in this decadent place with its mahogany walls, candles on every table. How refreshing to be in a place where everyone can have a seat.

'Dee, you look wonderful. This is a great look for you,' Miriam says.

My tweed skirt sits crumpled in the paper bag Ellen gave me, and I kick it further under the table.

'You do,' Indie agrees, Lola nodding beside her. 'You look beautiful.'

I reach a hand up to my hair. Ellen changed the parting, and it sweeps across my face, held in place with an intricate slide. I haven't changed my hair in years. The effect is quite altering. 'Thank you, everyone. And thank you for coming out to celebrate. Even if I am more adept at hibernating.' I have mixed feelings about my birthday. What with the date so close to Mum's, we'd enjoy joint celebrations. And then she was gone and Bertie's birthdays were so much more important and then—

Well. Other dates surpass.

'No hibernating tonight, my dear. The chef here is a friend, so we took the liberty of ordering the taster menu,' Shaun says, as a platter appears, looking better suited to an art gallery than a dining table.

Small bites of elaborate offerings balance on a candelabra-type ornament that grows up toward the crowning feature of a woman's face.

'Wow.' The waiter produces a blowtorch and scorches a selection of the morsels. 'This is spectacular.'

Goodness. Look at all this. This group, the faces of my new friends together on this high table, and—

There's a painting I know. A jovial scene, but in the centre of the frame is a woman, haunted by something. A Henri de Toulouse-Lautrec piece. *At The Moulin Rouge*?

Yes, that's right.

The painting is in two parts, as is this bar. Wasn't the canvas struck in two following the artist's death?

Gosh, yes. Shaun and Eric could be the aristocrats, Lola the woman preening in the mirror, Indie observing at her side. Isn't art funny? How extraordinary that I might remember the minutiae of a painting, and yet the memory of life is . . . a different mode. The lines blur, the oil smudges. Reality distorted. An Expressionist piece.

Reality distorted? Or heightened?

Rothko. What does he say? To paint a literal recital is to limit the viewer's response. Better to depict a biomorphic form.

Biomorphic form.

Photos do not capture the emotion conveyable in a painting. Miriam might snap this scene, but if I were to paint it, perhaps I'd exaggerate the way this silverware flashes, the mask of the candelabra not as a subsidiary detail, but as a vehicle to which I might attach this memory. Or would I attempt a more ambiguous Expressionist piece? 'Attempt' being the optimum word, of course. But the mask would feature, in whatever form or suggestion of form. The oddity of me being here in this scene, as the oddity of this mask being used to serve food. The mask is a woman, her face contorting, wondering how she got here, perhaps?

Yes, I like this detail. I would draw on this detail.

'Say cheese!'

And people. A painting can capture the character of a person, accentuating traits in a vivid and revealing manner. Unposed. Exposing the essence of that person in a portrait, perhaps, that's more truthful than a photo of the real thing. A person cannot fake a smile in a painting.

At The Moulin Rouge.

But. Am I the haunted green-faced woman staring out of the shot, or am I the entertaining red-haired woman in the centre of the circle?

Tonight, I suppose, I am both.

'Oh my goodness, I've forgotten I like food. Although, that wasn't food, was it?' I dab my mouth and turn to Miriam, who has moved onto the stool beside me. We have devoured dinner, and the others have moved deeper into the bar to *scout talent* on behalf of Lola and Indie. 'That was sensational.'

I close my eyes again, willing my mind to forever remember the flamed sashimi, the crunchy, sweet spring onion garnish like a firework in my mouth, lighting my taste buds like nothing I have experienced before. 'I didn't know food could be like that. I mean, I see those cookery shows where people create wonders but . . . The *taste.*'

'You've rediscovered baking; now you can rediscover food.' Miriam finishes her glass, and tops us both up with more. The sound of the chilled dance music (lounge music?) couples with my satiated belly and I feel . . . Heady. Pleasant.

'I was never *into* food, so this is a new discovery.'

Miriam lowers the bottle, raises her glass. But she doesn't

drink. 'You know,' she says, finally, 'I've been thinking about how this trip is about discovery. Discovering things you've always wanted to try, and rediscovering those things that were there but have, for whatever reason, been parked to one side . . .'

Miriam pulls an unusual expression - twisted, a hint of an interior battle? Her eyes fix on my scarf, scanning the pattern. Then, she looks at me square on. 'I've been thinking about this in relation to lovers . . .'

'Oh, gosh, Miriam . . . I told you about The Dee Dee man in trust.' I shake my head.

Miriam swigs from her glass. Another half gone, in one swoop.

She lowers the flute, a momentary pause, before her expression clears and she straightens in her seat. 'Have you thought about trying to contact him? This could be the perfect time.'

Ugh. Well, of course, I've looked before. Half-hearted, guilty, wondering . . . I've always closed down before it came to anything. 'What I did was not right, Miriam.'

'But you did it before you married David, before you were pregnant . . .'

I touch my scarf. 'Yes.' My heart, underneath my hand, is pounding. I have such mixed feelings on this matter. I hated myself for being like my father - for betraying David, but I always return to how it felt with Him. As Miriam said, our affair was before and then—

I chose David.

'What are you two talking about?' Lola is here. Miriam and I must look conspicuous, our heads leaning together, conversing in secrets.

'Darlings, why aren't you dancing?' And now Shaun joins, Eric at his side. The chilled beat of the music has become more insistent and a few people move to the dance floor.

'These two are exchanging something. Whispering . . .' Lola narrows her eyes.

'If it's a secret, let it be a secret,' Indie says, 'giving me eyes' in respect of Lola.

I look at Miriam, who shrugs.

Well, what have I got to lose? Tonight, I feel different. I want to be the woman in these clothes. The woman who tastes that food and drinks this champagne. 'Miriam wants me to contact an old flame, and I don't think it's right.'

'Goodness, darling, why would it be wrong?' Shaun waves his hand, as though batting away protestations.

'Because I'm married now. To someone else.'

'And where is that someone else?' This is Eric.

'He left her. On the aeroplane. On the way here.' Lola.

'Huh!' Shaun throws one hand to his heart and one to his forehead. He should be in amateur dramatics.

'He left you?' Eric again.

'We're meeting up again in ten days. It's just a short time out. A chance for us to . . . Regroup, I suppose.'

'Is that what you want? To *'regroup'*?' Eric's spindly fingers unfurl into air quotes.

I inspect the end of my scarf, where it pools in my lap. This conversation is not going as I expected. I am a fool. An even older fool, on today, this day. My day.

'Isn't the way to get over one person to get under another?' Lola says, with an exaggerated wink.

'It was a long time ago. And I'm not getting over David. I'm just waiting.'

'It was a long time ago in *real* time,' Miriam says, 'but in the time of your mind?'

I let myself picture Him. Gosh. Right there. The imagination immediately able to conjure his image with precision, the body so able to recall his touch. 'I . . . I guess.'

'Maybe it's time to give yourself a second chance?' Eric's voice is surprisingly gentle.

But I laugh. 'You don't get second chances at my age. You get ...' I splay my fingers.

'Hot flushes and bunions?' Miriam says.

'Precisely.'

Shaun lowers his chin. 'Darling, it seems obvious to me that if your husband is having a time-out you should do the same. Use it wisely and get in touch with the old lover. What have you got to lose?'

Ha! 'Dignity?'

Miriam puts a hand on my knee. 'The way you described him to me, Dee, with so much passion and lust . . . Don't you want a chance to have that in your life again?'

'I can't do it to David. Not again, I—'

Lola leans forward. 'David has abandoned you and all you're doing is contacting this other person. If anything, David is pushing you to it.'

I look at Lola. I look at all the other eyes in the group. Willing, wanting.

But...

What is it I want?

DAY TWELVE

Once again, I find myself a little foggy-headed today, the day I start my mission proper. Having chatted everything through with Alexandra, we now have a solid plan of action. Miriam and Alexandra are sorting the layout of the exhibition while I'm out collecting stories and profiling people. Miriam will then take the photos while I write everything up. Alexandra is in charge of marketing and everything finance-related.

Goodness. Just eight days to throw this thing together. A daunting thought, although I can't help but notice a little sizzle firing in the deepest part of my stomach. I catch sight of myself in the bakery window, and - do you know? - I actually lift my chin. I'm admiring my other new top - a soft pink blouse pressed upon me by Ellen yesterday - and my new hair complete with sparkly clip which flashes in the reflection.

My first appointment of the day is here at the bakery. I open the door, my chest swelling. Purpose?

Hm. I pause to inhale the scent of baked bread and coffee.

Heavenly.

'Dee, how lovely you look today.' Derrick's smile is broad, his beard spreading wide. Then he appears to remember something pressing as he fusses and mumbles, searching around his feet for some misplaced item.

'Thank you,' I say, but he's thrust his head deep into the display cabinet and is rearranging the sumptuous cream pies.

A young woman appears behind him, the one I've spotted here several times before, fastening a pinny behind her back. She is slender, her long hair secure in the hairnet, the tone of her skin as warm as Derrick's.

'Dad, are you not going to take the woman's order?' Her voice is soaked in that teen outrage reserved for parents. I remember Bertie doing the same, although we were fortunate that she grew out of it quickly.

'Oh, that's okay,' I say. 'When Derrick is ready, perhaps I could have a word with him? If he has time, of course. And a coffee too, please. That would be great.'

I scoot over to the last available table, the perfect spot to watch Byron wake up. Ellen is shuffling down the street towards her shop, the gallery door at the other end opens, eager tourists hunt out a breakfast spot.

'I could sit all day and watch the world run by,' Derick says, startling me from my reverie.

I indicate for him to take the seat opposite. 'Yes, and it's a lovely world to know.'

'Indeed, it is, Dee. I was very lucky to find it, the people kind enough to let an outsider set up business here. I've always felt very welcome, actually.'

'You know? I feel the same. Like I . . . fit . . . Well, I suppose, being a small town, it has that appeal for everyone.'

'Only those open to it.'

I clear my throat. 'Yes. Extraordinary, really, to think I've only been here for twelve days and feel that way.'

'Try being here for twenty years.'

I risk a peek at Derrick. Byron life does seem to suit him. He doesn't present as a man of stress with that skin that wrinkles well with age - thick, Mediterranean skin. 'Do you still enjoy living here? After all this time?'

'It's changed, you know. My . . . situation has changed, but . . . Yes. The place is perfect.'

'And how lucky you are to have your daughter here.'

'Yes, although I don't think it's healthy for her to hang around. I want her to get out and see the world, much as I'd miss her . . .'

I nod, glance down, give myself a moment to picture this feeling as a stone. Then I imagine myself bundling up the emotion onto the stone. Every scrap. I picture see the sea and I throw the stone far, far away.

'My wife passed, you see, a year ago. Annalys doesn't think I can cope, but—'

'Sometimes we surprise ourselves.'

Derrick surveys me for a moment, then: 'Yes. I do believe you're right.'

I open my mouth but, no—

I can't do this. How can I ask a widowed man to tell me, a stranger, his life story, and not give anything back?

The questions are inevitable. They always are . . .

And to explain everything . . . David, is—

I suppose it defies explanation. Right now, it's impossible.

And I'm not ready.

Inside the surf shack, Michael is talking to a customer. I mouth 'Tom', and he points me toward the storage room. I knock, seeing nobody present through the crack of the open door, but make out a muffled 'Yo!' from somewhere inside.

Hm. There are piles of boxes, some spilling bright-coloured clothing, a few board 'blanks' (as I now know to call them) resting against the far wall, but I'm at a loss as to where—

'Oh, hey.' Tom is balancing on the top shelf of a rather rickety looking wooden structure. A ladder rests against the far end, so he must have crawled along that shelf like a spider.

'Is that safe?'

'Probably not. Hey, watch out.' He throws down a plastic-covered piece of clothing which lands with a slap on the concrete floor.

'Don't you want to stand on the ladder?'

Tom turns his head to look at the ladder, as though seeing it for the first time. 'Hm. Yeah. This is the way my uncle did it, so . . . I don't know. Why change something that's working, right?'

'Is that your uncle?' I point to an enlarged photo of a man surfing in the barrel of a wave. You can see his huge smile, tanned skin, the sun glistening on the water. How lucky I am to understand a fraction of what that must feel like.

'Yeah. That photo was taken here, actually. I was just a boy. Man, I remember he would be so psyched after his surfs. The guy never grew up. I loved that about him.'

I study the photo, the differing shades of over-exposed blues, the whites luminous. 'Would you mind sharing this picture?'

Tom extends his body until he is lying prone on the shelf, his chin cupped in his hands. 'What do you mean?'

I take a steadying breath, and I pitch our exhibition idea.

Tom is all nods and smiles. 'Sounds great.'

Oh. 'And maybe you want to exhibit one of your own boards - show everyone the future of Byron?' I add, while I have the courage.

But at this, Tom freezes. After a moment his gaze drops, hands lowering. 'Oh, er . . . I don't have the logo defined yet, I—'

'Okay, well . . . If it's ready, you'd be welcome to include it. Is it okay to send Miriam back to take photos? And maybe we could meet for you to tell me more about your uncle and the history of the business?'

'Sure.' Tom pushes himself back up and swings his legs over the edge. 'I have time now?'

'Oh, okay, great.'

Eesh. My first interview. I can do this . . . Right?

Tom throws another bundle of clothing onto the floor, then turns his back to me and lowers himself down and—

Oh, goodness.

There. I see it.

'You have a tattoo,' I manage. Tom's t-shirt has gotten hooked on the shelf, the fabric pulling up to reveal a shape on his side.

He jumps to the floor, walks to me and lifts his t-shirt to unveil the palm-size marking that stretches across his ribs as my breath falters in my chest, like the wings of a new-born butterfly, fluttering as it tries to break free of its chrysalis.

'I got it a few years back.' He leans over to peer at it.

I too continue to look. But I already know every corner, every curve, every colour.

'My only one,' he adds.

And as he drops his t-shirt back down, I realise. The understanding dawns on me slowly, creeping into my consciousness. But once it is there, I realise I always knew. On some level.

And now the thought has fully settled into my awakened mind ...

I know who Tom is.

I walk in haste to Ellen's shop, glad of her friendly face. Someone I can confide in?

No, I'm—

No.

She embraces me, then pulls up a stool beside her at the till and regales me with her stories, thank goodness. I need distraction after scarpering from Tom.

Gosh. What must he think of me? Stuttering, flustered, falling . . . At home, I can keep tabs on this behaviour, but here?

Get yourself to a therapist, Francis would say. The American life has changed my sister, despite what she thinks. Even her hardened facade cracks sometimes. Though rarely. She has to keep it together for her brood of boys. Man children. Because they are still children. Replacing Francis with wives, returning to their mother at the mere hint of marital upset. And Francis, of course, complaining to me but secretly relishing the time.

My nephews - so different to Bertie. Instead of returning home, she freed herself.

Trying, at least.

What will Bertie say about Tom?

Talk to him. Tell him.

But I can't. Not yet.

'How long have you owned this place?' I ask Ellen as I open my notebook. Ellen has confirmed, as I expected, that she'd love to partake in the exhibit.

'Oh, well, I suppose it's nearly five years now, yes. I had some help from friends after the divorce. You know how these things can throw you, dear, but I did it eventually. This was my dream.' And she gestures around, breath wheezing through her beam.

I scrawl down some notes. I want to be sure Miriam catches

this woman's spirit. Ellen emanates warmth. Like a chocolate fondant that, when you open the tiniest of cracks, oozes chocolatey goodness all over the plate.

'A woman is nothing without her friends, am I right?' she says.

I nod politely, but—

Patricia. Is it strange not to have heard from her? I wonder if David has heard from Hugo. Do they know? Do the book club women know? Goodness. I'd be the talk of the town.

Just like—

Well.

I was always an outsider. David's family are part of a long line of relatives living in the village. As David's wife, people knew who I was before I even knew myself.

I hadn't realised that when I first moved there. The impact. The gossip. The knowing . . .

That's why I was so keen for Bertie to get out. To go to London. To find—

What I could not?

Stop it. Stop it, Diane.

Dee Dee.

'And your family? Are they here?' Focus. You've been doing so well.

Miriam is who I think of when I picture friends now, but . . . Miriam in my life at home? I just can't see it.

Hm. That's a troubling thought. I park it to one side. Besides, I doubt Miriam would want to be friends with me in 'real life'. Perhaps this current situation provides a mutual attraction - a mutual reliance. I'm the closest to her age and—

'My children are all grown up now. I'm actually about to be a grandmother,' Ellen says.

I offer a tight smile. Press my lips together. Nod.

'But my children live across Australia. One in Sydney, another in Melbourne, the third in Brisbane. Why they couldn't have all chosen the same city is beyond me.' The love is written all over her face, that glow, her body language – there's a lightness to her movements, despite her grandiose size.

'Three children? How lovely. You're very lucky, even though they're not right here.'

'I know, dear, and, to be honest, with grandchildren on the way, perhaps the distance is a blessing. I always thought I'd be the fun, jolly grannie. I'd hate to be one of those poor women used like a second mother or a maid, God forbid. I want to lavish them with treats and cakes and take them away from their parents for days of laughter and joy, you know?'

I nod, but I can't find any words. I watch a woman about my age walk hand-in-hand with a little girl past the shop door. The child fizzes with energy, jumping, chatting, pointing to something in the window display as they pass.

'Do you have any grandchildren, dear?'

'No. No, I've not been so fortunate.' I pull myself up straight. 'Can I ask you more about the business, Ellen? Are you the only one working here?'

'Funny you should ask that. I have an assistant but she told me only yesterday she's planning to go to Europe for a year so I should look for someone to replace her. Not ideal timing, if truth be told. That girl's extremely trustworthy, and I was hoping to leave her in charge for a month while I help my daughter with the new baby.'

'Ah. Yes, a dilemma.'

'If you hear of anyone looking for a job . . .' Ellen excuses herself to the bathroom, and I'm left with a strange feeling. A wondering, I suppose. *Alternate universe*, Bertie would say. I've never fully grasped her meaning.

Oh! The ding of the bell startles and the door opens. A woman enters. Mid-thirties, I would guess. A tall woman, strong - I can see that from the definition of her muscles through her leggings and tight vest top. Lean. Her hair is scraped back from her face, and she appears not to wear a scrap of makeup over that fresh skin.

Hm. Perhaps she's not even thirty.

'Oh, hello,' she says, her Australian accent thick.

'Hello.' I nod, and finish my tepid tea.

I try not to watch as the woman browses the aisles, selecting items, holding them up to herself in the mirror in a manner I could never. So . . . Un-self-conscious. I mean, she knows I'm sitting here.

'Is Ellen not here today?'

'Oh, no. I mean, yes. She's in the bathroom.'

I look at the woman's feet - bright pink toe nails rest pretty in 'thongs'.

'Okay, thanks.'

'The blue's lovely on you.' This is me. Speaking to this customer. Why? It's not my shop, for goodness sake.

'Really? I wasn't sure. The length . . . You know, with these legs.' This woman's scepticism is at odds with her upright exterior. Her manner, and—

Well. I suppose you never know what's really going on with someone. Isn't that what Bertie is always telling me? *Human interest, Mum. People differ from how they present,* she says, an edge of exasperation to her voice.

'And have you seen this one?' I'm standing, crossing the boutique to retrieve a mint green floaty shawl, which would look wonderful on this woman's long frame.

She tilts her head, considering. 'Oh, now that is nice. What a find.' She lets the material fall through her fingers.

I lift my face, silently urging her to try it on.

And when she does, of course, it looks phenomenal.

'I like it,' she says, taking a step back.

'It goes with what you're wearing.'

'You know? It feels lovely to be in something feminine. I'm

always in leggings.' She turns, casting her eye over either shoulder. 'You really think it goes?'

'Absolutely. I love the way—'

'Ah, Dee, I see you've met Kathryn. Wow, that looks beautiful on you, Kathy dear.' Ellen embraces the woman, holding her at arm's length to admire the look. 'Isn't Kathryn just adorable? Like a graceful gazelle who thinks she's a dormouse, for goodness sake. If I had legs like that I'd be parading Byron in my lacy smalls. Have you been to one of Kathryn's classes, Dee?'

'Classes?'

'I'm a yoga instructor. Kathryn.' Kathryn extends her hand, a strong shake.

'I'm Dee. And, yes, I think my friend Miriam has been attending your classes. She keeps on at me to join but . . . I don't know. All that . . . You know.' I flap my hands, hoping to indicate what I seem unable to convey in conversation.

'The classes are mixed ability so you'd be welcome anytime, if you change your mind.'

'And I'll come back, one day,' Ellen says, straightening something on a rack. 'Once I can fit into some leggings, my love.' She offers a laugh and Kathryn and I smile with her.

'You'd both be more than welcome anytime. I must be getting off to a class now, actually, but I think I'll have to take this with me.'

Ellen scans Kathryn's bank card and rings the order into the till. Then we both embrace the woman and watch her waft out of the shop in a cloud of elegance.

'Oh, darn, I should have asked Kathryn about the exhibition,' I say. 'Do you think she'd want to be featured?'

Ellen wheezes down onto the chair. 'For some reason that woman is seriously lacking in confidence, so she may take some persuasion.'

I pick up my bag.

'She didn't need much persuasion from you to buy that top though, did she?' Ellen is all smiles. 'I heard you, you know.'

'Oh, well, I had to suggest it. She looked remarkable.'

'Seems you might have a knack for clothes, Dee. You know I need an assistant . . .'

Ha! 'Thank you, Ellen. But I'm leaving soon.'

'Well . . . you know where to find me should anything change.' And she gives me a wink as I kiss her goodbye and I can't decide if I feel happy or sad. I suppose when you fall in love with a place like this, with the people in it, it's inevitably going to be hard to leave.

Miriam is back, and her presence immediately alters the atmosphere of the hostel lounge. I've been alone in here for hours, just watching the dust settle, feeling my thoughts settle in line with it.

But now?

I have to keep the dust down.

'Hey, how'd it go?' Miriam says.

I look down at my less-than-impressive notes spread out across the table. On Tom and Derrick, I have nothing. Just a blank piece of paper with their names written at the top. 'I think you might need to talk to them. I didn't really get to the nitty gritty of anyone. I . . . I don't know.'

'So, go back tomorrow.'

'Me?' I look away from Miriam, her body a silhouette against the light of the window behind her that hurts my eyes. 'Oh, er . . . No. Perhaps a fresh conversation would be better.'

'O-*kay*.'

I tidy up the pages, taking care not to fold them, and secure the lid on my pen.

'Is everything alright, Dee?'

'Yes, just . . . This is a tough task. What are we even doing?'

Miriam lowers herself into the adjacent seat. 'I thought you and Derrick got on well, but—'

'Not that. The exhibition. Who are we kidding?'

'What do you mean? Alexandra loves it. We're getting loads of stuff together. I'm enjoying it. Aren't you?'

'Yes, but—' Gosh. Derrick, Ellen. They have lives. They're moving forward. Every guest of this hostel - out and about. Living. They're not . . .

Goodness. Even Tom.

Miriam places a hand on my shoulder, and lowers her voice.

'It's tiring. Let's have a break tomorrow. Let's put the project aside and check out this flea market with Indie and Lola, yeah? Free some *creative space* in our minds.'

I laugh at Miriam's faux posh voice and, slowly, I nod. For now, all thoughts of exhibits and art can be shelved. Put it on the stone, and throw it away into the sea.

Keep the dust at bay.

DAY THIRTEEN

I had to haul myself from bed this morning. The temptation, as always, is to hide. But . . . *I'm* not in the exhibit, am I? I'm a mere curator. I don't have to tell my story. Tom doesn't know who I am, so maybe nothing need change.

Still. My mind needs to be occupied. As usual at this time of day, I am alone in the kitchen. I pull on the oven gloves (I treated Eric and Shaun to a new pink set, fed up as I was of burning my hands on their ghastly tea towels) and lift the bread from the oven. I breathe in the thick scent, my eyes closing upon an image of a ten-year-old Bertie. I'd been teaching her how to bake for the first time and I can recall her little face, shining up with such amazement as we took out our golden rolls. The wonder of the science behind baking, captured in her adorable peep. How many things have I seen anew through the eyes of my daughter?

And still now, being here in Byron. I'm here because she loves it, aren't I?

'Oh, wow, Dee, I hope you're bringing those for the road.' Miriam arrives, peering over my shoulder.

'Dee, how are we going to cope staying in any other hostel ever again?' Lola is vigorously applying sun cream to her face, rubbing it up and down with aggression as she enters the kitchen. This is a large space, but it suddenly feels rather crowded.

'What do you mean?' I say. I smile at Indie, standing back, in Lola's shadow.

'You're an asset to this place. Shaun should add you to his advertising: *Homemade bread baked on-site every day. Awake to the aroma of heaven!*' At this, Lola wafts her hands out to either side, and I remember what she'd said about wanting to be an actress. Something tells me if this girl wants anything badly enough, she'll achieve it.

'Somewhat melodramatic, dear,' I say. 'Are we ready?' I take off the oven gloves and wrap up the rolls.

'Absolutely.' Lola claps with excitement. 'Bangalow is supposed—'

'Banga—?' I can't say it. I can't bear to.

'Bangalow,' Lola repeats.

Gosh.

Someone has stuffed my mouth full of cotton wool. I wet my lips. 'It's near here?' I manage.

Lola frowns at Miriam.

'It's just twenty minutes or so,' Miriam says. 'The market is meant to be great, it—'

'It's . . . so close.' I draw the wrapped rolls into my chest. They're warm. Too hot, actually. But I hold on. 'I didn't realise . . .'

'Indie and I have been reading about it,' Lola says. 'Apparently there are loads of little boutiques and independent shops. They also have a farmer's market every Saturday. It looks super cute. You're gonna love it.'

I watch as the three of them leave the kitchen, the bread burning my hands.

But—

I can't move.

Miriam turns. 'Dee?'

I'm nodding. 'I'll give it a miss, I think.'

And I leave the kitchen and I'm retreating back to my room and—

'Dee?'

I keep walking. I'm almost at the door.

'*Dee.*' But Miriam has caught up. 'What's wrong? Why aren't you coming?'

I can't lift my head. I can't risk it. I am together here. I have it all together here.

'Just a funny turn. I'll be okay. Have a lovely day.' And I hand her the bread and I force myself to withdraw, despite her protestations. I close the bedroom door behind me, and I climb back under the blankets.

I am standing on the edge of a cliff. I couldn't stay in bed, I couldn't—

The sea rushes over rocks some fifty metres or more below. The roar washes dark blue waves in my mind.

'You're not going to jump, are you?'

Miriam's voice startles and I pull back from the edge. Hands on my knees, head lowered, colours washing through my rambling mind. I hiked up here at speed, needing the air, the wind.

My heart is pounding, breath heaving out of me. I want to cry; I want to scream, I—

I have to get myself together. I can't do this with a witness.

I turn to Miriam. She lifts her face to the sun, eyes closed, hair blowing back.

'You didn't go to the market?' I say.

'I thought I should find you. Sofia said you would be here.' Miriam opens her eyes, takes me in her sights. 'Do you mind if I join you?'

She doesn't wait for an answer. She sits on the step of the lighthouse, a few metres back from my position near the edge of the cliff.

After a moment, I join her. We look out to the sea, a hypnotic rise and fall of swell, a moveable canvas of dark, treacherous blue.

'Monet did a cliff painting,' I say. '*Cliff Walk at Pourville.* Three years after his wife died. Amazing, don't you think? That he could still see the beauty in nature, that he could observe at all. Goodness, to create ...'

Miriam offers nothing.

I continue: 'I believe his aim was to insert a person into a landscape without disturbing the integrity of the scene. But perhaps it was inevitable - make a subtle modification and you spawn an entirely different image.'

'Many find creativity aids their grief. Maybe this was the case for Monet.'

It's my turn to be silent. To this, I am blank.

A single blade of grass grows between the bricks. An intruder. A misplaced stroke.

'I thought I was doing okay by myself. I've been with David for so long. I've had responsibilities and Bertie to raise and—' I shake my head. What can I say? Who am I kidding? I can't do this alone. It was always going to come to this.

I pluck out the blade, tear it in two. Feed it to the wind.

'It must be a challenge when the children fly the nest. Starting again. Just the two of you - a new relationship with a different dynamic,' Miriam says. 'Did you ever want more kids? Or a career?'

'Yes, to both, I suppose. But David earns enough so I don't need to work. We weren't blessed with more children but to have enjoyed one healthy one . . .' I look at my hands: tight, interconnecting fists in my lap. 'Like you said; how can I complain? I had everything.'

'Unless it's not everything? Maybe you did need to work.'

A gull hovers on the wind in front of us, weightless, free, before it turns on a gust and soars out of view. 'I should have been different. In my marriage . . . I should have been . . . Better. I've been hiding, turning.'

'Stifled?'

Miriam is not listening. She can't see inside my brain. She can't—

'Thirty years is a long time to be silenced,' she adds.

'No. I need controlling. I can't act for myself, I can't . . . *Think*. Goddamn it.' I am on my feet.

Behind me, I sense Miriam sigh. 'When you stifle a strong desire, it doesn't go away. The urge keeps burning. Eventually, that flame finds a little oxygen, and it explodes. Now you can either be smothered in flames, or you can be lit up like a firecracker.'

The wind catches at the waves, white licks on blue triangles.

'I know you think I can rise out of this but . . . I'm not like Indie and Lola. I don't have brains or determination or fearlessness. They're young and I'm—'

'Just fifty-five, for God's sake. Stop writing yourself off, Dee. Have faith.'

I sit back down. 'I had faith.'

'Then what the hell eroded it? What happened to you?'

'I—'

'It's the marriage, isn't it? Look, I've broken out of mine and I've never felt freer.'

'You haven't broken out because you're still living together.'

'But I will, I—'

'You think you know David. You think you can write him off but you can't, Miriam. You don't know us. You don't know *me*.'

Miriam spins the wedding band on her big hand. 'Maybe that's because you don't let anyone in.'

I frown, rotate toward Miriam. 'I said I was *The Scream* but . . . Munch did another painting I remembered. *The Girl By The Window*. There is something here, Miriam. There's a window, but it's locked.'

'Can't you try to open it?'

'You see me, but—' My head is shaking. My eyes can't focus.

'Dee—'

'In that painting, the viewer can't see the girl's face. We cannot understand what she observes through the window. We cannot know her. We're not allowed. I am *The Girl By The Window*. I have to be.'

'Dee, please. Stop relating yourself to the external. Stop curating your persona. There is no perfect exterior. It's not real. Where's you genuine self? Where's your heart, Dee?'

'You think I have no heart? My heart got broken, Miriam. My heart *is* broken.'

Miriam grabs my hands, dips her head to meet my eye. 'But you're doing okay here alone. Can't you see that? You don't need him. He left you, Dee. If you could just let people in a little, take a risk, I think you'd reap the rewards. I know you and David have shared a life, and he's left you heartbroken, but you can survive and you can mend.'

'I can't mend.'

'You can. People get over break-ups, Dee. People deal with it.'

'*I* can't.'

'You can.' Miriam squeezes my hands, nods. 'And I will go home and tell people about my marriage. We can both do this.'

'I can't.' For God's *sake*.

'Why the hell not? Why can't you deal with David?'

'Because . . . David is not the one who broke my heart.'

DAY FOURTEEN

I dreamt of Bertie last night. A vivid portrayal. She was just a child. Five, maybe six years old. She came into my room in the night, just as she used to. David would always take her back to her own bed but this time, in my dream, I lifted the blanket, and I let her spoon in with me. A warm little nugget of flannelling, I could smell her baby shampoo and gentle, sweet breath.

When I woke this morning, in the haze of new light, I had to check whether she was still there.

But, of course, she was not.

I can't hide forever. Something draws me to him. He doesn't know who I am. He doesn't have to know. I can discover for myself.

Tom. Leading the surf excursion today.

I laugh as it is so obvious now. So different to David.

A different breed of man, of course.

I've checked where we're going on the map and I'm assured it's in the other direction to Banga—

Goodness. How could I not have even realised the proximity? Avoidance? Denial?

Francis will tell me, no doubt. Therapist-speak. She is well-versed.

Sometimes things just happen, I remember Francis saying once. It hadn't been a comfort. My sister has a rather masculine edge to her personality. She tries to fix while I—? Overdo it, apparently. I heard her talking to David once. An argument. When he got back from—

Well. She didn't agree that I should have stayed at home. She thinks it would have helped me to go.

Francis wants what's best for me. She worries. I know that.

But how can she think I should go home now?

Home.

Is home still a home when all the people have left?

There's a group of us going on this sunrise surf trip with Tom and Michael and at the moment, it's still dark. Too early to be up, yes, but after yesterday, I couldn't lie in bed again. I can't be alone. I need to keep busy. This sense of purpose, the exhibition, the activity, it's . . .

Something. Something good, I think.

Perhaps David was right. He never agreed with my staying in bed. And I got up, didn't I? Eventually. I resurfaced. Forced myself. Out. Onward.

Only before coming here did I relapse. The brain needing to pause, perhaps, before taking on such an experience. Perhaps David abandoned me because he was worried I'd retreat to bed while we were on our *trip of a lifetime.* Perhaps he's had enough of looking after me.

Michael is at the door of the minibus, ticking off our names as we step inside, holding a torch to illuminate the way. The helpful act seems incongruous with his rebellious look. I hadn't noticed the ear full of piercings before.

'I feel like I'm on a school trip,' I say, as I hoick myself into the bus.

I had been talking to Miriam ahead, but it's Michael who answers: 'Did you ever do a school trip like this?'

'Well, no.' Hm, my mood is surprisingly upbeat mood for this hour. I feel ... excited? Like I'm breaking the rules. This is not my typical behaviour. Well, not for a long time. 'Not much water in the middle of London,' I add, before I take a seat beside Miriam.

She and Lola have found common ground on the subject of some foreign film nobody else knows exist. I'm surprised by Lola - she seems to have good insights on the matter. Although, what do I know?

'Oh, hello, Jake.' I smile, surprised to see him boarding the bus. 'I thought you went up the coast?'

'Yes,' he says, ducking his stretched body down. He has left the gel out of his hair today and it looks good: relaxed, soft. 'I'm on my way back south, so I thought I'd stop in, you know ...'

And then Indie boards behind him, and they take a seat beside each other, exchanging subdued conversation.

Tom arrives, welcomes us aboard and hops into the driver's seat. The ignition of the engine flares brown in my mind. What was the last school trip I went on?

Oh, well, it was at college, actually, a trip to the Tate London.

Goodness. It's been too long. My father and David, well, they're not such art fans. I'd been so moved by the Van Gogh exhibit. Everyone else had gone for lunch but I sat, enraptured by his *Starry Night Over the Rhone*. I knew the painting was of the river Rhone in Arles but, for me, it conjured Paris - the stretch of water, lights signalling all that life underneath a sky full of twinkling stars, the lovers in the foreground ...

So much ... possibility.

I thought, one day, I'd go to Paris and create my own impression. The Seine, under the stars, a reflection of my life beginning. Didn't Van Gogh say the image of a night sky had haunted him? He felt compelled to paint, transcribe this from his brain lest it—

Well.

My night sky remains in my head. Although, of course, I would never expect it to be as bewitching as a Van Gogh. So different from my style. My art teacher, Mr Mathers, used to laugh, saying that my striking, colourful, abstract style seemed incongruous for such a quiet, reserved girl. What I could never express was that in my art I found an ... honesty? As though, in my painting, I was exactly as I should be.

Life, however, has always proved more difficult. Sticky. Like I could never wash the brushes completely clear.

And then, I guess, I spilt all the paint and nothing was clean again.

The minibus has left the straight line of the freeway and is bumping over a dirt track. Outside, dark shapes appear ominous in this low light. I hold onto the edges of my seat; the stability handles only reachable from the window position.

Goodness. Am I trying to meet Tom's eye in the rear-view mirror? Oh, what a clown. I draw myself deeper into the seat.

I consider Tom's story - taking over the shop, designing his own boards. And Derrick? Continuing to bake in the face of grief. Like Monet. All these people and their lives - the hurt is there and yet?

They have forward momentum.

While I ...

Miriam is right - David put me in this situation. Unkind, unfair and—

Did I spill the paint or was I prevented from getting anywhere near it? Lock the material away, and there won't be anything to clear up.

But what does he expect me to do now?

. . .

We arrive at the surf spot, parking in a secluded area in a forest. Through the spots of opening between branches, the sky is a dusty grey-blue. We use torches to help us put on wetsuits and choose boards, before we trample through the foliage. It's quiet and dark here in the trees, but not eerie.

Special. I have a sense of this being a special experience.

A short walk, then we break through the enclosure onto the most marvellous white sand beach, the sky and sea a landscape artwork, we the added after thought. To my left, I see no other person along the vast stretch, in the other direction, a singular lone tent. *Illegal*, Michael tells us.

Goodness. How strange that some people are living on top of skyscrapers in capital cities and others untraced on a desolate beach. *Not partaking in life,* David would say. *It's not real life.* But they're alive, aren't they? Happy in their own existence. Maybe they don't need . . . Everything else.

Is it these choices that Bertie struggles with? How do we know if we're making the correct ones? How do we know if we're making the right decisions for our children?

I wonder, had we had more babies, would the pressure have lifted off Bertie? Is that what she felt growing up? *It's too much,* she said once.

I must ask her.

The surf is a bit of a non-event, the waves coming in so sporadically we spend most of the time drifting on our boards.

But I don't mind. Being on the water is calming. The gentle rock of the board, the murky horizon, pink and orange striating in the cloud.

Impression, Sunrise.

Monet was criticised by some for his lack of form in that piece. The horizon merging with the water and sky, the shapes of the buildings and ships indistinct. But isn't that the beauty of art? The artist depicts their impression, their subjective take.

Gosh. What's happened to my brain? It's been sleeping in

monochrome, awoken now in a kaleidoscope. I'm living in an
art gallery and at every turn there's another relic of the past, a
reminder of a Great Work. Monet, Renoir, Van Gogh. The
gardens and flowers of the Impressionists, the sharp building
lines of cubism, while my mind is a mix of surrealism, as
confused as a Dali masterpiece.

There is comfort in this comparison. Perhaps I need not see
logic. In art college, I adored the abstract. As though, only in
the nonsensical can we find sense.

But what am I a fan of now?

Well, I suppose my canvas remains blank.

Through the clear water, a bright yellow fish circles my foot
before losing interest.

I watch the fish dart away, and— Gosh. Does it matter if I'm
not creating? Here, I am *in* the artwork. I am a stroke on the
landscape. I am, gosh, *at one.*

Yes, yes, Bertie, I know. *You've changed*, is what you'll tell me .
. .

Goodness. I could have chosen to not come here today.

David could have chosen not to have left.

But we have made those choices.

And the sun is rising and this is—

A new day.

Impression, Sunrise.

The last time I made a point of seeing the sunrise was
with Him.

Dee Dee.

Goodness. Again. My mind is going there?

I made my choice.

Didn't I?

'What?' Miriam has paddled up beside me, close enough to
see my expression. She is laughing. Kind eyes. Sometimes I feel
she knows what she's laughing at - a psychic, able to see into
my mind. Although, of course, this is a silly notion. A ridicu-

lous concept. I am *The Girl By The Window,* yet I sound like Bertie.

And even Bertie doesn't know—

Well.

Our group spreads out over the flat water. A collective of ants, minuscule in nature. I swish my feet forward and back, my toes beginning to numb. My spine is straight in this position on the board. I lift my face to the sky as the warmth of the sun builds.

A modern artist might use a myriad of tools to depict this scene. Acrylic, resin, screen prints. So much choice now. The artist free to fuse forms. There was once a formless free spirit to my abstract work. There was a ... freedom to my expression.

Freedom.

I turn my head to Miriam, and I don't hold on to the words: 'Let's try to find him.'

We return to the minibus in the forest. Damp, tired, happy. Miriam pauses to speak to Tom, who is waiting at the door. Then she hops up onto the bus in the same manner as Lola and Indie. She doesn't look desperate or mutton-esque. She looks like ... Miriam. A youthful energy.

'Dee,' Tom says, as I step forward. He's holding a clipboard, scanning the page.

Funny, really, that he doesn't understand our invisible connection. 'Counting us all back in from our day release, are you?'

Tom smiles, nods. 'Gotta make sure we have you all.'

I open my mouth, but I find I can't speak.

'It seems you don't exist, Dee.' He scans the pen down the list a second time.

'Oh, it's Diane.'

'Ah, right. Diane .. ?'

I clear my throat, take a moment. 'Diane Bridges.'

I note Tom's raised chest; the loaded pause of his inhalation. Slowly, his eyes lift to mine. An extended exhale.

Michael calls out something from the back of the bus but we ignore him. Tom, eventually, returns attention to his clipboard.

'This must be you,' he says. 'We had you down as *Brides*.' He finds my misspelt name on the list, holds the nib over it, and ticks.

His focus remains on the paper but he speaks, his voice coiled, bound, like the exposed roots of the trees here, growing into daylight when they should be underground. 'Thanks.'

Only as I move away do I sense his gaze lift.

DAY FIFTEEN

My interview with Derrick. I have to do this. I made a promise to Alexandra and Miriam and, besides, I want to capture him in our show. There's a particular warmth that emanates from Derrick. He has his own brand of gentleness. A lone candle in a window on a dark night. No ego, perhaps. I'm so used to David and his ... ways, but—

Perhaps I'm simply enjoying having a male friend. And, well, David is not here to stop me.

When Derrick's daughter heard of my interview request, she said we should go on a hike. Annalys insisted I wouldn't get any decent insights into her father if we sat in his cafe with him able to fuss over what she was and was not doing, so here we are, embarking on a trip to Minyon Falls. Annalys' friend runs day trips, and she got us two seats on the excursion.

'Way to feel old,' I say, as we board the bus amongst a swarm of identikit Indie and Lola's.

'They've got nothing on our wisdom,' Derrick replies, his voice bouncing, jaunty. He's following me onto the bus and as I point to a couple of spare places at the front, he nods, consistently genial. There's no criticism of our surroundings, the heat, my choice of seat ...

Maybe I don't mind taking the bus, after all.

We observe the other passengers as they board: a lairy group of lads who look as though they'd be better placed in one of those awful reality TV shows about Brits abroad, a number of solo travellers and, finally, an older couple. The man is gangly and hunched, but he helps the tiny woman up the high step into the bus, and Derrick rushes to aid her at the top, gently helping her into the seat across from us. She's wearing a camera like Miriam's around her neck but she's so small, I'm surprised she can bear the weight.

'Thank you for your help, dear,' she says. 'I struggle with the large steps, but my legs will be fine once we get moving.'

Goodness. I would estimate the age of these two to be at least eighty and yet here they are about to trek the rainforest?

'See,' Derrick says, returning to his seat beside me. 'We're spring chickens.'

At this, I can't help but laugh.

'Age is whatever you make of it,' he adds. The bus engine rumbles and we set off.

'Or whatever your body makes of it.' I think of David. A man of aches and pains. I get the odd niggle but with my regular workouts, even if only in my living room, my body is in relatively good condition.

And, when you look at this older couple beside us, relatively young.

What a thought . . . Me: Still young.

'So, should I tell you my life story now?' Derrick inclines his head toward me.

The scenery outside turns increasingly green, and I settle back. 'Yes,' I say. 'I think I'm ready.'

Derrick and I have broken from the group - the lads bounding away like excitable puppies to find a waterfall to jump off, the elderly couple searching a paved path, and we're taking the hike at our own pace, trekking through the trees. My mind is clear here. The foliage underfoot is cushioning and the blanket of trees above deadens any noise, so no colours flood my mind. Sunlight dapples the tranquil scene. Quiet, still, calm.

We walk and talk and I'm not worrying about where the conversation is going, or whether I should be witty or ensure that Derrick has a moment to feel witty. I'm just . . . Here. I'm out of puff but I'm . . . exhilarated. I'm so far out of my life in a way I never would have let myself imagine. This is more than just a holiday. This is—

Like the sunrise surf: This is an experience.

And from what Derrick has told me about his life, today is just one more to add to the list. I mean, the man has seen the world.

Hm. My exhilaration has faded to melancholy.

Just like that.

Alternate universe, I suppose.

'Do you find Annalys pushes you? You know, to think about . . . Your life now? How you're living it?' I have stopped. I reach out to touch a leaf. This shade of green is magnificent: luminous and . . . Cheering. I feel a desire to create the colour myself. A canvas, a streak, jagged lines and—

Goodness. An urge.

'Annalys is always pushing me.' Derrick has stopped a little way above, one foot resting on a fallen tree. 'But I think I'd prefer a cup of tea and a sit down.' He smiles. 'No chance of that, of course.'

'You'll miss her, if she goes?'

Derrick walks down to where I stand. He too holds a leaf and we watch as a drop of dew rolls down the length, lingers at the edge, and then drops. 'She needs to go. It's her time.'

I gulp in a lung full of moist jungle air.

We continue hiking and eventually break out of the coverage, stepping up to a wooden platform which juts out across the roof of the jungle.

A lookout.

I walk to the edge, squinting against the glare of the sun. I raise my hand to shield my eyes, my scalp beginning to burn under the intense heat.

But. I am here. A different feeling to those times near the road at home, beside the train track. Here, I'm—

Happy to be on the edge, I suppose. I'm happy to be here.

Derrick leans on the railing beside me. 'Beautiful, isn't it?'

And it is. On this clear day we can see right out to the coast, above the line of the trees. The view is vast and expansive, and we're standing on top of the forest. It's quiet and breezy and—

Perfect. This is perfect.

After a time, we retreat to a bench at the back of the platform. On an adjacent seat, another couple eat sandwiches in peace.

'You told me about your experiences, the world you've seen but . . . I'd like to know more about your family. Is Annalys your only child?'

'No, I have a son.' His chest rises, he sits taller. 'He's gone back to his roots.'

'To baking?'

'To Greece. He runs a yacht for tourists.'

'That must be fun. Have you been to visit him there?'

'No. It was planned but—' He looks down.

After a moment, I find my hand reaching out, touching his arm. 'I'm sorry.'

He offers up his palms, then interlaces his fingers, nods. There's a calm about Derrick. I feel at peace in his presence. 'One day I'll get there.'

Is he—? Oh, he's talking about Greece. 'Does your son visit here often?'

'It's difficult for him. He came back for a time last year when

—' Another nod. The full stop to the sentence I don't need him to finish. 'Like I keep telling Annalys, it's important for them to move on. What's that quote? Erm ... Yes—' He opens his hands to the sky: '"*Death is not the greatest loss in life. The greatest loss is what dies inside us while we live.*" Norman Cousins.'

I kick at a piece of mud on my shoe. Or, rather, Miriam's shoes. My own walkers are in my luggage. Safely packed away with ... Everything else. 'Hard to know how to conquer that, I should think.'

'Moving on doesn't have to mean forgetting.'

I think of Francis. 'For some people, perhaps it's easier ...'

'Perhaps. And what else can we do but move on?'

I force my gaze up. Try to smile. 'The hard bit. When everyone else does.'

'Yes.' The lads have arrived, but they move swiftly to the lookout edge to take selfies, larking about in various poses, their cries incongruous with the surroundings like a sharp knife piercing into a tropical fish tank. Most of the boys are shirtless, spiked hair, tattooed arms. Trying to find their place in the world, I imagine.

We watch for a while, observing this seemingly foreign species, before Derrick speaks: 'You've known loss?'

One of the group pretends to fall off the edge, leaning too far over for my liking. I avert my eyes.

'I guess we have to find something to hold on to,' Derrick continues, his voice soothing, 'so we can move with them but still be here. For some, it's baloney - angels and the like – but—'

'What if you don't have a faith? What then?'

'Even without religion, I should think it's ignorant if we write everything off that can't be understood, solely because it can't be intellectualised. Some things are simply meant to be felt, not reasoned.'

'Like ... intuition?'

'If we let it drive us, we'll arrive as we're meant to.'

'You think your wife is meant to no longer be here?'

'She's not here in this world - The one we can see.'

I swallow. The lads run to the far side, moving en masse, a soaring flock of birds.

When Derrick speaks again, his voice is low, quiet: 'Love doesn't have to be the thing that is over, Dee. Love is a fluid entity, an energy that shifts, like sand dunes, it shifts and alters with the weather. Sometimes the tide is covering the sand, then it washes it away, but it's always there, scattered, and before long it's returned and rebuilt. Sometimes in another form, sometimes unrecognisable from the original structure.'

A comfort settles, a calm. Peculiar, for me. David is so . . . black and white. A man of reason. Fairness. He should know that life is not fair.

Maybe that's why he fights for his place. The chip on his shoulder about his education. His background. Never accepting, always trying so damn hard. Trying to find his place, just like those lads.

How tired he must be.

But—

Acceptance?

This is a fight that's mine alone. And it's a fight I am a long way off winning.

DAY SIXTEEN

'Okay, that's great, thank you so much, Kathryn.'

The sweet yoga instructor embraces me and then leaves the gallery café. I find my head shaking as I watch her depart. A formidable woman and yet—?

Why can't she believe in her own beauty?

'Finished?' Miriam arrives, her self-assured spirit transforming the space from shaky to set. After asking Kathryn to tell me her story, the stop-start of her faltering voice a distraction from the content, Miriam's calm is a welcome juxtaposition.

'What are Kathryn's classes like?' I don't want to be mean about the woman but . . . Surely a temperament such as that can't create a relaxing environment?

'Great.' Miriam collapses into the chair opposite. 'She has a very soothing voice. Steady, rhythmic. It's quite transformative. You should come.'

I open my mouth to voice my rebuttal but—

Well. Today, it doesn't come.

'Maybe,' I say, surprising myself.

Miriam waves at a woman I don't know on an adjacent table. 'Did you get everything you need?'

I scan my scrawling words. 'I told her you'd be round in the morning to take the photos and she was reluctant, but agreed.'

'Reluctant?'

'She's shy. Which is a shame, as I liked the idea of her as a sort of live installation. I thought she could hold a headstand or something, create a more animated part of the exhibit.'

'I love that idea.' Miriam thanks the waitress who places her tea on the table between us.

'I doubt she'd be keen.'

Miriam makes a murmuring noise.

'What is it?' I say.

'I may have a weapon in my armour that could convince her . . .'

'And?'

'You'll have to wait and see . . .' And with that Miriam lets a sly, knowing smirk spread across her face and she reaches for her drink.

Out of the window, the usual scene slides by. I am an observer, content to watch the pigments mix, dilute, then separate.

'I'm glad we have a moment, actually.' Miriam lifts her phone. 'I'm ready.'

'Ready?'

'It's time for action.' She taps in her passcode and opens the Facebook app.

'Action?' I release the word slowly, nerves tightening my throat. What if Miriam looks at my profile page? I haven't checked it for ages. What if there are giveaways? Why didn't I think of this? My whole facade could—

Ah. She has clicked on the search bar.

'His name?'

Oh, goodness.

'I don't know, I—'

'*Dee.*'

Under Miriam's stare, I feel like one of her pupils. No doubt she is a firm but fair teacher. A memorable type. 'I'm not sure . . .'

'You're worried about David?'

'Obviously.' I waft my top. The air conditioning may have just broken or something . . . 'It's not fair.' I reach for a napkin, dab at my forehead.

Ugh. No relief.

Goodness. I can't contact the artist when David is still part of my life. It's wrong. All over again. Bringing the tainted past into my present . . . 'I should leave him behind.'

'Don't you want to know about him?'

The question is, does he want to know about me? Does he want to know about what he left behind?

But I'm not ready to tell Miriam that. About any of that. It's too . . .

Too much.

'It didn't end well.' I focus on my hands, intertwine my fingers, and keep them locked. Secure.

Goodness. Only moments before I felt so . . . Together. 'Why would he want to hear from me?'

'Dee, if your relationship was as passionate as you described, why wouldn't he?'

I nod but . . . I don't know. The tiny glint of light that draws me to giving the go-ahead is a sense of duty. Duty to tell him something he should have known a long time ago.

Unless, some part of him already knows . . . My reasons for ending it. Did he sense a change and take the opportunity to run?

Either way, my conscience will not be clear until I confess to the truth.

And it's a big truth.

Oh, *gosh*.

The waitress is clearing my empty cup, but I can't smile.

Annalys passes the window but I can't bring myself to catch her attention.

Rise and fall.

It's time, isn't it?

It's been a long time.

Too long.

'Okay.' My head nods a fraction, the force of physical action needed to support this mental decision. 'Okay.'

DAY SEVENTEEN

I hold the door open for Miriam, and as she steps through she pauses, meets my gaze, inhaling one quick, sharp breath, which she holds until I give her a nod, and we enter the studio.

I suppose it's a little ridiculous that we should be consumed by such nerves. It's only a local exhibit, and it's only Alexandra, for goodness sake. We know this woman. We like this woman.

I place my notebook on the central workbench and straighten my top unnecessarily. Miriam takes a seat on one of those uncomfortable high stools, and unpacks her camera.

I clear my throat.

Alexandra has arrived. We can hear her talking on the phone in the corridor; the words are muffled, but the tone sounds angry. And I suppose her voice must be raised if it's managing to travel through the heavy door.

My eyes close to waves of dark blue. I put my hand on my abdomen, and picture Derrick's bearded smile. He'd been so kind to answer my questions with such searing honesty. Ellen, too.

But Tom? I'm afraid to say I have not made it there yet. I will, but—

No. Not yet.

The door makes a sucking noise as it opens and Alexandra paces in. I try to catch Miriam's eye, but her stare is fixed on Alexandra, watching her every move as she places her bag and another lovely scarf on the sideboard.

'Okay, tell me, guys. What have you got for me?'

Hm. No, *How was your weekend? How are you feeling?*

What was a flutter of anticipation has morphed into a thrum of anxiety.

I clear my throat again and place a hand on my notebook. My notes - they're very . . . Vague. They're not prying, not journalistic. It may be of interest to me how these people set up a new life in this beautiful place but is that going to be of interest in an exhibition aimed at the people who already live here?

Goodness. Alexandra is sure to think me a fool.

'I've got some great shots,' Miriam says, flicking through her camera roll, glasses balanced on the end of her nose as she studies the small screen. 'Some fabulous ones of Kathryn. I should sell them as marketing material for Byron.'

I peer over Miriam's shoulder - the image she has paused on is one of Kathryn bent over in a - goodness - rather provocative yoga pose. Unintentional, I should think but, still, I'm not sure that one is appropriate for marketing.

Well, for a certain type of marketing, I suppose . . .

Miriam flicks on to less suggestive shots.

'I still need to have my talk with Tom,' I say, moving away, 'and type up the other conversations.' I can't show my notes. My scrawled comments, my—

Drawl.

'Okay.' Alexandra takes her phone from her pocket, frowns at the screen, then puts it away again.

'And we've got an idea for Derrick,' Miriam says, nodding.

I find I am smiling. 'Derrick The Baker.'

'Pies.'

'Pies.' I lean my bottom on a high stool.

Alexandra walks to an opposite stool. 'Pies?'

'A stack of them.' Miriam.

'A food sculpture,' I add. 'A big one.'

It was actually Annalys' idea. She saw something online about this huge food installation that garnered a lot of press interest. It had *gone viral*, apparently.

Alexandra looks from me to Miriam, and back again.

'You Aussies love a pie.' Miriam shrugs.

'Right. What else?' Alexandra crosses her arms.

'Tom's boards.' Miriam lifts her chin, pulling herself up straight on the stool. 'I thought we could stack them somehow, maybe hang them?'

'I'm not sure he'll be keen,' I say. 'He seems a little . . . precious of his designs.' I pick at a fingernail. 'But Shaun and Eric were keen to tell their story. Well, Shaun more so . . .'

'Yes, he's digging out some old photos of the original hostel,' Miriam says.

Alexandra is again looking at her phone. Is she even listening? She must have had a haircut as her slick bob is extra sharp today. The corners cut at a perfect right angle to her jaw. I touch a hand to my own hair, loose and already at my shoulders. How freeing it has been to not need 'do it'. The curlers and hairdryer are tucked away in the lost luggage, so I tie a scarf around my head on those days my barnet misunderstands 'no fuss' to mean 'unkempt'.

'Can I see the photos?' Alexandra says suddenly, leaving her seat to take Miriam's camera.

I've already seen what Miriam has there - a selection of wonderfully vivid yet intimate portraits of our candidates in their work environment. It's not Hockney, but they're inspiring.

To me, anyway.

Alexandra flicks through at speed, not bothering to hide a sigh. Finally, she looks up at us both. 'Thank you, guys. You've been working hard, but—' She looks at the camera in her hand.

'Vinnie is on her way here and I wanted to have something to show her, to prove that we can do this exhibit without her influence, to show that I'm capable of running the gallery alone, but …'

'But what?' Miriam's eyebrows quiver into a questioning expression.

'Are we just … Amateurs?' Alexandra looks up, holding my gaze. Finally, she nods and returns the camera to Miriam. 'I have to see Vinnie now.'

Miriam stands. 'Why are you even bothering to meet her?' She stares at Alexandra, but then busies herself, shoving the camera back into the case, her head shaking.

'What do you mean?'

'She …' Miriam pauses, fixes on Alexandra. Eventually, she drops her glare. 'Nothing.'

Alexandra stays next to Miriam for a time, watching her every move, then she steps away. 'It will be okay,' she says to me, retreating. 'You're doing great, thank you.'

And she nods and leaves, but it's only me who says goodbye.

I have to give myself a moment, surveying the door through which Alexandra has retreated, before I turn back to Miriam. She is slumped over the worktop, head in her hands.

I walk over, place my hand on her back. 'You okay?'

'We failed her.' Miriam's head stays down. 'Did you see her face? Gosh, she's so disappointed.'

'She was nervous. She's worried about seeing Vinnie. It wasn't personal.'

'It was.'

I take an adjacent seat. 'I saw the posters. Alexandra is putting money and time into this. She's worried. And, I mean, she has reason to be.'

'Thanks.' Miriam laughs.

'Well, wouldn't you be? Your first exhibition as a solo person? Goodness knows when I—' I look at my hands.

'What?'

'It's nerve racking. Art. It's . . . Exposing.'

'It's not her art we're showing, though.'

'Even if you're not the artist, I imagine it's tough, you know? Her name is on the line and she has this pressure . . . It's understandable.'

Miriam looks at the ceiling, then back to me. 'Dee?'

I smile at my friend.

But she simply nods, and places a hand on my shoulder. 'I'm going to the cafe to edit these, and then I'm going to the printers to talk about sizing.'

Miriam stands, camera bag over her shoulder. 'Let's make this exhibition as flipping good as we can, okay? For amateurs everywhere.'

And I laugh, and I watch Miriam stride out of the room.

I'm not sure how much time passes with me sat alone in the space. The peace I find in the studio is so . . .

Restorative.

I've been working nonstop, using Alexandra's laptop to type up the details of our candidates, creating bite-size morsels of information to bullet point around the photos Miriam will have printed. It's so lovely to have a task - a job, I suppose. The joy of distraction? Perhaps. Maybe it's healthy to have something to occupy our minds, a purpose, something to resist the inevitable spiral . . .

Goodness. Look at our art therapy over there. I'm not sure we achieved anything. The mess I created - the awful striping of blue and—

Just one blob of yellow. Still at my heart. Singular.

My feet are walking me over to the creation and I have somehow got a paintbrush and—

Ah. There - the pink.

I dab my brush into the pink and I dot it all over the picture, obliterating the awful blue.

'Well, that looks a lot better.'

The door makes that sucking noise and I turn to find Alexandra behind me.

'Pink for joy, wasn't it?' she says.

I turn back to the painting - pink spots scattered all over the blue, my blob of Bertie remaining strong in the middle.

'It was long overdue,' I say, stepping back from the creation. 'I couldn't leave you with that awful other thing.'

At the sink, I wash the brushes, the pink diluting with the water, a musk river escaping down the plug.

'Is Miriam here?' Alexandra asks.

'She's finishing the photos.' I lay out the brush to drain and return to the workstation to pack up the laptop.

'Listen.' Alexandra approaches. 'I'm sorry. I shouldn't have been so negative about the exhibition. What you're doing is great, both of you. I'm so grateful for your help.'

'You don't need to thank us. If anything, I need to thank you. This whole thing has . . . Well. It's been good for me.'

Alexandra nods. Slow, considered. 'I put Vinnie in her place. I thought of Miriam wanting to stand up for me and . . . I don't want to upset her. I like her and . . . I suppose I shouldn't let my feelings get—'

'She likes you too,' I interrupt, wanting to stick up for Miriam. 'We all do. Everyone I speak to in town is willing to help with this show, because they know it's related to you.'

Alexandra's face clears. She pulls her shoulders back and her chin lifts a fraction. Rebuilding herself to stoic?

'Oh, I—' Ah. I have dropped my notebook.

Alexandra bends to help, her hand resting on the page that has fallen open. 'Those doodles,' she says, crouching down. 'These are quite something.'

I look at the page. The design. Over and over again I have sketched it.

'This.' Alexandra rests her fingers on the paper. 'This means something?'

I don't have to check to know what Alexandra is looking at. If I close my eyes, I can see the doodle, imprinted on my retina, some small pattern I have created and which I draw, instinctively, whenever I have a blank page.

'Yes.' It's a bird, but from its tail shoots stars - small, intricate, flying.

Magic.

I take the notebook from Alexandra and close it.

'We should do something with that in the exhibition,' she says, but I can only look down. 'It's really beautiful.'

My head lifts a fraction. Slow. Eventually, I meet Alexandra's eye. This is genuine. She wants my sketch.

Oh. Yes. *I* want my sketch. Because I know what it means, and I need to remember this meaning forever.

Something in me pulls. A need. A desire to go immediately. To do this thing, before I have anyone to talk me out of it.

———

'Yay, you're here,' Lola says, pulling Miriam and I in for a dual hug. We've just arrived at the local bar near the hostel where Lola has invited everyone to join us for her and Indie's send off. The bar is quiet; no one else from our hostel is here yet. Lola drags Miriam and me over to the bar where we find Indie chatting to the barman. Cocktails are ordered. *Sex on the beach.*

Goodness.

'We're so sad not to be staying for your exhibition,' Lola says, sticking out her bottom lip.

Oh. I am smiling at the mention: *Exhibition.*

My exhibition.

Kathryn has agreed to be part of a live installation and Miriam had a message that Hans is coming back to Byron and he too wants to take part. Apparently, he and Kathryn 'hooked up' before, and he's returning to see her before he flies home. The two of them will perform something called 'acro yoga'. I don't know what it entails, but I think it requires muscle.

So. Hans will amaze, I expect. Kathryn, too.

Miriam has been to the printers today and the photos look fantastic. Derrick is really rather photogenic, his beard extraordinarily glossy. Ellen, too, her plump face shining with a joy that, even in the photos, you can see emanates from the inside out. She practically begged me to stay when I saw her again earlier, telling me I must look after the shop for her, that Byron is my place now . . .

Well.

Alternate universe, right, Bertie?

I exchange a hug with Indie, whose disappointment manifests in a gentler way to Lola. There is a genuine warmth to Indie's embrace, those big eyes dipping at the edges, searching mine.

'The exhibition will be great,' Indie says.

I inhale through my mouth, emotion building behind my eyes.

Clamp it in, Dee. Breathe. Control.

Goodness. Out of nowhere . . .

'I did something today,' I say, holding Indie at arm's length.

I step back and roll my shirt sleeve up a fraction.

'You're happy about an injury?' Lola says, as I reveal the bandage on my wrist.

I lift a corner of the white material.

'Oh. My. God.' Indie clamps a hand over her mouth.

Lola grabs my hand and takes a closer inspection. 'No *way*. What does it mean?'

'Oh, it's . . . sort of personal.'

Miriam takes the tray of cocktails from the barman. 'I see you've met Dee's latest addition?'

'Ha. You say that as though I'll have more.' I cover my tattoo back up and we move over to a booth.

Indie squeezes my hand. 'It's really beautiful.'

I know, I know. I got a tattoo.

Something . . . drew me in. My design. I had to . . . Remember this, I suppose. I want to crystallise this feeling of—

This.

Me. Here. Doing this. Being this person.

'So, Dee, does this new inking have any relation to Mr Lover Lover?' Lola winks.

'No,' I say. Although when I think of being with Him . . . Is this feeling the same?

Same realm, I guess. Optimism, opportunity . . .

'Have you had any word back from him?' Indie asks.

I look at Miriam, and we shake our heads. After my giving her the go-ahead, we found Him on Facebook and Miriam sent him a message from my account. I couldn't do it myself. I just . .

.

I couldn't summon the words. But Miriam? She was ace. She kept it polite, short, to the point. Did he remember me - *us* - and how had he been?

Simple.

Yet every time I think of it my stomach feels as though it will fall out of my bottom.

'What will be, will be,' I say with a confidence I am far from possessing.

Goodness. The message is out there. Flying, irreversible, through the ether of the internet, the words whizzing from my soul. A little heavy, perhaps. But what I do know is that it doesn't feel as straightforward as simply sending words through a machine. Instead, parts of my structure, my bricks, flecks of my concrete are flaking off, moving back in time to Him.

Then just as I think I might implode with excitement— Boom. I fall all the way back down to regret. What about David? For goodness sake. It's all so . . . Irresponsible. Juvenile. Yes, I had only been twenty or so then but—

'What will be, is that you will hook up with that man and have the—'

'No no no,' I cut Lola off, waving my hand. 'I don't know what I want but . . . Not that.' I think of us then. The storage cupboard. Illicit, *hot*, as these girls would say.

Goodness. So hot.

But I have David and—

I suppose I just want to find out how He is, how He remembers me and . . .

Everything else.

'Let's have a toast.' Thank goodness. Miriam to the rescue. 'To new friends and new beginnings.'

'To new friends and new beginnings,' we repeat, clinking glasses and—

Goodness.

Happiness.

New friends.

New beginnings.

The party has ramped up, the bar now busy, music chiming behind conversation, which chimes even louder. I am standing at the bar with Alexandra, whose guilt over her negative response to our work on the exhibit is causing her to be overly nice.

'I wasn't kidding yesterday, Dee. The stuff in your sketch-book is great.'

Hm. When I look at Alexandra's face, she is clear, considered, neutral.

She does seem genuine.

'Would you consider doing something for the exhibition?' she adds. 'You never know, maybe you could sell something.'

I pick at the label on my beer bottle. 'Oh, I don't know, it's .. . personal.'

Alexandra laughs. 'Isn't that the point of art? To reveal something of yourself?'

'Perhaps that's why I haven't done anything for so long.'

'That must be hard.'

'What do you mean?'

Alexandra waves to someone across the room, tilts her head back to me. 'To keep it in. Your art is . . . On lockdown.'

And I open my mouth but— It has been on lockdown. Out of necessity, otherwise—?

I nod, shrug, pick at my bandaged arm.

'Oh, my darling girls, I'm sorry to interrupt but I have to thank Dee here.' Shaun kisses Alexandra before embracing me, his stomach pressing against mine and I can feel the sweat beneath his floral shirt.

Sofia is beside him and we say hello before she's lost in conversation with Alexandra.

'What have I done?' I narrow my eyes.

'Darling, Eric has been asking me about prices for flights back to the UK.'

'And why are you thanking me?'

'Because he said when you interviewed him for this exhibit thingy-ma-jig, he asked you about your home in England and you made the countryside sound delectable, apparently.'

'Well, I—' When I think of England, the countryside is indeed delectable. Beautiful, but—

Home?

Only four days left.

'So, you think he'll finally go back with you?' I ask.

'Well, I told him Sofia here has agreed to run the place and . . . I think he's close to agreeing.' At this, Shaun puts his hands on his belly and laughs a huge guffaw and I can't help but share in his happiness. Then he takes me by the shoulders and spins round to order more drinks at the bar.

'How are we going to let this go?' Miriam says as I squeeze into the booth beside her.

'You know? I'm not too sure.' I look out to the people in the establishment, chattering, smiling, escaping.

'It's been a great trip, hasn't it?'

Miriam's face is bare, glowing with a gentle suntan, windswept hair.

'The best.'

Her eyes rest on me for a moment before she sighs and looks across to the bar. 'Alexandra has been talking to Sofia for a while.'

Hm. Am I imagining a tone of annoyance?

I follow her eye line to see Sofia resting a hand on Alexandra's forearm, and then they both laugh at whatever Sofia has just said. 'I suppose they're friends.'

Miriam nods, looks at her lap.

'She can have other friends.' Gosh. If I didn't know better, I'd say Miriam was sulking. Her bottom lip is quivering, and that frown is furrowing, creating wrinkles on her forehead.

Alexandra appears immaculate as always, this evening in her crisp clothing, sartorially incongruous to the other patrons, her head lifted in a way only a self-assured person can.

'You like her,' I say.

I look at Miriam and—

Goodness.

'More . . ?'

Miriam's eyes widen.

'More than just as a friend,' I say. 'The reason you're not with your husband . . ?'

Her expression, slowly, clears. 'Yes.'

Gosh. The thing about Miriam I have been too tardy to realise. 'Does your husband know?'

'He's the only one who does.'

'And this is the reason you don't want to tell your children you've split up?'

She shakes her head. 'They're teenage boys, Dee. They won't understand; they'll be ridiculed and . . . For what? So I can pursue some selfish desire?' Her eyes flick up to Alexandra, and then immediately back to me. 'I'll just wait until . . . Well.'

'I'm sure if this conversation were to be reversed, you would not be accepting that this is a mere *selfish desire*.'

She studies the table. Touches at something on her neck.

'You must live up to your truth,' I hear myself say.

Miriam lifts her head. 'Like you are, you mean?'

Her words land atop of me, a wall of bricks, collapsing. I sit back under their weight. Because, to this, I have no answer.

. . .

It's midnight. I'm trying to leave the bar when I bump into Michael at the door. I immediately tense, but - thank goodness - Tom is not with him. Back in the bar, Alexandra and Miriam remain chatting as they have been for the past hour. Shaun and Eric sit at the table with Lola and Sofia, and Indie disappeared with Jake a while ago. There are crowds of people in various arrangements scattered throughout the space, but nobody has yet taken to dancing.

'You're arriving late?' I say to Michael, who raises a smile as he clocks my presence. That retro moustache he sports is well oiled today, and I wonder how much time he spends perfecting the ends in the mirror. He rubs at his heavily inked arm, and—

Well. I can no longer make any judgement.

'Or are you leaving early?' he quips back.

To this, I laugh. 'I'm allowed. I'm old.'

'You're only as old as you feel, right?'

'Hm. Say that when you get to my age.'

'You don't seem old, Dee,' he says, winking. He steps toward the bannister, leans against it. I suspect this is not the first bar he's been to this evening. 'You said you had a daughter here, but how is it possible you have a child old enough to travel alone?'

At this, I swallow. I had been feeling somewhat lightheaded with the booze myself, but I am instantly brought back to sober.

'Oh. Did I make a mistake? You said your daughter came here, right?'

My focus stays down. 'Yes.'

'So, maybe I met her. What's her name?'

'Liberty.' This is okay. She wouldn't have referred to herself as Liberty.

'Oh. Unusual.'

Didn't Michael once tell me he's relatively new to town? Yes, that's right. He wouldn't have been here seven years ago. 'Actually, we call her—'

'Bertie.' Goodness. Tom. I didn't see him there. He must have come in through the door as I turned my back and—

Well.

I run my hand over my tattoo, and I force my eyes to meet his.

———

'I need to talk to you,' Tom says.

But I'm already through the door of the bar, out into the open, dark night. 'I'm leaving, I can't—'

I can't do this. Not now.

He knows. Of course, he knows. How could I possibly think he wouldn't work me out?

'We need to—'

'Tom, I think you've had too much to drink. Besides, I know . . . I don't really want to—'

'Bertie.'

I stop still. It's cold out here and my body tenses. I wrap my arms around myself.

This is not how I wanted this to go with Tom. I just wanted to get to know him. I needed to discover for myself what kept her here, understand the person he is to everyone else, before he learned this about me and began treating me as people do when they find—

I lower my head. 'Tom, please. I just—'

'Bertie was your daughter, wasn't she? She was here and—'

'Tom, I—' I don't enjoy hearing her name in other people's voices. It's not theirs to say. It belongs to nobody but me.

I begin my walk back to the hostel.

But Tom continues, his voice slicing through the darkness: 'I've been waiting for you. For seven years. I always expected you to come.'

'I couldn't. I . . . I can't go there.'

'*Please*, Dee.' Something about Tom's tone. Like seeing an animal on the motorway. I swerve. And I stop. 'I have to say how sorry I am. I am . . . Sorry.' I have my back to him, but I can imagine how he looks as he scrabbles for words. He shouldn't bother. He'll find nothing of use. 'I am sorry.'

My vision is blurring because my head is shaking. Slowly, then faster. Repeating. 'No, Tom. It's fine—'

'*Dee*.' A hand reaches, fingers outstretching to my arm, and he tries to turn me toward him. 'Diane, let me—'

'*No*, Tom.' I pull away. I don't want to hear people's sorrow. I don't want their platitudes because nobody can understand. Nobody knows what I feel or how I feel it. Not Tom, not David. This . . . *Pain*. This utter utter devastation. I carry it with me every day, and no sympathetic words are of use to me.

I step away from Tom but something moves in the distance and I look back to where I came from and I see Miriam there, outside, streaked in the bar's light, watching. Her eyes lock with mine, and there is the pitying look I so despise, painted all over her face.

And now my secret is out.

And now, I know, everything will be different.

———

I enter the hostel. Nobody is here. Everyone is still at the party in the bar. Something has come over me and if I don't let it out, I fear I'll implode with this . . . Ugh. *Feeling.*

Alexandra is right. I have been on lockdown and, my gosh, I can't hold it in any longer. This must be why people turn to drugs or sex or alcohol or *something.* Finding some way to release.

Well, this is my release.

And I can't believe I didn't do it sooner.

DAY EIGHTEEN

I am in the hostel kitchen. I had to get up. I couldn't lie there, knowing what I've done, waiting for—

My secret.

I peer into the oven. The bread needs a few more minutes. I dry the mixing bowl, the utensils.

Rise and fall.

Voices outside the door. 'Have you seen it?' Eric.

'Oh, I mean—' Sofia. I can imagine the pinched expression, head shaking . . .

'Do you think it was the youths again?'

I look at my hands. I pick at the colour but—

I need a strong product.

'It can't have been one of the tagsters because whoever did it used the cans I'd stored under the reception. I found them empty in my bin. Unless it was a break and enter as well?'

'What? Break and enter and do some art in apology for pissing me off with your awful graffiti for so long?'

I open the oven, closing my eyes against the heat that whooshes up into my face.

'But what's out there is not awful, that's—'

'Modern art, my darlings.' Shaun.

I throw the bread on the side. I didn't use the glove. My hands are burning. I hold them under the cold tap.

Goodness. I am so stupid. Accessing that part which I should keep locked up.

I don't want to step outside. I can't bear to see the monstrosity. I mean, it must be awful, I haven't created in years and—

'You're right. It is modern, and it is fantastic,' I hear Eric say. *Fantastic?*

I'm not sure I've heard Eric talk of anything in the positive.

And now the kitchen door is open and the three of them - Shaun, Eric and Sofia - enter.

'Oh, darling, you won't believe what's happened,' Shaun says, coming over to where I stand, still rinsing my hands at the sink.

'Dee, this smells phenomenal. May I?' Sofia has picked up a knife. The bread should really sit for longer, but—

Well. We all need longer.

Shaun puts a hand on my shoulder. 'That bugger Eric there let me drink all those drinks last night knowing he was going to surprise me today, because he's booked us flights to England. Can you believe it? Today! We're heading to Sydney this afternoon and then our flight is at some godawful hour in the morning.' He squeezes my shoulders and I turn to hug him properly. Wow, this is great for Shaun.

'Darling,' he says as I wipe my hands on the towel. 'Is that paint on your hand? And—' He stops, his gaze down at my tattoo, now uncovered, the bandage removed. Exposed. He lifts his eyes to mine. 'Oh.'

I look at Eric. Sofia. Shaun. My hands.

'I'm sorry.' I've let too much out. I can't . . . be here.

I cannot be here.

And as I run from the room, my phone vibrates with a Facebook alert, and it seems the parts I've kept buried for so many years are all coming back to haunt me at once. Because there's a message.

And it's from Him.

———

A knock at my bedroom door.

Miriam.

We make eye contact, then I step back, let her in.

I keep my focus down. I feel her assessing me. Wanting—
What?

All is different. It will always be different now.

'Dee—'

I shake my head. I sit on the chair.

Miriam moves to the bed where my things are scattered. Disarray. Trying to make sense of a mess.

'Where are you going?' she says.

'The wedding. I'm leaving a few days early. I can't . . . Stay here, anymore.' I clasp my hands together.

'But—' I sense her darkening expression. Without looking, I know. 'The mural, Dee. It's brilliant.'

'It's just paint, Miriam. It doesn't mean anything.'

'I think it does.'

'Well then, you're dumber than you look.' I stand, look, lower my chin.

'Dee, I—' She steps forward, hand on my arm. Just like the first time we met. Except now? 'I'm sorry.'

'I know.'

'You didn't say, you . . .'

No. No no no no no.

She doesn't stop: 'I'm so sorry. I wish I'd known.'

'Why? So you can change it? So you can pity me? Whisper? Make me feel *safe* like everyone else does?' I step to the bed.

'No. So I could . . . Be a better friend.'

I throw my scarf with all its ridiculous colours into the suitcase, the new clothes which somehow, I believed— What? That they would make me a different person? I am a silly old fool. I should have stayed in my tweed skirt. Plain. Nondescript. Anonymous. 'You haven't stopped pushing me since we got here, Miriam. I told you I wasn't like them. I'm not like anyone.'

'Dee—'

'I'm so stupid. My name is Diane. I am *Diane*.'

'Diane. Everyone has issues. It's not a sin. For goodness sake, don't undo all you've achieved here,' she says, gesturing toward my mess of belongings.

'What?' *Achieved?* I have achieved nothing.

'Be light with love, with forgiveness. You obviously need to forgive yourself for something.'

My head is shaking independently of my body. 'Do you believe this pop psych you drone on about?'

'*Drone on*?'

'I don't want to continue. I am not one to argue. I like quiet. I enjoy a quiet life at home. No confrontation.' I grab the tweed skirt.

Miriam's head is down, but when she lifts it, her expression has altered, twisted, and she opens her mouth and I know—

'Liberty Bridges,' she says. 'Tom told me everything . . . Why didn't you say anything?'

I look up. Connecting with the eyes of this woman, just a stranger, really, and I hope she never has to understand why I don't tell people. I give a pathetic shrug. Pathetic, because everything pales in comparison. Nothing does my pain justice. Nothing can convey my grief, the depth of my utter sorrow, just—

At the airport. Her face. If I'd known that would be the last time, I—

I pick at the paint under my nail. 'We were supposed to avoid this place, David and I. We were supposed to go everywhere but here and then you said it and . . . Something . . . I felt I had to join you.'

'I'm sorry, I—'

'I couldn't come at the time. Not then. David came alone. Identified her. Brought her home.' My saviour. Our saviour.

'How could he leave you alone here this time? To deal with this by yourself?'

I step to the window. In the box, the wild gum blossom has, at last, given up the fight.

'Maybe it was too hard for him to return. I'm not sure he could handle my emotions alongside his own. Not again.'

'But he's your *husband*.' Miriam searches my face, unable to work it out.

And, for a long time, I've felt the same. But now? I think I understand why he would abandon me here. The obvious reason, really.

Because maybe, at last, he knows the truth.

I haul my large shopping bag outside and let the taxi driver lift it into the boot.

'He left you to handle coming here alone and now you're running back to him?' Miriam has followed me out. 'What about the exhibition, Dee? *Diane*. You've worked so hard.'

'I can understand why David did it.' I nod at the taxi driver and stand beside the car.

'He should have been there for you. We've both worked so hard. It's just two more days, Dee.'

I open the door. 'No.'

'How can you defend him?'

'You don't know us, Miriam. David did what he thought was right.' I lift a leg into the car.

'Like you did what you thought was right when you denied yourself the love of your life for that man?'

I shake my head, both feet back on the ground. 'Oh, that's rich from—'

'What?'

'You, too, are living a lie. But I'm not ruining your life like you did mine.'

'What do you mean?'

'The artist replied, Miriam. He wants nothing to do with me. He doesn't even remember me, for God's sake. And you and Alexandra will be fine doing the exhibition without me. You'll all be better off without me.' I get into the taxi.

'I'm sorry, I—'

His words. That message. *Cut throat*, as Bertie would say.

'No. I was okay before this. I had myself together. Yes, of course, I am deep in grief, but I could dream, Miriam. I had my dream. I could think of Him and dream of what was and what could have been and—'

She puts a hand on top of the open door and leans in. 'Can you hear yourself, Dee? You are living in a dream. That's precisely what's wrong. Okay, so, evidently, I don't know you very well, but what I do know is that when I met you, you were not fully engrossed in your life. You were on the side line, observing, judging everyone else. Well? Now you're exposed.'

My worst fear. I look up to the mural. Loud, large . . .

Exposed.

'So instead of running from that,' she continues, 'why not embrace it? Deal with your grief. Use it. Stop living in your head and get into life, Dee. Look at that art you've created, that's part of you, it's—'

'I'm too old for all that. Graffiti art? For God's sake.' I put my head in my hands, grab my hair.

'You're alive. Don't you see? More than anyone, what this is? What life is?'

I have no breath. I have no words.

'There's a story that has been created about you - by David, by yourself, your history . . . I don't know - but you can change your story at any point. You have the power to do that, Dee.'

'I can't. I can't change what happened to Bertie.'

'No.' She stands straight and drops her hand away from the door. 'But you can change what will happen to you from now on. The question is, do you want to?'

'I—' I pick at my hands. Paint-stained. An embarrassment. Grotesque humiliation. This whole thing. 'How could I be so stupid as to think I can survive alone? I haven't ever been alone. David cared for me, supported me, let me go on talking to my daughter but she's not here, Miriam. It's time I face up to that and get back to the real world. Because this, Byron, is all make believe. This is not real life, Miriam. Everyone is running from something. It can't be sustained. We have to face facts - our life is at home, waiting for us.'

A glare. I don't want to question it.

'Will you continue to paint at home?'

My head shakes with startling violence. 'Art is just . . . It means nothing. It's just paint, for goodness sake. Pointless paint.'

'I'm sorry to hear you think that.'

'Yes, well—'

'For the record, I love your painting. I think it's transformative.'

'People see what they want to see.'

'I see art transformed you, but what do I know?'

'It was really great to meet you, and I thank you for letting me join in—'

Miriam tuts. 'I didn't *let you join*, Dee. You were there, with as much right as anyone. This wasn't my journey on which you tagged along. This was your journey. The exhibition was your idea, remember?'

My idea. I let her words settle. My idea.

Finally, she sighs. Softens. 'I won't forget you, Dee.'

And at that, she closes the door and I nod to the driver and I drive back to the life I have made. My life, with my husband.

The entire car journey I've been wondering, thinking, avoiding. The road - *that* road - is parallel to here, my driver having to take a diversion so as not to pass it. Goodness. What could have been if Bertie had not come, if we'd stopped her . . . ? Or did she feel she had to come because we *did* try to stop her? We prevented her from doing what she always wanted and she had to break out from the result of that. We pushed her and—

And now we are here.

And she is not.

But my therapist used to say it doesn't serve to think that way.

Some things, though. I could have changed some things.

We arrive at the hotel and I don't know if David will be here. I am two days early and—

Goodness. There he is. Drinking some exotic-looking drink on the terrace, facing out to the sea beyond.

I pay the driver and let him set my bag on the veranda. I would like to take a moment to appreciate the incredible potted plants that adorn the area - spiky green things interspersed with orange and purple flowers, but—

David. He has lost weight. Still him. The familiarity of his shape. And without that weight, the neck sags from his jaw even more than before. It brings to mind a . . . turkey?

Goodness.

Not that I can talk about weight. I know I have put it on. These leggings have become a little tight.

He hears my step.

'Goodness, Diane. You're here.' He moves towards me, falters with an almost imperceptible shift of his weight to the back foot and, finally, leans forward. A kiss on the cheek. 'You look . . . Of course, your luggage. It's in the room.'

'Yes.'

David is here, and he is real. This is my life. No more dreaming. No more reminiscing. David is my husband and I must live in the real world with him because he helps me. He knows what we have been through. It's vital I go back to therapy when we get home and work through this together.

He continues the scrutiny. I suddenly think of Derrick, the gaze never staying on me for long; dropping quickly, shy. But David? I am his wife. I suppose he can stare.

'Your scarf is—'

'It's new. A birthday present.' I took the scarf out at the last moment. Armour?

'I'm sorry I missed it.'

'That's okay.'

A pause. 'Is it?'

I look at my hands. I cover the paint. 'I suppose that is to be decided.'

David takes me up to his room but— Can this be right? Wet shorts drape over the chair, a tell-tale damp patch spreads on the carpet below; toiletries scatter across the leather-covered desk; the lid of his roll-on deodorant is missing and a single hair wraps itself round the wet ball; his charcoal toothpaste, also without a lid, seeps out like lava, pooling into a hardened grey penny.

I avert my eyes.

'They upgraded you?' This room does not resemble the one we saw online - the room David had been so unwilling to accept.

He clears his throat. 'Yes. An anniversary gift, they said.'

My mouth frames a question, but I don't ask it.

'Happy anniversary.' His tone is incongruous with the content. Like trying to lift sand out of a bucket of water.

On the large bed; the covers scramble. He must have put up the *Do not disturb* sign.

'We should celebrate.' He steps toward me.

I look at the window. The sea is sparkling. I step toward it. 'Yes.'

I reach over the desk, open the window, close my eyes to the oncoming breeze that, if visible, we'd see snaking through the gap, leaping and spinning into the room.

I inhale the sea air.

'Have you been okay?' I ask, over my shoulder. There is an original artwork on the wall. I think of the framed wallpaper in the hostel. Smile.

A set of car keys sit on the sideboard, a hire-company tag attached. I wonder how far David has driven in it.

'I missed you,' he says. 'But you look well. Although . . . Here—' He moves across the room, takes my suitcase out of the wardrobe and places it on the bed.

I open it. There - my things. Untouched. The box nestles into the corner. Secure. Waiting.

I clutch it to my chest.

The clothes align in neat squares. Muted tones. Sensible. It should relieve me to see these too - the items I have been hankering over, thinking all would be okay if I had them . . .

What did Miriam say once? *Treat your past like your luggage: lose it.*

David removes the box from my grasp, places it back in the bag, takes my hands. 'I'm glad you're okay. I'm glad you made it in time for today. They have a hairdresser downstairs. Do you want me to make you an appointment?'

I drop his hands. Touch my longer do. Well, 'do' is generous.

David picks up the phone, fat fingers over small buttons, punching in the three digit code, connecting to the hair-dressers, his voice deepening in response to their lack of appointments left today, the clenched fist, neck wobble as he speaks.

I close my eyes. Dark blue washes in my mind.

'Can you believe an in-house service such as that has no space left to cater for their own patrons?' He has put the phone down. He stands in front of me.

I try to smile. Nod.

'They can fit you in tomorrow, but it will have to be at six in the morning.'

'Six?' I rub my temples.

'Maybe you could tie it up or something for the family dinner tonight and—'

David has spotted it. Eyes to my wrist. He looks tired, I notice. Dark rings. The glaze of anger as his jaw clenches. But he readjusts, clears, looks back to me. 'Is this a midlife thing?'

I can't help but laugh. How would I even begin to—? 'No.'

'A little . . . common, don't you think?'

I step back. He must have shaved just before I arrived. Spots of dried blood on his still-pale skin.

'Diane?'

'Does it matter? It's not hurting anyone.'

A silence. Another clench.

'You should cover it up for dinner.' David's stare is firm, unyielding.

Eventually, I drop my gaze. I pull out the dress I had planned for this evening's dinner. David's family will all be in attendance.

Goodness.

Here are the matching shoes. Dancing shoes?

I look at David.

Well—

'Should we have a drink in the bar first? I assume dinner is not for another hour?' I say.

'I don't think you should drink too much before eating,

Diane. We have the champagne reception before the meal already.'

'Right.'

'You'll need time to iron that outfit, I imagine? Fix the hair? Do something about—' His lip curls, eyes darting toward my wrist.

He turns his back. Pours himself a whiskey from a bottle he must have bought in the duty free. Of course, David would not be so stupid as to access the minibar. Not at those *inflated prices*.

I pull the ironing board down from the wall, plug in the iron. The dress is thick. Too thick. What was I thinking packing this?

I picture Elaine's store full of floaty, soft clothing.

'Don't burn it.'

'Oh!' I lift the iron just in time. Hm. Maybe I should have let it ruin.

David sits in the chair facing out to the sea. I don't suppose this is the first time he has sat in that spot, contemplating.

Or, perhaps, he thinks nothing.

'How have you been?' I say.

He seems to need to physically haul himself out of whatever mind tunnel down which he has fallen. His deep inhale locating him here with me, in this moment.

He tilts his head in my direction, but he doesn't turn. 'I had to do what I did, Diane.'

I am nodding.

And yet—? I am always nodding. For David . . .

'It seemed a little harsh.'

At this, his head does turn. Lola's word: *harsh*. I don't know if David's surprised by the language or the rebuke. Both, I suppose, are not becoming of the woman he knows.

And he cannot answer her. This unknown. I'm not playing to the script, and he does not know how to improvise.

'You needed to be on your own,' he says finally.

I look at my tattoo.
And I am unable to summon a disagreement.

―――――

I nod at David's sister, and reach out to grab another flute from a passing waiter. As I turn back, I meet David's stare from across the room. He's looking out from his huddle, eyes on me. His focus shifts to the glass in my hand before, slowly, he returns to his conversation with his nephew and brother-in-law.

'The flowers arrived just in time,' my sister-in-law, Cecelia, says. 'We'd been so worried as the florist rang the day before and was talking nonsense about an entire display which none of us knew anything about, and then, after about ten minutes and a lot of confused back and forth, we realised she had phoned the wrong client! Can you imagine? If we'd not worked that out? We could now be in a sea of purple instead of the sophisticated cream. I mean, I didn't like to say to the woman but . . . *purple*.' Cecelia pulls a face of disgust. I remember now that, just like her brother, she too has a desire to propel herself *above her station*. A David phrase, which I've never questioned as odd, but—

Isn't this exactly what he tries to do? What happened in their family to make these siblings desperately want to better themselves?

Cecelia is gabbling on about the flowers in the church and I should listen, I know . . .

I know this is exciting. A Big Day. One we will never have, but for once I have a sense of— Something that isn't envy. I am happy for Cecelia and her family but—

I am not interested.

Goodness. I am just not interested.

Then again, David says I've not been interested in anything of late.

I think of the art exhibition. I wonder if Miriam managed to pull off her surprise for yogi Kathryn . . .

'Diane?'

'I'm sorry?'

'Your house,' Cecelia says, scanning my face. Would she have questioned my whereabouts over the last few days? Well. Of course, I am the woman David presents me to be. Here - I am his wife. 'In England, all is fine?'

'I should think so, yes.' I finish my drink, pull at my dress. It's gotten too tight. I expect David will reprimand me later. *Inappropriate.*

Did he pack it for me? Holding items up while I gave a minuscule nod?

His choice.

This was his choice.

We are seated at a table with Cecelia and her husband Clark, the bride and groom, the bride's parents, and the bride's aunt and uncle. I paint a smile on my face. Make an effort to nod where appropriate. But I am a boat, grounded. Tugging, pulling, aggravating.

I don't know these people. Isn't it strange that this - their most personal family occasion - should be enjoyed by me, a virtual stranger? A relation, yes, but—

David has not seen his nephew in five years, for goodness sake.

'Cecelia tells me it's your thirty-year anniversary today, guys? Congratulations.' Clark moves focus to us.

'Wow.' The groom raises his glass. 'I hope we can still be as happy together as you guys in thirty years.'

I look at my napkin. Fold it. Refold it.

'Do you have any advice for us?' The bride seems sweet - a bright, open face. She reminds me of Indie. I must reply to Indie's message. She wanted to see how the exhibition was going, said they'd stopped at a spot up the coast which she thought I'd love.

'Advice? I suppose just look after one another,' David says. 'And be loyal.'

My plate sways. *Look after one another*? How is leaving me on the plane looking after me?

And ... *loyalty*?

Well, an affront to me, yes. But I have the sudden image of us in thirty more years. Will he still be angry then? Will he still be 'looking after me' in this way?

David is telling the story of how we first met. I force my eyes up, smile, nod. Laugh on cue.

I've heard this story before, of course. The jokes never change, the teasing of me as a *ditsy being who didn't know her right from her left*. He still sees himself as my saviour.

And he is.

He was.

But this story is thirty years old. How many times have I heard it replayed? The same telling. And I am still the butt of the joke.

Where are our new stories?

Well. Mine are in Byron. But to tell them here - surfing, climbing, dancing - seems inappropriate.

Goodness. I am inappropriate. My tattoo. My dishevelled hair.

I excuse myself to the toilet. My reflection, I notice, has altered. My hair is longer, lighter, my skin tanned, my face has filled out. I have put on weight but I feel somehow ... Lighter.

Better.

But not in these clothes. In this outfit I am pretending. I have been pretending.

And after thirty years?

Goodness.

———

'Where did you go?'

I left the dinner. I am in the room. I am taking off the dress, and as David comes in I cover my chest. Ridiculous, really, to feel exposed. My own husband.

I face the wall and pull on the top. The one from Elaine's shop. It drapes over my skin, settles.

'Diane? Do you not feel well?'

I can't help but laugh. Shouldn't David be explaining himself? Shouldn't I be demanding an explanation for why he left? I know it wasn't because he simply didn't feel well.

And yet—

I can't be bothered to listen. I don't need it. What I do wonder is why he didn't do it sooner?

'Why don't you just tell me what you think of me?' My voice is measured, steady, landing as I aimed.

Arguing doesn't have to be negative, I realise. To exchange opinion, to *have it out*, as Bertie would say. There were many late night tirades amongst our hostel group. Debating, conflicting. My opinion respected, considered. And then in the morning? All as normal. Let's share a loaf of bread . . .

At home, people stopped letting me know their opinion, and I stopped asking. Instead? Polite nods, suffused feelings.

Patricia. Goodness. She's been out of my mind of late. And wasn't she the worst for this? The smug face. Hushed tones as I left the room.

I'm fine! I'd want to shout.

At least Francis is always open with me. I may not agree, but I know what she thinks. The others? Nothing . . . *real*. Nothing is goddamn real.

I think of Miriam. What was the word she used?

Stifled.

Hm.

David moves toward me. 'I'll tell you what I think is that . . . tattoo—' it clearly pains him to say the word, so foreign to his mouth, his lip curling at the transmission - 'is ridiculous. I mean, honestly, *Diane*. What are you trying to do? I let you go for a short time and . . .' His voice trails off.

I survey the image I created. Run my finger along it. My doodle. Put there as a permanent mark, so I don't forget the meaning: Liberty. 'I was free in Byron.'

'Free from responsibility. Hiding.' David sits on the bed. A sigh. A change of approach. 'She's not there, Diane.' His voice is low. Gravelly. Tired.

And now it's my turn to clench my jaw because this is not about Bertie. This is not about hiding. For once, after all this time, this is about freedom.

My freedom.

I lift the box from the suitcase, comforted by its familiarity. The wood is soft, in a way. The plaque on top still shiny, the print exactly as I recall. Etched in my mind for eternity.

'David, you left me on that plane because you knew, somewhere, you had to do it.'

'What are you doing?'

Maybe I don't need an alternate universe. Maybe my world can be just as I design it. 'You should look up Fauvism.'

Impatience. 'What?'

'The first painters to break tradition regarding perception. Painting straight from the tube, bold strokes. Subjective responses that changed the viewer's opinion. Change your perception of me, David.'

'Diane, please.'

'Or maybe it's me that needs to break perception. Either way. Change.'

Change.

I am a Surrealist.

I step toward the sideboard.

'So, what? You're not coming to the wedding? What will I tell my sister?'

I consider David over the last few months, years, putting on a 'brave face' to people, making excuses for my behaviour, my *upset*, as he called it. 'I'm sure you'll think of something.'

I grab the hire-car keys, and I leave the hotel.

To: Liberty.Bridges@icloud.com
Subject: The Truth Between Us
From: MrsDBridges@outlook.com

Dear Bertie,

I did it. I got the tattoo! You'll laugh, I'm
sure, but I think you'll like it. It's a bird
- a doodle that won't leave me alone. I've
been doing some painting of late and I feel
enlivened by it. Someone from the local
gallery even thinks they could sell some of
my pieces. Can you believe it? Me - a professional artist at fifty-five.

Never too late for your dreams to come to
fruition, I can hear you say. You used to
love painting with me when you were little
but the artistry petered out. Not productive,
Dad would say. Maybe I shouldn't have
listened. Still, we can't change the past,
much as I think about it . . .

Because I have been thinking about our past.
The truths I spoke of. I can say this to you,
because I sense you'll understand, but I feel
art has a way of accessing our truths. I
suspect we can only be creative when we are
at our most truthful, accessing that part of
us which is beyond our conscience, the higher
being, perhaps. I suspect that's why I have
not created for so long - because I'm not

sure I have been living in truth, Bertie.
This trip is making me see that.

Something has been lost, over the years. A
sense of fun, which I thought of as youth -
that element we enjoy when we have no responsibility - was actually my essence. What made
me, me. That has been smothered, but something about being here is uncovering that
truth, like a relic buried under the desert,
the sand slowly blowing off to uncover that
which was always there. Not youth but . . .
Me. Vitally, intrinsically, me.

I stopped painting. Your dad didn't see the
value in it, no, but he also knew I connected
art to not only myself, but to my memory of
another man.

Eduardo.

I can't quite believe I am typing his name,
whispering it in my conscious mind, releasing
it to the ether, transcribing it here on the
keyboard . . .

Eduardo.

Please don't think ill of me, Bertie, but we
had something when I was engaged to Dad. A
fling, I suppose, although that word doesn't
do it justice. It felt like the deepest
connection - souls? Can I say that? Again, I
think you would understand this - and it was

complete love and lust and everything that
makes a person feel utterly alive, simultane-
ously of their body and not of their body. I
want to say transformative but he didn't
transform me into something I was not,
instead he transported me into the ultimate
being I was capable of becoming. Fulfilling
my ability; me at my best. My best self, I
can hear you say, but so very much more. My
best self if my insides were made of stars
and every morning I could stretch my sleepy
arms up to tickle the moon.

Goodness, listen to me . . .

But. I was already with your father. It is
not like now. I know that's hard to understand. Everyone has a choice, I can hear you
say, but I felt I did not. Eduardo could
offer me nothing, and David was offering the
world. He promised me art and travel and
galleries and maybe my own gallery one
day and—

That all changed. Slowly at first, but as you
grew the changes in him became more
entrenched because we could see the changes
in you. We never spoke of it - David never
asked - but you are the spit of him, Bertie.
And although I should have been ashamed I
also knew I had a piece of Eduardo with me
forever. And that makes me love you even
more. I loved David, I did, but with your
biological father . . . Indescribable.

From the deepest part of me, I have to tell
you I am so sorry I kept this from you. I am
desperately sorry you were never told because
maybe that would have solved some feelings
for you - confusion, not fitting in - but you
did what Eduardo did, it must be innate, part
of your fabric, because you followed your
gut, anyway. And I let myself be confined,
narrowed, dreams forgotten. You honoured
yours and I cannot tell you how admirable
that is.

Only now, here in Byron, am I fully coming to
terms with what that meant, Bertie. For you
to turn your back on something secure, struc-
tured, and to follow your passion. It's what
I should have done. It's what I should be
doing.

And that's why I got the tattoo - a permanent
reminder. A reminder to fly, just like
you did.

All my love,
Mum x

———

I don't need a map. Somehow, I know. A feeling, a guidance, something outside of myself?

Still. Just as I begin to question whether David was right all along and I am insane, the sign: Bangalow.

I slow the car down. Breathe.

It was the main road. I remember that much. A junction. An oncoming lorry.

She wouldn't have known anything about it.

I clamp my fingers around the wheel, lean forward. There are no cars coming or going.

Rise and fall.

An expanse of flat grass, nothing for miles and then—

There. A cross. Flowers.

David—?

Somehow, I pull over. I hear only my heart. Hammering. But I see no colour. I have no connection to sound, to anything.

I leave the box on the front seat. My feet take me. I don't know . . . I . . . I can't . . .

Her face. Her beautiful *beautiful* face. The image of her at the airport, smiling, waving, leaving us . . . I wish I could go back to that moment and—

Had I known that was the last time I'd see her, I'd—

Why her?

Why? She had so much hope.

Potential.

Potential.

Goddamn it.

I bend. Cowering. I can't . . .

'Francis, it's me.' I hear the rustle of a duvet from the other end, whispers. 'I'm sorry to call at . . . I don't know what time it—'

'Diane. What's wrong?' My sister's voice is steady, reassuring.

'I—' My breath shudders and I hear myself make a noise. I clamp my hand over my mouth.

'It's okay, Diane. It's okay. Take your time.'

I nod, but she can't see me. My nod turns to a shake. The grass in front of me blurs, a light green sea and this solid, wooden cross adorned with yellow flowers. I can't breathe evenly and I can't keep a lid on this and I am pinching my face and—

I can't keep it in any longer. I can't hold it in. I can't be here and have her not here and—

'I'm here,' I manage.

'Oh, Diane, my love, I—'

'Why did it have to be this way? If I could change a—'

'Diane, you know there is nothing you can—'

'But, Francis, I can't—'

'No, Diane. No.'

I hold my breath. 'It's too hard.'

'For her, Diane. For her. Think of Bertie.'

'But—' The cross. Reduced to this. I can't bear that this image is all I have now. That whatever I do, however I behave, I can't escape it because—

'She's gone,' I whisper. 'She's gone,' I say again, my head dropping as I feel my knees hit the earth and pain sears into my bones. 'She's gone.'

And I lower the phone and I shudder over my body.

Bertie was here. And this is the last place she ever was.

She's not coming back, is she?

DAY NINETEEN

I am in my bed, but I am also on the beach. Slow to rise from slumber, unconsciousness keeps pulling me back. I feel in my body but my mind is stuck in the halfway house and—

Bertie. I see her here. In my dream state. She seems so real. I must stay here. I have to see her for as long as I am able. I submerge into the dream.

'He was my love,' I say to her. 'My initial, my absolute. Can anybody touch us in that way of the discovering first time? Exciting, ready, yielding. Never felt like that before, overwhelming love and lust. Maybe the first love is perfection. Because you haven't yet learnt to hold anything back, haven't been educated in heartbreak. You give your full self entirely, and you receive that in return. Everything, unencumbered.'

'Everything.' Bertie can only whisper in my dream. It sounds like butter melting through a hot crumpet. Liquid, warm, inviting.

'Once we've faced rejection, humiliation, we can never throw ourselves into love in the same way. Experience underlies all our decisions, taunting us. Knowledge jarring the present.'

'Unless we don't let it.' She has a smile that changes her entire face.

'How can you ignore what you've learnt? There is only one first time.'

'Or you give in to it. Ignore the knowledge, retrain your mind to think this won't be the same. And maybe it won't. Because if you give your all, maybe this is the last love, and maybe that is greater than the first. Maybe it's the love you die with. Perhaps there is a power in that.'

'You have a power,' I say.

'You have a power. I think you've found your power. Here, in Australia.'

A pause.

She is floating. 'This is what you always needed, isn't it?' she says.

I look out to the horizon, the salt of the sea breeze settling on my skin. I wrap my cardigan tighter around my chest. 'Perhaps. But I doubt I would have been ready before now.'

'Your first love - the artist - it's not a waste. It was not an illusion. If it was real to you, then it was real. Because you felt it. It changed you.'

'But—' I see him in her. Even now, here. And for that, I can't help but feel anything but positivity towards him. And who knows, perhaps he is protecting what he has now. Perhaps he can't let himself go back there.

Wasn't that my reason for staying away so long?

Bertie's hands are on my shoulders, the tattoo exposed on her ribs. The same tattoo I saw on Tom. Here, she seems taller than me. 'Do you remember what you told me about Michelangelo?'

'Mm.' Like Bertie, I am light here, content.

'In every block of stone there is a statue, and it is the sculptor who must discover it. You are the block *and* the sculptor. So carve, Mum. Be your own first love. Fall head over heels entirely and absolutely with your creation.'

I look at my daughter and I wonder. Shouldn't I be giving advice? Me - the mother? I should be the wise one.

Michelangelo. He said it was an angel he set free.

Bertie's face is different. Evanescent. 'Tom was your first love, wasn't he?'

A chin dip, that side of her lip teasing at a lift. Her eyes flick up to mine in confirmation.

'And your last, my angel. Fly.' I picture the love between Bertie and Tom – a life-changing love that lasts, a love from which they both can soar. I look at my own new inking. I run a finger over the bird. Swooping, soaring. Free.

Liberty.

Alternate universe.

'You too, Mum. It's your turn to fly.'

My daughter grips my arm lightly, strokes her thumb over the bird. And then we look up at one another, lightness reflected in light, and we laugh.

'Tom?' I give a brief rap on the door. Michael sent me back here to the storage room. I know he's here and—

His head sticks up from a box in the corner.

'Dee.' He stands and we look at one another. Take it in. Unsure what is appropriate.

After a moment, he points me to a beanbag and sits on the floor beside me.

I look at the boards. 'You're working on a new one?' He has coloured one of the blanks. Bright yellow.

He nods, then lowers his head between his knees, exhaling with a groan. 'Why didn't you say anything?'

I look at my wrist. 'Sometimes denial is the easier path.'

His head stays down. I'm not sure he agrees with my choice. Most people don't.

'She told me about you,' I say.

At this, he can't help but engage. A flick of his chin. 'Oh yeah?'

'I didn't recognise you at first. She said she'd met someone whom I would completely disapprove of - an unkempt surfer, long hair, beads.'

A half smile. 'Well, I've smartened up. You know, age.'

'Yeah, I guess that's it. In my mind, everything is as she told me. You should be in your early twenties, as Bertie . . . Still is.'

He hugs his armpits. Rocks back.

'Can you tell me about her? About what she was like when she was here?' I say.

Another smile. Bigger. A small laugh. 'She was . . . joyous.'

'Yes.' I think of photos – Her getting the tattoo, playing on the beach, partying with new friends. She looked so relaxed, unencumbered. Unlike any time I'd seen her in London.

'She put everyone at ease, you know? Sociable, caring. One

of life's good people.' His voice cracks and he looks down, clenches his jaw, hugs tighter.

After a pause, his voice whispers into the space between us: 'I'm sorry.'

I can't look up. 'I know.'

I sense him move closer. 'No, I'm sorry because . . . I was meant to go with her that night.' Another pause. An audible inhale. 'It was my van she was driving, but I was here, setting up in the shop. I didn't think I could run the business, I was nervous, and she wanted to go to this party so I told her to take the van and I'd catch her up and I thought she would leave straight away but she must have waited until dusk and then the light was dropping and—' Another deep breath, uneven. 'I'm so sorry, Dee. If I'd known, I—'

I shake my head. I can't engage. I can't take this in. I don't want to listen but also, I want to know. I *must* know.

'I could have stopped her, if I'd known . . .'

'Tom.' I try to spark authority in my voice but it won't—

'I wish I could go back. I wouldn't let her get in the van—'

'Tom,' I repeat, gathering myself. 'This is enough now.' I move in front of him, my hands on his arms, my head dips to make eye contact. 'It's not your fault, okay?'

He won't meet my gaze.

'You're not to blame, Tom, and nobody holds you accountable, okay? It was an accident. A tragic, *tragic* accident, but you're not to blame.'

Slowly, he raises his face. Red-rimmed eyes.

'It's not your fault,' I repeat.

After a time, gently, his face clears. An indecipherable shift underneath all that masculine front. I drop my hands and move back, kneeling, hugging my own arms around myself. I nod, and he nods, and we share an understanding. Perhaps it's that we can't alter the pain, but we can alter our perception. Manifest it to aid?

Maybe. One day.

'I know I have not dealt with her passing well, but I'm changing,' I say. The box. I will bring it here. Tom can help me scatter her into the sea, fly into the breeze. 'Maybe you need to do the same? Move on with your life, take her inspiration with you.'

'She was inspiring.' He looks at his boards. 'You know, only people of a certain privilege can speak about anything being possible, usually because they get what they want, but she did it with subtlety. She encouraged me, made me see what could be. She made me believe, like she believed.'

'Bertie didn't get what she wanted.' Why did I encourage her to be in London? Why did I—?

'No,' Tom says.

I don't want to give advice, because I don't want to risk sounding like David but—

I *have* to say this. 'Maybe you could do what you want in her memory . . .' I heave down a breath, force myself to look at Tom. 'If she'd stayed, she would have helped you.' And I realise now that this is exactly what she'd been trying to tell me she wanted. She was doing architecture for us, but it wasn't her. It wasn't her passion. She loved the beach. She loved being outdoors. She loved the sunshine.

She loved Tom.

'Would you help me?' Tom asks.

'Oh, I don't know anything about surfboards or running a business.'

He sits up straight. 'The artwork. The logo.'

'Well, I—' I have no experience. I can't possibly . . .

And yet—

Bertie. Brave. Miriam. *Just say yes.* 'Have you got anything started?'

'I've just been playing with ideas, names and stuff. I've been brainstorming but I'm not sure and ... Here.' He passes me a piece of paper with various brand name ideas scrawled in different sizes and fonts and I scan the offering but this is not for me and—

Wait.

I pick up a pen, and I write out my word, drawing in a font I believe would suit the lettering.

I pass Tom the paper and I watch, tense. He studies it, narrows his eyes, then breaks into a full face-shifting smile.

'Bertie's,' he says.

'Your freedom.'

'You're not going to put that there, are you?' I say, a mocking tone to my voice as I enter the gallery.

Miriam spins, her face fluttering from a frown to that grin of hers, eyes alight. 'You're here!' She runs over to hug me.

I, too, beam in return. My insides are swelling. A hot-air balloon, lifting into the sky.

The exhibition looks phenomenal. Miriam's photos hang along the white walls - fantastic, colourful landscape shots of Byron scenery, close up portraits in black and white.

'And David?'

I shake my head. 'I'm so sorry, Miriam. I shouldn't have—'

We are interrupted as the main door swings abruptly open. Alexandra enters and opens her mouth, then drops her gaze, a redness to her cheeks. 'I'll leave you two to . . .'

Alexandra leaves. I tilt my head to Miriam.

She presses her lips together, shrugs.

'Oh, Miriam. I wish you'd told me.'

'Of course I couldn't tell you. Do you remember how you reacted to Eric and Shaun? Jeez, Dee.' She lifts the print she's holding onto a stand and folds her arms.

'That's not fair.' I reach forward, but drop my hand. 'Okay, so I was a little judgmental. I'm sorry.' Goodness. How have I let myself become this . . . Blinkered? *Wrong*. So goddamn wrong.

Miriam looks down. 'I'm sorry, too.'

I move closer to her.

'For David,' she adds. 'For the artist.'

'I suspect David and I were over a long time ago. I just haven't wanted to see it.'

'Because of the artist?'

'Everything,' I say. 'We weren't strong enough to survive Bertie's death. And, actually, we were over a long time before that. But I'm not regretful. We built a life together, but now I realise that's not a reason to stay in the marriage. Besides, the artist . . .'

'Maybe he's still upset that you didn't choose him.'

'No. I've been imagining him as something he's not. He was mesmerising, yes, intoxicating, actually, but he was unreliable. A typical tortured artist . . . I suppose that's why I didn't put up too much of a fight when David thought it would be wise to wipe that part of my life away. I was pregnant. I needed to be responsible. I couldn't sleep all day and paint at night. I had to change, forget him. And so? I did.'

'But you don't need to keep changing. Not now, surely?'

'Well now, finally, I think I know myself.'

'I do believe we only get one major love in our life.'

'Great,' I laugh. 'So it's over for me?'

'No, the love is with yourself.' I think of Bertie. The dream. She would have liked Miriam. 'Anything else is a bonus.'

I turn my palms up. 'You know, Miriam. I have a piece of heart for you. I'm sorry it's only in friendship.'

'Hey, they can be the best pieces. They're the pieces that keep us afloat when everything else is sinking.'

And with this, I take Miriam's hands in mine, and kiss her gently on the cheek.

To: Liberty.Bridges@icloud.com
Subject: Goodbye
From: MrsDBridges@outlook.com

Dear Bertie,

I wanted to say how sorry I am not to have
told you - about everything - sooner. I have
been feeling so guilty but - after I wrote
those words - I wondered if, somehow, you
already knew. Because you were wise. Always
so much wiser than I . . .

When you were just three years old you told
me you were an angel and - you know what? - I
believed you. You were always an angel and
now you have returned home. And I know you
are there, and one day I will be with you
again. You remember I have had my doubts
about this, but a friend has made me see it
differently. I'm softening to the idea. Does
it matter either way? If it helps? That's
what you would say.

And so, my darling girl, this is my last
email. Not because I am not thinking of you,
but because I am incorporating you into all
that I do, seeing you in all the light, the
colours, the dreams of all the young people
here. I feel connected to you here, your
happy place.

But I'm not staying for that reason alone. I

don't feel morbid. Instead, in Byron, I feel
more in touch with myself. My true self. And
I suspect this is the only time in my life
when this has been so, after all these years.
You, my darling Bertie, have brought me home.
I remember your love and I feel it here.

You wanted to fly, and now you always will.

My Liberty, eternally free.
I love you.

Mum x

DAY TWENTY

The day of the exhibition and I am standing outside of the gallery. I couldn't sleep. Nerves, excitement, *something*, coursing through me, making me feel . . .

Alive.

Goodness. I am alive.

The sun has now lifted, the early morning heat ramping up already, but the breeze provides a refreshing reprieve. I suppose, here, spring is on the way. It was lurking all along, waiting in the wings to offer its blessing of bloom and warmth.

I enter the gallery. Take a moment to absorb the space. My kind of space.

The exhibit looks brilliant. Alexandra, Miriam and I worked all day yesterday, putting up the last of the photos, assembling the board on which Derrick and Annalys' food sculpture will sit, and here, in front of me, Tom's surfboard. The first in the 'Bertie' range. Bright, bold, yellow.

Amazing.

'You sure you don't want to add a piece to the collection?' Miriam says, balancing another stack of prints in her arms as she squeezes through the heavy door. I hurry over to help.

'Well, miracles happen. Look at you - up before eight.' I smirk, wink.

'Big day.' Her voice is measured, stable. Like me, I suspect, trying to cover a flailing underside.

We carry the stack of prints through to the studio and place them with care on the workbench.

'You took it down?' Miriam is looking over at the wall where once hung my atrocious art therapy piece.

'I'm starting again.'

'With more therapy?'

'Goodness, no. I've done enough of that. Therapy is valuable but . . . Only if you can take what you learn and apply it.'

'Oh? How?'

I smile. 'By living.'

On the empty wall, I notice a spot of pink I must have missed.

'Well, seeing as you're not willing to put the therapy piece into the exhibit, it's a good job you did this.' And from the stack of large prints, Miriam pulls out a photo.

'What—?' Wow. It's a photo of the mural. *My* mural.

'It's beautiful, Dee.'

Goodness. I am nodding, agreeing, because, well, it is beautiful. Somehow, I scaled up my doodle - my flying bird - in perfect proportion. The bird swirling in an array of bright colours - pinks, yellows, purples, bright blues - the star crisp and poignant. 'It's so . . . Uplifting.'

'Enlightening.'

'Free.'

'And it's taking a central position in the exhibition.'

'What? Oh, no, I—'

'Dee, this picture represents what travellers find here in Byron. It captures the essence of the town.'

'What? The waifs and strays running away?' I think of the people here - Shaun, Eric, Ellen, Tom . . .

'No, running *toward*. Running to something else. Searching. *Hope*. There is hope in this image, Dee.'

'I—'

'This is freedom. Making your life whatever you want it to be. Ignoring naysayers, embracing your truth.'

'A little heavy, perhaps?'

'No, Dee. This is art. *Your* art. And it's phenomenal.'

The exhibition has opened and - can you believe it? - people are here. People we don't know who have paid to come in. Scores of them. Travellers in couples, small groups of local business people on their work breaks, singles . . .

Goodness.

Miriam squeezes my hand, the two of us huddled in the corner next to the food sculpture. Cowering, I expect. We watch as Alexandra welcomes a woman in a skirt suit, clipboard in hand.

'The grant?' I say.

'Gosh. I hope Alexandra is okay.'

I squeeze Miriam's hand back. Alexandra was nervous this morning. She gets tetchy when she's nervous, I've noticed, yet Miriam has a way of calming her. Enabling her to see the pressure for what it is - a challenge to overcome. To see that, one way or another, everything is doable.

'She'll be fine,' I say. 'Oh, Ellen, thank you so much for coming.' I greet Ellen with a squeeze. 'You look fabulous, as always.' Today's ensemble is a bright pink maxi dress worn with a deeper pink blazer. 'I do love your clothes.'

'Well, my dear, you know what I'm going to say. If you ever want a discount on clothes, you just need to work for me.'

'Work?' Miriam chirps in, greeting Ellen. 'That's exactly what Dee will need round here, right?'

'What do you mean? Are you staying, dear?' Ellen grabs both of my hands.

Gosh. Look at this woman's happy-go-lucky face, the light shining off her cheeks . . . I can't do anything but beam back.

'Oh, darling, I'm so happy for you,' she says. 'And if you need a place to stay, you know I'm looking for a house sitter whilst I go down to Sydney to help my daughter?'

'Dee, it's your lucky day,' Miriam says.

I open my mouth. I want to express my gratitude to this woman, this luck, this place—

All I can do is hug her. Hug her and hope she understands what I am unable to convey with words.

'Now I'm going to browse this fabulous show,' Ellen says, straightening her clothes, 'and check out that marvellous mural I've heard so much about. You know I've been looking for an artist to commission? I'm on the council and I've proposed we do something similar down at the beach. Maybe get the young tagsters involved, keep them busy. Anyway, fabulous work, ladies. You're the talk of the town!' And with that she moves away in a flurry of pink positive perfection.

'I . . . Wow,' I say to Miriam. 'I can't believe my luck.'

'I've always said that when something is meant to be, the universe aligns to make it happen with ease.'

'Well, this is—'

'And here's your next piece of the puzzle. Ready to slot right into place . . .' Miriam takes a small step back as I turn to—

'Derrick. Hi.'

'Well, Dee. Aren't you a surprise?' We embrace and his beard feels as soft on my skin as it looks.

'Oh my gosh, Dee Dee, you are a legend! I love this stuff.' Annalys.

Dee Dee. I like the sound of my name from her mouth. I find myself not disturbed, but instead I'm—

At peace. It makes me feel warm, but not desperate.

Reframed. At last.

'I don't know about that,' I laugh, brushing my thumb over my tattoo. Even when I'm wearing a long sleeve top as I am now, I'm aware of the presence of ink on my skin. It's comforting. 'The food installation is a tremendous hit. Such a fabulous idea, Annalys.' I glance over to the pile of donuts, a huge tower of glistening pink icing - beautiful in its audacity. It's comical, teasing, tongue-in-cheek art and I love it.

'It is the inspired who give inspiration, Dee.' I scan Derrick's face for signs of an undercurrent of something sinister - a mocking, perhaps?

But there's nothing. He is genuine.

Hm. Maybe I would like to have him as a friend.

Perhaps. Over time . . .

'Well, I don't know—'

'You inspired my daughter to book her flights, didn't she, Annalys?' With this, Derrick's voice alters pitch. A subtle change, noticeable on the wave of pink it projects in my mind.

'You did?'

Annalys beams at us, her body twitching, the excitement a palpable thing, something I could touch. A bubble, a cocoon, a possibility. A world of possibilities. 'I'm starting in South-East Asia and then I'm heading to Europe. I'd love to see England, too. Maybe I could come visit you there?'

'Oh, well, I could certainly give you recommendations but I probably won't be around.'

'You're moving?' Derrick says.

'No . . . I think I'll stay here, actually. For a while.'

'Whaaaaaaat?' Annalys drops her mouth open and I have to resist the urge to reach out and close it for her.

I look at Derrick. He doesn't need to say anything. I don't need him to say anything.

Maybe I don't need anyone to say anything anymore. Not now.

Now, at last, I am authentic.

And I am happy.

Yes.

I am happy.

The End.

ACKNOWLEDGMENTS

For eighteen years, I've envisioned writing an acknowledgments page. Some people believe them to be excessive but ever since I enrolled on a creative writing module at University and fell in love with the craft, I have wanted to publish a novel. I didn't realise quite how long it would take me to achieve that goal so, screw it, I'm going to indulge myself!

After plenty of 'failures', I took the decision to take control of my career and self publish THE WOMAN WHO LOST HER LOVE. So, after much dreaming and wishing and working, in amongst the lovely messy jumble of life, here is my debut and thus, this page.

Firstly, I'd like to thank my writer's group. In particular, Joe, Brad and Gemma for all their advice and reading.

My advance readers, who consist mostly of friends I have begged to help. I'd also like to apologise to any friends who received earlier (TERRIBLE) books. Thanks for not telling me I was crap.

My dad, for always telling me anything is possible.

My mum, to whom this book is dedicated, who has been reading my work ever since that first time I wrote a poem - pen in one hand, thesaurus in the other. I was the original Joey from *Friends*.

My children, for being epic Lego players, thus allowing me plenty of opportunity to work.

And finally, Dan. I am a writer, yes, but I find no words to convey how blimmin' wonderful you are. Even the thesaurus won't suffice on this one. My team mate. My husband. My love.

Thank you.

ABOUT THE AUTHOR

Jo Lobato grew up in Cornwall, and now lives in Spain with her husband and two children. She has a Masters in Creative Writing, and writes a blog on creativity and the writing process.

Stay up to date with pre-release news by signing up at
JoLobato.co.uk/subscribe

Read the blog at:
JoLobato.co.uk/blog-news

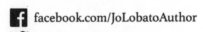 facebook.com/JoLobatoAuthor
twitter.com/jolodisco
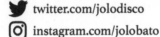 instagram.com/jolobato

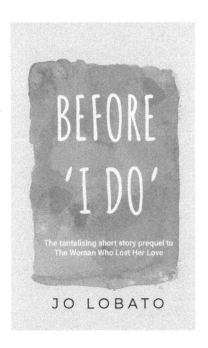

**Want to find out how it all began for
Diane, David & the artist?**

When Diane begins seeing David, little does she know how a
moment of illicit passion will impact her entire life.
Will she tell the artist her news?
And will David ever find out the truth?

Join Diane in her first encounter with the love of her life, and
discover the truth behind those life-changing choices in this
fascinating short story prequel to
The Woman Who Lost Her Love.

Available now at:
JoLobato.co.uk/books

Lightning Source UK Ltd.
Milton Keynes UK
UKHW041014210620
365346UK00001B/10/J